THE FRAGILE LIGHT

To the Balmuth-Loris
family

[signature]

THE FRAGILE LIGHT

A Herotown Novel

DAVID NURENBERG

To order additional copies of this book, contact:
Xlibris Corporation
1-888-795-4274
www.Xlibris.com
Orders@Xlibris.com
27320

This book is dedicated to a number of people: to my wife Liana, who stubbornly refused to stop believing in me. To Tom Hart, who was willing to take a chance, and to Dave Prifti and Monika Andersson, allies in art and in politics. To my parents, who taught me all about truth and justice. Finally, to my friends in the Marvel Roleplaying Club—we brought out the heroes in one another, and continue to save the universe every few weeks, one way or another.

But the wish of lesser people to secure themselves against interference from those who are better gives rise to a false sense of moral responsibility. The natural fear of being overwhelmed by a superior foe becomes internalized as the self-generated sense of guilt, and individual conscience places severe limits on the normal exercise of human desire. If truth can be achieved at all, it can come only from an individual who purposefully disregards everything that is traditionally taken to be "important." Such a super-human person, an Ubermensch, Nietzsche supposed, can live an authentic and successful human life.

—Garth Kemerling, *Nietzsche: Beyond Morality*

"Go ahead, scoff," he said, petulant. "Except in the life of a hero, the whole world's meaningless. The hero sees values beyond what's possible. That is the nature of a hero. It kills him, of course, ultimately. But it makes the whole struggle of humanity worthwhile."

I nodded in the darkness. "And breaks up the boredom," I said.

—John Gardner, *Grendel*

PRELUDE

"Please don't hurt me again."

"We're not here to hurt you, Ma'am. We're superheroes."

"Since when," the Doctor protected her face with her arm, white sleeve torn and tattered, "do superheroes steal mementos from widows?"

"Whoever did that, he wasn't one of ours."

"And the ones that followed him? Who tore my office to shreds looking for what he had taken?"

"Not ours either."

"How am I supposed to keep track?" She wiped a trickle of blood from her lip. "From what I remember before I left the State for good, all the Supers there are just puppets of the government. Either puppets, or prisoners."

"We're not from the State."

"Well, you're not Bulravian. I can see that."

"We're from Superion City."

"*Free* Supers, then?" She spoke the word "free" as if it was "pink polka dotted", "three-armed" or some other adjective that seemed irrationally inappropriate. "I've never met a free Super who wasn't Bulravian before."

"Doctor Michelis, we don't have time for this."

Doctor Michelis tried to bring their image into focus, but with her glasses shattered, she could make out only three humanoid shapes. They seemed tall, but then, anyone looked tall when you were lying sprawled on the ground, in a pile of broken glass and spilled fluids.

The man in the center stood the tallest, a hazy smudge of yellow and cobalt blue. Either his words crackled with electric static, or something in the Doctor's hearing had been damaged by her previous visitors.

"Doctor Michelis," his voice thundered (or was it just the blood in her head?), "it is imperative that we find your attaché."

"Ehat? You mean Ehat?"

"Yes," said the figure to his left. He was bald. No, not just bald—a gross exaggeration of baldness, a head ballooned and stretched to funhouse proportions.

"I don't know," said the Doctor. "Ever since the transmission, Ehat had been . . . had been . . . ."

"Acting strangely?"

She remained silent.

"We believe he's been *infected* with something, Ma'am," said the man in blue.

"That's ridiculous. I'm a doctor, I would have been able to tell—"

"Not a disease *per se*. But something that may be altering him as a person."

"That's ridiculous."

"How much did your late husband tell you about his space mission?"

"Not much," she lied.

The three shapes around her conferred, hummed. The bald one touched his grotesque forehead, and a buzz, like an electric shock, took fire in the doctor's brain. As impossible as she knew that it was, she could feel her ganglia on fire.

"The package," said the one with the finger to his temple. "It's arrived intact. The Bulravian attaché is the vector."

"That's just splen," said the blue one with the booming voice, "except we have no idea where he's fled to."

"She knows," said his partner.

"Ehat left with the first Super that came," said the doctor. "The one who made me sign the release forms, to give away the last memory I have of my husband."

"She knows more than that," the bald one tattled.

Doctor Michelis remained silent.

8

"I can't bear to watch this," the third one finally spoke, a woman painted in silver tones, although the edges of her form seemed to bleed and cocoon, almost as if they formed wings.

"Then leave the room, Sarah. You know what's at stake here. The lives of billions. Nothing can measure against that. We do what we have to."

"Would Captain Omega approve of this, I wonder?"

"Leave him out of this."

The silvery woman lingered a moment, then withdrew, and something in the doctor's stomach dropped as the sound of her footfalls died out. Doctor Michelis tried to shut her mind, to think about anything else—medical school, her wedding, the war, even Trinity—but as the fires scorched her brain cells again, they burned away entire chunks of gray matter to reveal a graven image of the spires of Mesopolopolis, capital city of the State . . .

Traditional scholars attribute the success of the First Heroic Age fifty years ago to an elevated moral standard among the Metahuman community, a "people of gold," so to speak, that walked in the wake of the very first mutations. Somehow, they would have us believe, these people of gold have in subsequent generations degenerated into baser metals; such an analysis smacks painfully of "good old days" illusionism. Contemporary sociologists have come to the painful realization that the people of the State in those days simply abdicated too much of their moral responsibility, expecting Metahumans to "pick up the slack," to become their own personified superego. Thus we share some modicum of blame for conditions that led to Trinity, if only in that the crimes of the wicked always depend upon the failure of the righteous to act . . .

—President Augustus Lee, *Mending the Breach*

GAYLE

Night fell across the spires of Mesopolopolis, laughing at the tiny neon spears that rose from the city to challenge it. Small flecks of black snow rained down upon Gayle, who pulled the torn folds of her leather jacket closer as a sudden wind flung candy wrappers and styrofoam hamburger containers at her knees. She ignored the barrage, gritted her teeth against the cold, and pressed onward, along the gates that divided Herotown from the other boroughs. On warmer nights, she would crane her neck up, follow the metal lattice of the gates dozens of meters, all the way to their barbed-wire tips, and snicker silently.

Given the number of us who can fly, why bother?

Sneakers worn and bending with each footfall (she refused to let George buy her new ones; he had given her so much already, asking so little in return), Gayle hurried down Guardian Boulevard, past the silent rows of parked trucks and the flickering streetlamps that played sentinel to the warehouse district. The occasional clatter of metal or the tortured cry of a stray cat would give her mind pause, but not her legs.

Why, why, why did I have to wait until the buses stopped running, and why didn't I want to spend money on a cab?

10

Waley always laughed at her for being afraid of the streets at night.

"Fine," Gayle told him once, "let's wait until Friday. Then I'll walk naked through Desperation Flats."

"That I'd like to see," Waley had licked his lips, but of course they hadn't followed through. Waley never followed through. Well, maybe he did now, but Gayle wouldn't know—they hadn't spoken in years.

Gayle's feet felt as if they had been walking for three years. Her muscles still ached from this morning's exercise regimen. Twice a week, she added more repetitions. Today was Wednesday.

The muffled thup-a-thup of a patrol helicopter passed overhead. Gayle tensed, ducked into an alleyway, waited for the telltale searchlights to sweep the streets for curfew. The darkness above revealed nothing, though—only dim streetlight casting shadows on speckled gray water towers.

A poster draped down across the full height of one of those towers, a poster of a bald head, red face mask framing charcoal black eyes that, in the dim light, pretended to be holes in the poster itself. The man's mouth neither smiled nor frowned, occupying some nebulous middle ground that had always looked to Gayle like teeth gritted against pain. Darkness obscured the caption below, but Gayle and every other resident of Herotown had seen the letters every day of their lives.

Captain Omega says, "Villains can't hide."

Another poster, a few buildings down: *"Do your duty. We are all one humanity."*

The wind picked up again as Gayle reached the door to warehouse number 18, unburied her hands from her armpits, and gingerly pulled off one worn purple mitten. Slim but solid fingers tapped out a pattern on the keypad.

After a small eternity, the door slid open to reveal a hulking man-shaped metal statue, casting a shadow that engulfed Gayle in a sudden bout of darkness, save for the red flare from its eye-sockets. Teeth chattering, Gayle craned her neck up to meet that crimson gaze.

"Sorry I'm late," she muttered.

"It's all right, Gayle," boomed a megaphone voice. "Better late than caught by the Peace Officers for breaking curfew. Come on in."

11

With a series of loud hydraulic hisses that shot darts of pain into Gayle's burgeoning headache, the metal man twisted, turned and began a slow series of stomps away from the door, into the light (and warmth!) of the warehouse interior.

"I've got news," the boom went on. "We've picked a site. Come take a look." Mechanized feet pounded towards a desk at the far side of the room.

"Hi George," Gayle hurried in, depressing a switch to close the door behind her. "I'm great, how are you? No, you don't have to take my coat, I can hang it myself. Yes, I'd love a hot mug of tea, it's freezing out."

The iron giant swiveled again. "Oops. Sorry. Just got excited—'

"No worries." Gayle unpeeled herself from her small cowhide prison and hung it on a nearby coat rack, alongside a weathered looking Australian outback vest and a slinky black vinyl overcoat.

"Everyone else is here, I take it?"

"We saved the best for last," said the metal man, and lumbered forward, arms outstretched.

"Uh-uh," she held up a finger.

"Oh. The suit. Right. Forgot."

A hum issued forth and the metal man's chest cavity irised open, revealing a tall, ursine man who clawed his way out with a practiced discomfort. At least a day's growth of stubble lined his chin, but only a day's worth. Noctyrne was apparently working her magic on him. The evidence lay everywhere: George's faded yellow tee-shirt looked washed for a change, his patchwork dungarees replaced with new denim trousers, and his black sneakers, will wonders never cease, looked polished. He still didn't look like the millionaire he was, but at least now he didn't look like a vagabond.

Of course, Gayle had always kind of *liked* the old vagabond look . . .

George threw his meaty arms around her, and she returned the hug as best she could. Even without the GAP suit, hugging George was like hugging the base of a soft, hairy oak tree. Her arms just didn't reach. The smell of insulation from the GAP suit's interior still clung to him. Gayle took some strange pleasure in that. Noctyrne hadn't changed *everything* about this man Gayle had known since childhood.

"You look tired." George's eyes seemed to widen to fill the horn-rimmed glasses he wore.

"I'm ok, George."

"You sure?"

"Mm-hm," she lied, but with a pleasant smile. His chivalric instincts satisfied, George released her and bounded back to the table.

Gayle surveyed the room—yes, Noctyrne had been busy. The marble floors looked freshly waxed, the chandeliers dusted, the fireplace logs all arranged in a perfect crackling pyramid and the mirrors polished to spotlessness. Gayle caught a look at herself in one of them, and wondered if Noctyrne could work any magic on *her*.

Gayle's shaggy bob of dirty blonde hair hadn't held up well in the winds, scattered and frazzled like some over-petted lapdog. Gray-purple bibs ringed her brown eyes, and chapped whiteness pockmarked her lips. Gayle had never been a tall woman, but she saw her posture hunched, and she arched back a bit to correct it. Without her superhero costume, she had to admit the motivation to stand erect tended to flee.

"The city gardens."

"Hrm?" Gayle snapped around.

"Our site. For the wedding ceremony. Eight months and 4 days from today." Gayle forced her eyes to brighten. "That's wonderful," she brought her hands together. "Still going with the medieval theme?"

"Now we're thinking `Under the Sea.' Naomi's designing the costumes herself. I get to wear Neptune's Crown, and she gets to hold a pitchfork."

"We're still working on a design for our `best man.'" George punched Gayle playfully in the arm. Although she barely felt the impact, it gave her shivers.

"No spandex," she reminded him. "I don't wear it on the job, and I certainly won't wear it to a wedding."

"Don't worry," said George. "You have full veto power on anything we pick for you."

Gayle rubbed her eyes with a bunched fist. "This is charming, George, but if the reason you signaled me was for a consult on wedding themes, couldn't it have waited until morning?"

"Yeah," he rubbed his chin, "but I figured as long as we had you here for business, we'd let you in on our latest. You're the first to know."

She smiled. She had been the first to know about their engagement, and about George's plan to propose, and, two years earlier, George's plan to start a super-team of his own. Gayle had been his first recruit, if you could honestly call it recruitment, and not charity.

Why did charity come easily to George? Was it because he viewed it as paying back a debt? But which debt? Was it that, after what his father was unwittingly responsible for, he couldn't help but become a superhero? Was the kindness he showed her in recompense for what she had done for him back in childhood?

George hadn't met Noctyrne in childhood, but rather last year, on the streets of Herotown. He and the team had freed her from the Blood Chains of her "Vampire Lord" (how melodramatic—the man had some Class A-3 psionic abilities, a disturbing case of hemotophilia, and had read a few too many gothic novels). That was how it was supposed to work, right? The hero saves the damsel and they fall in love?

Gayle had saved George once. Maybe men just made for poor damsels.

"About that business."

"Yeah," George's face drew tautly into into his professional stare. Everyone in the business needed a professional stare, as well as a posturing stare, a pensive stare, and of course the stare of fighting against unbelievable pain. The fact that no one ever saw George's face beneath the GAP suit didn't change the principle of the thing.

"This way, Gayle. Or, since we're now officially on-duty, Gal Friday."

"Costume's in the wash back home."

"No problem. I had a few spares made for you. Extra-durable fabric, with the new hidden pocket design and microchip communications device woven into the cuff link."

Sigh. That was George. Gayle had almost learned to not feel guilty anymore. Almost.

"George, you didn't have to—"

14

"Oh, and guaranteed non-slip traction pads on the boots," George's face was lit like a child's on Christmas. "Naomi—I mean, Noctyrne—tried hers out this morning. They're absolutely splen!"

"Thanks," Gayle gave up. "I'll change before we go."

"Sure," George didn't miss a beat as he approached the fireplace. "Do you want the honors?"

"All yours," Gayle beckoned.

With a swift and savage motion, George pulled on the positively ancient bust of old President Stevenson on the mantle. The hearth, flames and logs and all, rotated out to reveal a staircase. George ducked and bent, and Gayle always held her breath at this point, wondering if he would fit. He always did, and the darkness swallowed him.

She glanced back to his hulking metal GAP suit, empty, standing patient sentinel in the waiting room. Sooner or later, George would remember and activate the remote control to send it on down to meet them.

Taking a deep breath, Gayle launched herself into the tube. She could have just crawled in slowly, but some decorum had to be maintained.

*　　*　　*

"Ok, team, this is our biggest break in months," George drove the Stallion through the empty streets of Herotown. The late hour made a rapid pace easy. The only autos on the roads would be owned either by curfew violators or other contracted heroes, on their way to the outside world to fight the Normals' crime for them. Call it an honor or call it a living, it was the only job that paid anything above subsistence level for residents of Herotown.

"We've petitioned and received permission to aid the Mesopolopolis police in an investigation they've dubbed the `Georgie Porgie' case."

"What?" Craig, in the back of the Stallion, brought his feet down from the headrest of George's seat. "This is the best you could do? What's next, a secret mission to put Humpty Dumpty back together again?"

"Easy, Craig." Gayle, seated in the back of the van beside him, put a hand on his the furry gauntlet that covered the man's wrist, careful to avoid the stainless steel claws housed within. "A job's a job, right?"

"If you say so," Craig yanked away from her touch. "Personally, I'd prefer a little more dignity."

"This from a man who wears a paper mache rodent on his head?" Noctyrne snickered from the shotgun seat up front.

"Hey!" Craig's face, two beady eyes and a flat nose staring above a bush of red beard on a nearly-square head, grimaced from between the jaws of his helmet. "How many times do I have to tell you? It's a wombat, not a rodent! Wombats are marsupials! I'm not Combat Mouse. I'm not Combat Squirrel. I'm *Combat Wombat.*"

"Oh, please. If you want people to take you seriously, Craig, for Spirit's sake get a new codename. You think your foes are going laugh themselves into submission?"

"It shouldn't be about codenames. Why should my name matter? A hero's actions should speak for themselves."

"But it *is* about names. Names and images. If you ever hope to be a public figure—"

"I don't . . . *need* . . . a new codename," Craig surged, claws springing out with a loud *shink.* "These claws helped earn me that M-2 on my ID card—that's M, as in, Mutation, as in all real, baby. If big boy's willing to stop the van, I'll show you just how real."

"Spirit above." Noctyrne rolled her eyes from the shotgun seat up front, sending a smooth white hand through her cascade of midnight-black hair. "We're not even five minutes into the mission and already Craig's going to bust up another van. You want to try slashing apart some supervillains for once, instead of our equipment?"

"I haven't *seen* any supervillains in months." Craig thrust the top half of his body into the front seat. "You know how I've been paying the bills? Demolition work. I come home every day sneezing with soot and brick dust, knowing the whole damn time that if I wanted to I could just pick up my computer, hack into a bank, and withdraw myself a few million."

"Only if you wanted to become a villain yourself," said Noctyrne.

"Well, I just might one of these days," said Craig, "unless our fearless leader, your boyfriend, could find us better gigs than automobile washes and shopping mart dedications—"

"He's my *fiancée*, not my boyfriend," Noctyrne, met him eye to eye, hands falling towards her shapely hips to draw a sai blade from her slinky costume, "and I don't see you complaining about the free room and board he's giving us—"

"Guys, settle down," George tried to say, but the words drowned in the roar Craig let loose, a guttural howl ending in a high pitched wine that brought Gayle's hands to her ears.

"Oh, shut up," Noctyrne squirmed around in the front seat, throwing out a clawed hand that hit him square in the jaws of his Wombat helm, bending one of the plastic teeth inward.

"Oh, you've done it now, Naomi," Craig growled. "Oh, you've done it now . . ."

He reared on his haunches, knocking into George's elbow, sending the Stallion swerving around the road. George shouted protests, pulling the van up against the curb with a violent shudder.

Noctyrne egged him on. "What are you going to do, growl and spit at me?"

"I'll do worse than that, girly. Prepare to face my—eeek!"

Craig's voice vanished. His freckled face had puffed up like a fish, his eyes bulging wide. A thin whistle escaped from pursed lips.

"What did you do?" George turned to his fiancée.

Her blemishless face wore a look of surprise beneath all the mascara and foundation. "*I* didn't do anything. That leaves—"

All eyes turned to Gayle. She sat calmly in her Gal Friday costume, a simple yet elegant noir trenchcoat and fedora, one gloved hand resting on the armrest . . . and one hand missing. George and Noctyrne followed the arm down and across, where it vanished under the shaggy, baggy leg of Craig's Wombat costume.

"Craig," Gayle said softly and evenly, "cool it. Or I squeeze harder."

"Eek," Craig hissed in a frustrated falsetto. "You'll feel my wrath for this—"

"Your wrath doesn't feel very terrible," Gayle's arm shook at the shoulder, and Craig winced. "In fact, it feels pretty fragile. Let's call it a truce for now, ok? George promised there'd be bad guys to fight?"

Gayle looked to George hopefully.

"Um, yeah," George blinked, recovering. His face was as white as Craig's. Hmph. Men. "As I was, um, saying, we have a case now."

"Go on."

"Aren't you going to, um—"

"I'll let him go when we hear the whole mission," said Gayle.

"Aak," Craig tried to shift away, and apparently failed. "Speak . . . quickly . . ." he squeaked.

Noctyrne's smile shone like a beacon in Gayle's direction.

"All right," George eased back into character, "as I was saying, the Police have dubbed it the Georgie Porgie case. They wanted to call him a serial rapist, but, well, they're not sure what he's doing qualifies."

Noctyrne and Gayle's faces darkened as one.

"What do you mean?" Noctyrne asked, brows creased.

"On four separate occasions, a man in a dark cloak has shown up at crowded events—two parties, a carnival, and just recently a dance club—hung around for awhile, walked up to a woman seemingly at random, and kissed her."

George paused.

"Well?" Gayle tapped the armrest with her free hand.

"That's it," said George. "He kisses them. Not just pecks on the cheek, either—we're talking deep, full, romance novel kisses."

"Tongue . . . or no tongue?" Craig gasped, before something made him squeak. Noctyrne punched him in the arm for good measure.

"Then, just like Georgie Porgie, he runs away, only to appear days later and do the same thing."

"Sounds more like a fraternity initiation prank than a super villain," Noctyrne folded her lithe arms. "Why the need for us?"

"Because in each case, witnesses say the woman didn't fight him off, didn't object, didn't even seem capable of independent action. He had them completely under his power."

"Wow, and all he did was kiss them?" said Craig. "What a loser."

Gayle seriously contemplated ridding the gene pool of Craig's contributions, then decided she was better than that. "You're thinking a telepath, then, George? Or maybe a mystic hypnotist?"

"My thoughts exactly, Gal Friday. Maybe *you're* the mind reader."

Gayle harrumphed, but she couldn't deny the rush of blood through her arteries, the pounding in her chest, that breath of "alive" reawakening in her lungs. After so long, a real, honest case!

"All right, so he kisses people," said Craig. "That hardly makes him a threat to world peace. Is this really a job for heroes?"

"Maybe he's really a subterranean life form come up to harvest the breath of human women," Noctyrne sat up eagerly on her knees. "Maybe he's the point man for an entire invasion from beneath the Earth, and only we can stop them!"

"Yeah," the blaze in Craig's eyes finally began to kindle, "I gotta admit, ain't nothin' better than smashing subterranean mole armies. Even better than killer robot armies. Robots don't scream. Molemen do. Sometimes they even bleed green goo."

"Easy, gang," said George. "All we know is a basic physical description, and eyewitness accounts that he speaks with a thick Bulravian accent."

"Bulravian? He's far from home. And how did he get here, what with the war and all?"

"I told you, Combat Wombat, we really don't know much about the situation yet, and we won't ever unless we get back on the road and go talk to the Detective on the case."

"This Detective," asked Gayle, "is he the one who gave you the tip?"

"Um, not exactly," said George, putting the Stallion into drive again, pulling the van away from the curb.

"What do you mean, not exactly?"

"Well," George's forehead creased whenever he attempted to assemble a lie. "What I mean is, not directly."

"Did he put a note in a bottle for you, then?" asked Noctyrne.

"If by note you mean an all-points-bulletin, and for me you mean the entire precinct, then, um, yes."

"Dammit!" Craig roared, "I knew it!"

Someone seemed to have dropped a three ton weight down Gayle's esophagus, and she felt it pull her down from the shoulders. She forgot about her "restraining hand" on Craig altogether, letting it fall limp.

"A normal police case," she muttered. "Cruiser-chasing."

Noctyrne collapsed back into a pile of shapely limbs. "Splen. Positively splen."

"Look, it *could* be a super villain." George fought to keep his voice from sounding like a whine. "It's work, ok? It gets our name in the spotlight—"

"If you call a paragraph on page 12 of the late edition spotlight—"

"Don't you start too, Naomi—"

"Noctyrne. We're on duty now. Such as it is."

"Oh, like you ever let anyone call you anything else *off* duty either—"

"It wasn't big enough for them to call in a *real* super team," Craig finally bellowed. "That's the only reason we're—"

"No!" Gayle suddenly found her grip again, and Craig's sentence ended in a wince.

George and Noctyrne snapped around to see.

"We *are* a real super team," said Gayle. "GAP, Noctyrne, Combat Wombat, and Gal Friday. Don't ever forget that. People need our help, either from a super menace or a run of the mill pervert. If we can make a difference, no job's too small, right?"

Everyone paused, waiting for someone else to speak.

Gayle finally released Craig entirely and pointed towards the windshield. "Eyes on the road."

George turned back just in time to avoid a head-on collision with the checkpoint tower.

Two Peace Officers approached, armor clanking. In the dim light, Gayle might almost mistake them for George's GAP suit. For all she knew, George's father probably designed them, maybe even financed their construction. If irony were edible, she would have choked.

An Officer took each side of the van, shining spotlights inside, bathing everyone in a blinding glare. Gayle brought a hand up to her face in a futile attempt to shield her eyes, wondering how necessary any of this was.

"Name, identicard, travel papers."

George had it all at the ready. The Officer passed it on to a third, unseen comrade, or maybe to two, or three of them. Everything outside the Stallion's windows lay obscured in a white bath. There could be an army waiting beyond, or just a wicker rocking chair with some lemonade.

"Mister Snordwell," the Officer's voice warbled slightly. Respect? Or contempt? "Didn't expect to see you out here this time of night."

"I don't like to advertise my movements," George said, lowering his glasses conspiratorially.

Gayle gave him credit. His voice never shook, his posture never slouched. Even Noctyrne was flinching from the light, hissing, and Craig's characteristic boiling rage dropped to a low simmer the second he saw the plasma rifle the second officer had trained on the vehicle. Gayle didn't blame Craig one bit.

"Well, your papers check out," said Officer number two. When had the third Officer returned? Or was it all done via hidden radio?

"Six hour post-curfew visa is in effect starting from now. You keep your noses clean and don't cause any fuss, you got that?"

George tossed an exasperated look at Officer number one. Although his face of course remained unreadable beneath the combat suit, Gayle thought she could detect the hints of nasal congestion in the officer's voice, perhaps the beginnings of a headcold.

"We're just doing our jobs, Mister Snordwell. Nothing more or less."

"You don't have to do them so well," Gayle mumbled, but the Stallion was already away, through the swiftly opening electrified gates, over the imaginary border that separated Herotown from the rest of Mesopolopolis. Gayle turned in her seat, tried to watch the checkpoint and guard tower and Peace Officers through the back windshield as they receded, but her vision was still marred by flashing halos of whiteness.

If only Friday wasn't four days away, she told herself, *then I wouldn't have been so shaken. I would have told them exactly where they could have shoved those plasma rifles. Shown them even, if necessary.*

Wow. That was impressive. For a moment, she had almost believed it.

The Stallion drove on through the night, its occupants uncharacteristically silent.

Without the law, we are nothing. I tell you this again—whether we are able to lift a mountain or shatter it to dust with our fists, whether we can boil off its snow with our vision or freeze it to crystals with our breath—without the law, we are no more than forces of nature, deaf to the will of our own humanity.

—Captain Omega, Address to the Allied Forces at the
Battle of Annihilus Bay

MARLA

"Commander, you have to give me something to work with here."

Marla Arliss didn't even try to sound convincing any more. She had spoken herself hoarse for the past week, and Neville Shandon still wouldn't open his mouth.

Marla's family hadn't wanted her to go into law. Public defense had never been profitable, especially since the Trinity Disaster. Biotech, they assured her, was the up-and-coming field. Genetics, metahumanics. Put that expensive education we gave you to some real use, put that head to good ends, instead of knocking it against walls.

Well, Mom and Dad, "knock knock." 'Cept no one's answering today.

"Commander, please. You've been charged with criminal negligence, and given the severity of the disaster, never mind the recent toughening of the Space Acts, you're looking at fifty years minimum, and that's if I wear a really short skirt in front of the judge."

A pause.

"That was a joke. You could at least smile."

Commander Neville Shandon looked nothing like an astronaut. Marla's college dorm room had been plastered with posters of astronauts, all well groomed and erect and smiling paternally, even the female ones. A woman could employ a paternal smile. Marla was using one right now, in fact.

But nothing in Neville Shandon's eyes looked warm or fatherly. They were small and brown and beady, weasel eyes, and they never left the small plastic table—perhaps he was counting the decades worth of stained coffee rings. Shandon's small mop of brown hair almost drooped, as if wilting under the pale halogens flickering along the ceiling. Had his frame always looked so gaunt? Marla had seen enough prisoners to hardly consider three months, even in a maximum security facility like the Mesopolopolis Penal Dome, sufficient to denude a person's body quite so much. Then again, the first three months were always the hardest . . . .

"Look, you can't possibly like your living arrangements, and if you go to trial next week like this, they won't change for a very, very long time. Let's at least review the details of the case, ok?"

Shandon's nose twitched slightly. Marla settled for that as a sign.

"You commanded the *Santa Maria* on a geological study mission to Europa. Three man crew, fairly low profile—that moon's been landed on twice before. Didn't even make the evening newsbytes."

At least, not at first, Marla added silently.

"You began drilling at Rhadamanthus Planum for subterranean water samples."

"Now here," Marla said, "is where things get sketchy. Sensor logs register an explosion. Your two crewmates, Lieutenants Michelis and Al Awadi, killed by electrocution. You radio in a report that their deaths are `under investigation,' and finally conclude `conduit malfunction in the drilling mechanism.' Of course, you left the drill on Europa, and all the maintenance logs have somehow been wiped— due to the explosion, you say."

Marla sighed, pushing back a persistent forelock of black hair that had broken loose from her bun. "I've got to tell you, the State will eat you for breakfast unless you come up with something pretty spectacular."

Shandon's shoulders heaved slightly. He remained silent.

Marla tapped her unpainted fingernails against the plastic table between them. "Now, you have no prior criminal record, not even a speeding ticket."

The media wouldn't care, of course. "It's always the ones you least suspect," they'd say. She could see the headlines now: *Are our tax dollars sending homicidal lunatics into space?* Ever since last year's Metahuman Services Expansion Act created three new Herotowns in the Territories, the Forum had been on the lookout for programs from which to make cuts.

"You had no motive," she continued speaking into the silence. "Maybe, maybe, that's all that'll keep you from a Murder charge. I might be able to give you criminal negligence. That's fifty years, Commander. I can't even guarantee that, though, unless you can give me something. Anything."

Silence. Ok, time for something different.

"It's not just you on the line here," she darkened. "The corporate sponsors are already talking about pulling their investments from the Europa project. Several corporations are getting more cautious about space in general. They don't want the liability. Michelis and Al Awadi's families are already suing the Space Exploration Corps for wrongful death. The SEC's put a temporary halt to all new missions.

"Commander, you might single-handedly derail the entire space program here. I can't—"

She bit her tongue. How had that slipped out?"

"*You* can't," she began again, "let that happen. You can't."

Marla's wide blue eyes swept Shandon like searchlights. "Please," she whispered.

Shandon remained silent.

Sighing, Marla left the room. The guard buzzed her out, and for a moment she wondered if she had taken a wrong turn, if someone had replaced the prison's dull gray wall with a dark cobalt blue one. Then she realized she was staring at someone's massive torso.

Marla craned upwards, following the muscular neckline and jutting chin, all the way to seven feet high, where two onyx eyes shimmered beneath a yellow visor. Lightning bolt wing-tips topped off the helmet, their tips nearly scraping the hallway ceiling.

"Oh, excuse me," she mumbled, trying to slink around, forgetting that she was wearing a business suit and that lawyers weren't supposed to slink. But then, members of the Superior Squad had a way of making anyone feel like a criminal around them. Particularly Thunderbolt.

"I wanted to speak with you, counselor," the hero's voice echoed like his namesake, each consonant a staccato pound at Marla's eardrums. The voice itself seemed to crackle with electricity, giving her clothes a static bounce with each syllable.

Marla drew herself up, arms crossed defensively before her, wishing she could put them to her ears. She hoped this conversation was short.

"Shandon's not just a murderer, he's a coward."

"A jury will decide that, Mister . . . ah . . . Thunderbolt." Why did her voice sound so tiny?

"You know he hid out in Superion City on the moon for weeks until I caught him. He then had the audacity to seek asylum." Something like a chuckle bubbled up in Thunderbolt's throat. It sounded more like a busted gasket. "Asylum, from Captain Omega."

Marla didn't need to ask why it wasn't granted. No normal humans lived in Superion City.

"The criminal element is always cowardly," said Thunderbolt. "They always think they can escape justice if they run fast enough, if they hide behind a big enough rock . . . or lawyer."

Goosepimples made their way across Marla's back. Despite herself, she glanced left and right, to the guards. As if they even mattered—what could two little men with handguns do to someone like Thunderbolt, who could juggle tow trucks and electrocute a man fifty feet away? It didn't seem fair at all. It didn't seem like justice. What *did* this man in yellow spandex know about justice, other than might making right? Supers from Superion City were all like that, Marla had been told. They're different from the Supers back on Earth, in Herotowns. Marla never believed that until she met a few.

"Commander Shandon will get a fair trial." Marla tried to stand her ground, but instead her voice peeped like a schoolgirl's. "He's entitled to that, like everyone else."

Thunderbolt snorted, and Marla detected the faint smell of ozone. "Captain Omega has decided that Superion City will launch its own investigation of this matter."

"The State has already launched robotic probes towards Europa to gather data—"

"In case you've forgotten," Thunderbolt spoke over her, as it was so easy for him to do, "Superion City is a sovereign power, free of the influence of any terrestrial government—including your State. Furthermore, we have the technology to reach to Europa weeks before your probes arrive. We will conduct our own investigation to acquire the proof necessary for his conviction in this . . . fair trial you say he is due."

Or, failing in that, manufacture it? Part of Marla wanted to squirm away and run, and part of her, like a cat backed against a wall, wanted to hiss and spit and fight. It was a natural reflex, like when she saw a snake. This wasn't a human in front of her. Thunderbolt's eyes were glowing, for pity's sake. He lived on the moon.

Why would some alien thing from the moon care so much about the fate of a single, normal human accused of murdering two other normal humans? She wanted to ask what his motives were, his interests . . . but this was not a courtroom, not a cross-examination. He was seven feet tall and had her squeezed up against a wall.

Then, just as capriciously as he had cornered her, he turned and strode down the hallway. Marla heard the guards a few feet away echo her own sigh of relief.

"Damned Supers," one of them said. ""If you ask me, the Lee Act didn't go far enough. If Trinity didn't teach us you can't trust them, what will?"

"We should just nuke that moonbase of theirs," said the other. "It can't help but give the ones in Herotowns ideas."

Giving people ideas . . . thought Marla. Maybe that was it. Maybe that was why Thunderbolt was so angry. Normal humans having the audacity to build machines so they could fly alongside Supers, who could do it naturally. Soaring into space, landing, heaven forfend, on their precious moonbase.

That was what the space program was all about, after all. Space was still a place where normal humans could be heroes. Normal humans needed normal heroes. Heroes like astronauts. Even astronauts like Shandon.

Commander Neville Shandon, first human to walk on Ganymede, Gold Phoenix medal recipient for bravery in the Battle of Annihilus Bay, following the Trinity disaster. Heroism couldn't be allowed to die that easily.

"I'm going to get him off the hook," Marla told the guards, who stared at her, puzzled. She didn't care. She was going to get Shandon off. She only wished she had the slightest idea how.

"When the First Heroic Age dawned half a century ago, visionaries proclaimed that the police would soon become superfluous and obsolete, in the same way that the dawn of the computer was supposed to eliminate books and pocket calculators. Ironically, new advances often tend to reveal the heretofore unappreciated value of their tried-and-true antecedents . . . "

—President Augustus Lee, *Mending the Breach*

GAYLE

Kevin's Place wasn't so much a "place" as a pit, a hole someone had dug into the reluctant concrete of Downtown, reinforced with some steel beams and girders, then decorated with fluorescent lights and reflective streamers. Gayle squinted and wished for Noctyrne's "vampiric" night vision (ahem—Class A-1 perceptive enhancement). If this was how well-lit the club was with all the lights on, she was amazed anyone could dance without smacking into six other people with the lights dimmed. Judging from the flesh-revealing outfits of the patrons behind the police tape, maybe that was the point.

The team let George as GAP take the vanguard, as always. It spoke highly of George's skills in diplomacy when he could still express himself eloquently when encased within an eight foot tall metal battlesuit. Or maybe it was just that no one argued with him.

Of course, George's life hadn't always been like that. Gayle remembered meeting him at age ten, when he was an awkward twiggy thing and she was an angry twiggy thing, angry with good reasons. When the Relocation forced Gayle's family to move to Herotown, and the debt from her mother's funeral expenses had forced her father and her to live in Desperation Flats, ten year old Gayle made a promise to herself that, although she would consent to go to the stupid "super-school" and eat the disgusting "Trinity foods," she would never, ever grow to like this walled-in section of streets and overgrown greenery claiming to be parks, and would certainly never talk to any of the freaky creatures who lived there. The Lee Act, which forced so much on her, didn't force her to do that.

So she walked silently through hallways of the school building (actually a barely refurbished bunker that had, years ago, housed support troops for the Battle of Annihilus Bay), learning how you didn't even need invisibility power to vanish. She was smarter, quicker, and quieter than almost anyone else there, so she escaped notice, which was fine. All of the lessons the teachers gave her had been covered positively years ago back in her old school, so the work wasn't a problem. The worst part was finding something to do.

Watching George finally became her favorite pastime, and that was only because she couldn't figure him out. Why couldn't he have tied his shoes with laces instead of using those weird magnetic metal straps that his dad invented? And those stupid baggy silver jumpsuit pants that made him look like a radiation diver from the Trinity Disaster salvage teams! She almost couldn't blame the others for making fun of him as he sat there oblivious to the first snow of the year, covering the jagged scrap-piles metal and wood with a thick layer of black cushioning that the kids always used to play "king of the hill."

During her first few days at school, Gayle had tried to play, but of course she was a girl, and what's more, didn't have a reliable superpower (class A-5V, and that one letter suffix, V for "variable," made all the difference). They wouldn't let her play, and she quickly stopped asking. But George? What was his problem? Those goofy gadgets of his could probably let him fight as well as anyone else.

Gayle would often sit on a tire or in the shadow of the schoolyard's one tree and do her homework, occasionally looking up to see which ragamuffins were pounding, clawing, or laser-blasting their fellows this moment. They all ran amok like little rabid squirrels, and even Gayle admitted a guilty inner rush when one or another would ascend and wave the mottled rag that served as the victory flag. But George didn't play. He walked around in circles by himself and took notes, and Gayle soon found his wandering paths more interesting to watch.

Not that she liked him, of course. And he had no one to blame but himself, when on a perfectly roaring winter day, when everyone else tossed their chores aside to play, he stayed inside with his books. Gayle had watched him, seen the white pages reflected in George's coal black eyes as they communed with him in their secret language, watched as he drew traces in the snow of some formula or other. Who did George think he was? Why wasn't he satisfied with snow forts and ice balls?

He would draw the occasional crowd of onlookers, who, when they grew bored of onlooking, would jeer, and when jeering ceased to satisfy them, they would trample his snow diagrams, steal and shred his notebooks, break his slide rules over their knees, and shove him to the ground. But he never cried. He never complained. He just picked up the pieces and began again.

It wasn't until the day of the big fight that Gayle really grew to know the real George William Snordwell, and if she hadn't taken so long to actually realize the implications, if her Waley hadn't come along before that happened, then maybe . . . maybe . . .

The flashlight of the police officer outside Kevin's Place jarred Gayle back to the present.

"I've never heard of the Friday Knights," the officer on duty shook his head. "But your papers check out, so someone must want you here."

Gayle judged the man's age to be less than her own—he probably wasn't old enough to remember the days when police were grateful when anyone with a cape and tights swooped down to help them. Nowadays, anyone in a cape and tights who swooped down without the proper authorization tended to get shot. Even those who had permission got dirty looks.

Of course, heroes still did what heroes did. For Gayle and her friends, anyway, refraining from Superheroing just because of the Lee Act would be like an artist giving up painting just because of a high tax on canvas and acrylics. No, you could still be a superhero these days—burning buildings still needed extinguishing, drug kingpins still needed overthrowing, and of course, most supervillians didn't care any more about the Lee Act than they did the more liberal laws that preceded it. Oh yes, you could still be a superhero. You just had to sign a lot of forms in triplicate. And never, ever, make a mistake.

The officer lifted the yellow cordon tape, and GAP stared for a moment before taking a giant stride *over* it.

Combat Wombat followed, snarling once for good measure and looking immensely satisfied with himself when the officer inched away, hand falling instinctively to his sidearm. Gayle went next, tipping the brim of her hat, smiling an apology. Noctyrne slunk back into the shadows and vanished—she would explore on her own, as she always did.

"Detective Roland," GAP's synthesized voice called over to a figure squatting by the DJ's station.

The figure turned, and Gayle felt her breath catch. If Heaven came in brown, Detective Roland was it. Brown hair (neatly combed, ruffled *just* enough for that quietly rugged look), brown eyes, brown suit, brown tie . . . brown bag lunch in his hand. Wasn't it a little late for lunch, or even dinner, for that matter?

Nothing specific screamed "attractive" in his features—his nose seemed blunted, if anything, his cheeks slightly wan and drawn, his right eye prone to some sort of tic. But something about the way he stood, the way he gestured, the way he spoke . . . . was it confidence? Was it poise?

Was it of any import? Focus, Gayle. Thinking about George earlier must have ignited all the wrong neurotransmitters (it was all just neurotransmitters, right, and hormones? Yes, easily controllable). Focus on the crime scene. Such as it was.

Confetti littered the floor, half-filled beer glasses populated the chairs and bar tops, spills in various colors pooled on the floor, the origins of which Gayle chose not to speculate on. And this was only after a few hours of operation—the cops had shut the place down at 1 AM.

There, seated between stereo-mixers, ringed by the lights from their console, sat the young woman Detective Roland was asking questions. She couldn't have been more than twenty, dark hair coiled into ringlets that flopped like hastily dumped spaghetti off her scalp. Gayle had seen assault victims before, and this one wore none of the blankness, the shock, the distance from reality. In fact, she looked more annoyed than anything else.

"What, more questions? Am I on *Hidden Camera* or something?"

"Ma'am," Detective Roland held up a hand, his voice struggling like a frustrated schoolteacher's, "if you could please just bear with me a few moments—"

GAP suddenly caught his attention, and Roland thrust himself forward.

"Who the hell are you people?" the Detective demanded. Hmm, he had guts, too. Not everyone told off a hulking robot monster. "I didn't call for any backup."

"My name is GAP. I lead the Friday Knights. We're here to investigate the potential superhuman nature of the crime."

"Spirit abooove," the girl rolled her eyes, doe-like if deer ever used methamphetamines, "it was just a kiss. Losers come up to you all the time in clubs. You shove them away and you keep dancing. I don't see what the big deal is—"

"According to the security tapes," said Roland, "you entered some sort of trance the moment the perpetrator approached you, and remained in that state throughout the, ah, period of physical contact, as well as the next five minutes. When the bouncers approached him, he apparently entranced them in the same manner."

"Well, then, the bouncers here aren't worth splen, that's all," said the girl, tugging her micro-short skirt down past her upper thigh in frustration. "Can I go now?"

"If I might for a moment?" GAP beckoned.

Roland studied GAP, looked him up and down with tired eyes that Gayle wasn't sure actually saw anything in the dim light. Whatever he saw or didn't see, it must have been enough.

"What the hell," Roland sighed, stepping aside. "Be my guest. Maybe you'll have more luck."

"Good evening, citizen," GAP called out, approaching the detective, and Gayle took a step back, embarrassed, wanting to melt into the greasy floor.

Where were Roland's eyes? On Combat Wombat, naturally. Craig was off sniffing empty drink containers, downing the contents of any partially full ones he found. Well, what did Gayle expect? He *was* part animal, and he seemed immune to hangovers. But still, it was a pretty poor showing in front of the detective—

The detective. Roland's gaze had finally landed on her. Gayle smiled weakly, then remembered she was on duty, darkened her face, and nodded with professional solemnity. Roland had already turned away. What the hell was that? Since when had she become the invisible woman?

Oh. GAP was scanning. Yes, that usually caught someone's attention. Beams of multicolored light flashed across the face of the young woman in the chair, up and down the curves of her lycra clad body, across the dance hall to the floor below.

"Now wait," Roland began, "just what are you—"

"Done," said GAP. "Thank you for your cooperation."

"I didn't do anything," the girl scowled.

GAP turned to Gayle and Roland. "My scanners definitely detect residual psychoempathic reverberations."

"Say again?"

"Some telepath's given her the workover, Detective," Gayle stepped in.

"Hold on," Roland kept his back to her, still talking to GAP—the nerve of him!—"You mean to tell me that by flashing multicolored lights, you can tell that some . . . mind reader . . . worked some mental mumbo jumbo on her?"

"Yes," said GAP, but Gayle found her attention being drawn to the whispers of two of the uniformed policemen behind them. They were staring at Combat Wombat. One of them pointed and said, "Isn't that . . . you know . . . . one of *his* relatives?"

Gayle snapped around. She had to intercept this before Craig did—at least, if she wanted to avoid blood.

"I assume, officers," she shot the sharpest daggers she could their way (better than Craig's sharp claws!), "that you're referring to Combat Wombat being the nephew of Twister. When last I checked, that wasn't a crime."

"No," said one of the cops, sounding not quite sure.

"H-hey," said the other cop, hands raised in a conciliatory gesture, "we don't mean no harm, lady. A fellah can't choose his family. Why, I bet he was probably even proud to call Twister his uncle, before . . . before . . ."

No one ever had to finish that sentence. Until Twister went bad, turned traitor, held the Trinity nuclear plant hostage. The State refused to accede to his demands, and the rest of his team, the Amazing Elite, rushed in to try and stop him—he blew up the plant, along with half of the southern seaboard. Hundreds of thousands died, most of the Amazing Elite included. Only two members survived—Twister himself, who had an escape route all along . . . and Captain Omega. Twister fled to Annihilus Bay, the so-called supervillian colony. Omega rallied all the superheroes he could find, but it was the world's armed forces that really decided the day.

Annihilus Bay finally proved that all the warring factions of humanity could indeed come together against a common threat—superhumans. The battle lasted six days, and on the seventh, Twister was dead at Omega's hands, one more body amidst a pile of over two hundred superhuman corpses, "heroes" and "villains" alike. In the aftermath, of course, came the Lee Act, the Relocations, the Herotowns . . .

The clarion of GAP's synthesized voice called out. "Gal Friday, Combat Wombat, to me. I've tagged the mental emanations, and the trail's still warm."

"Hey wait," Detective Roland was calling, and Gayle took full, guilty pleasure in seeing him in the lurch. Arrogant pig. No, that was too harsh. Maybe he was stressed, maybe he was dealing with—

"Trouble," Noctyrne's voice came from nowhere, and both the Detective and the girl jumped.

The final member of the team did not so much walk as slink out of the darkness, long slender legs cutting a swath through the smoky air. Her eyes glowed crimson through black eyemask on her face.

"I've got a scent. Buzz is here."

"What? Who? Lady, you can't just walk in here like that," Roland approached. "Are you part of this team, too?"

"Why do you ask, Detective?" Noctyrne's voice warbled melodiously. "Looking for a date?" With each word, fluorescent light glinted off the tiny fangs in her mouth. When Roland saw them, he took a step back.

"No, Ma'am." He recovered quite nicely, and the mercury in Gayle's opinion thermometer rose again slightly. "I'm trying to keep this crime scene from getting any more befuddled than it already is. Now, if you'll kindly take your flashing lights and bloodhound women away here, I've got a job to do."

"We share the same job, Detective." Gayle finally found her voice. "Just thought I'd remind you."

"Lady," Roland finally turned to meet her gaze, finally spoke to her. His teeth fell just a little uneven when they met. "As far as I'm concerned, your job is to protect the planet from evil death rays and zombie hordes. My job is to deal with the real, honest threats to the city, the stuff you people overlook when flying by. Capice?"

Someone may as well have punched Gayle in the gut. She opened her mouth, searching for breath, and felt lithe fingers brush over her shoulder.

"Let it go, Gal Friday," said Noctyrne. "We have bigger problems on our hands. Buzz is nearby. We can't just let him—"

"No," Gayle shook her off, straightening her posture, adjusting her fedora. "I want to say something first." She took a step forward. "You, Detective."

"Yeah?" Roland dropped his hands to his hips.

"You . . . you . . ."

The words all rushed Gayle at once. They jockeyed for position, begged her to lay into him, to tell about the years of hard work and sleepless nights she put into supercriminology school, of the ache in her feet from practice patrols, the rejection letters she'd received from every super team in the city . . . how she'd never seen a death ray or a zombie horde, or a 50 foot tall rampaging insect or even a gang of honest to goodness, old-school bank robbers. No, she'd rescued cats from trees and helped sandbag floods and once, once, broken up a riot over the new Captain Omega action figures, and felt pretty damned good about it all, too, because people had needed her and the Superior Squad sure as hell wouldn't have deigned to lend a hand. And every night she ate lettuce sandwiches and read by candlelight because she resisted taking any more money than absolutely necessary from the millionaire friend who had given her a job when no one else would take her, all because of this inane superpower of hers . . . and how she didn't, hadn't ever, and most likely would never, fly.

"I have nothing to say to you," Gayle said at last, shoulders sinking, and turned to join the team.

"Hmph," said Roland, "women." He then turned back to interrogating his witness.

Gayle should have stayed and argued, she knew, but suddenly found she had too much anger at herself to spare any for Roland. Why was she always attracted to men who infuriated her? What pheromone did they exude, and how did it entirely bypass the same mind that earned *summa cum laude* with bronze clusters from the University's Criminal Justice program five years ago? Two minutes, two minutes of actual interaction with Roland, had revealed his jerk nature, and yet those first few instants seeing him all cloaked in brown had snagged her.

Beer goggles, Craig would say, except Gayle didn't drink. Maybe she should start.

"Buzz is nearby," the nostrils of Noctyrne's perfectly shaped nose fluttered as the four heroes left the club and took to the streets beyond. "I'd smell his cologne-drenched ass anywhere."

"Now, Dear," said GAP, scanning beams sweeping the adjoining alleyways, "I'm sure even Buzz doesn't wear cologne there."

"He will by the time *I'm* done with him," Combat Wombat snarled, then paused, realizing that hadn't made a whole lot of sense.

Gayle produced a flashlight from the folds of her trenchcoat and held it overhand, police style, sweeping the streets. Grime and detritus coated the sidewalks of Downtown, the same as in the Herotown that adjoined it. If anything, there seemed to be more soda cans, more plastic wrappers, more abandoned tire rims and torn newspaper pages. If you dropped someone down to street level in any of the Downtown boroughs, Gayle wondered, could they tell the difference?

"Got something," said GAP. "Ten meters and closing . . . seven meters . . . three meters . . ."

"Gotcha!" a voice like leather rubbing against a washboard careened out of the night, followed by the soft thud of flesh against metal. The natural human instinct, at least for Gayle, was to expect a shout of pain from owner of the flesh. But as the Church of Humanity pamphlets were quick to remind, there was nothing natural or human about people like Buzz.

A male figure stood with one leg perched on each of GAP's giant metal shoulders, hands up in a what was most likely a fake martial arts stance (Gayle knew Kung Fu, Tae Kwan Do, Jujitsu, and Chung do Quan—Buzz wasn't emulating any of them). His black hair (dyed, Gayle knew), black pants, black undershirt, black blazer, and opaque sunglasses would have camouflaged the man completely if not for the streetlamp haze, light which reflected off Buzz's ivory belt buckle and perfectly white teeth, bared in the most devilish of smiles.

"Heyyy, gang," he cried, "miss me? Miss me? Now you wanna kiss me?"

"I'll kiss you all right," Combat Wombat crouched, taking the bait—Gayle could have smacked him—coiling his legs and launching himself up, up towards Buzz. Or rather, towards where Buzz *used* to be. Quicker than Gayle's eye could follow, Buzz leapt off GAP's shoulders, while Combat Wombat's own jump led him crashing into the robot-man's giant frame. Muttering curses, Craig slid down the metal surface like a character in a cartoon show, and GAP wobbled, pinwheeling his arms, desperately trying not to fall over.

"Aww, I can't resist," Buzz called from somewhere, and the next thing Gayle saw, he flung himself, shoulder first, into the two heroes, providing the extra push to send them both clattering to the ground.

"Fall down, go boom!" he cackled. "Oooh, ain't I a stinker?"

Gayle felt her breath catch—Craig's skin and bones were tougher than a normal human's, to be sure, but if two tons of George's suit fell on him . . .

"You guys never change," Buzz sighed. "You take yourselves soooo seriously." He shifted his weight, balancing in an exaggerated karate crane posture. Then something in his face darkened. "As much as

I'm enjoying this reunion, we need to talk. There's some real serious splen going down right now."

"Yeah," Noctyrne approached, "and you're gonna be hip deep in it."

"For once, I'm serious, Naomi," he said. "The guy you're after . . . he's involved something serious. You been reading the papers? The Shandon Space Murder trial? Something intense is going down between the headlines, even steamier than what went on between you and me."

Noctyrne screeched, throwing her arms wide. A thin membrane stretched from her slender limbs to her hourglass figure, billowing into wings. Unseen winds picked her up off the ground up into the shadows where Gayle lost sight of her. Then down, down in a dive that set nearby building awnings flapping with the force of her speed.

But Buzz, his M-4 agility making him impossibly faster, seized hold of her arms as she strafed him, then swung, using her momentum against her. Noctyrne barely had time to shriek in frustration.

"That eager to be back in my arms again?"

"Only . . . to . . . tear . . . you . . . . apart . . ."

"Ooh, wound me," Buzz made kissing noises.

"I . . . will . . . the . . . second . . . you . . . let . . . . me . . . . go!"

"Anything you say," said Buzz, and released her, sending her spinning in uncontrolled flight until she crashed through the window of a nearby storefront. Glass flew everywhere, forcing Gayle to shield her face with a trenchcoated arm. Alarm bells sounded everywhere. Cops were just around the corner, back at the club. This would not look good.

"Oh, baby, baby. This didn't go like I planned at all."

"What?" Gayle approached cautiously. "You had planned a different brand of chaos entirely? Do you even have a permit to be here?"

"*Permit?*" Buzz shook his head. "Gayle, you're thinking about permits? This is much, much bigger."

"A shame I can't stay to dance with you too," Buzz was suddenly right beside her, one arm slung around her shoulder, the other resting meditatively on a lamppost. He gave her a quick kiss on the cheek, then darted away before Gayle's fist could even begin to rise.

As she punched air, Gayle whirled around, not knowing where to turn first. Across the street, Noctyrne could have been hurt by all that glass. A few meters away, GAP and Combat Wombat were still untangling themselves. Footsteps from behind meant the police were coming to investigate. And Buzz . . . Buzz . . .

"I'll find you again!"

Gayle heard his voice's distant echo as she saw him receding into the distance, scaling the wall of an apartment building as if his hands had suction cups.

Well, Gayle had a few tricks of her own. Drawing a small pistol from the holster inside her coat, she took aim and fired.

"Drop it!" came a voice from behind. Roland's. Terrific.

"It's not lethal," Gayle raised her hands, letting the gun droop and fall to the ground with a clatter. "It's not even a gun."

"Sure looks like one to me, sister," Roland approached, his own weapon drawn, flanked by two uniformed patrolmen, neither of whom looked very accommodating.

"It launches homing devices," said Gayle. "Microscopically small. If I managed to tag Buzz, we can follow his moves."

"Tag who?"

"Buzz," said Gayle as Roland approached, his nearness casting off the smell of pizza and denim. Eew. She had been attracted to this?

"I don't see anyone here but you and your troublemaking friends," said the detective. "Now, hands behind your back."

"What?" cried Gayle. "I'm under arrest? For what?"

"Property damage," he chucked a finger at the shop across the street where one of the patrolmen was already drawing near. "Disturbing the peace."

"That was all Buzz's doing," said Gayle. "He's an ex-hero, now a rogue . . . he's probably here without—"

She stopped herself. Without authorization? Was she about to turn the Peace Officers onto Buzz's tail? The man was a jerk, and deserved a good slap in the face, but Gayle wouldn't wish a Bloodhound Gang on anyone, even Buzz.

"Detective!" GAP's synthesized voice rose up, even as his body flailed helplessly on the ground, an upturned tortoise—no one had helped him up after all this time? "We were attempting to apprehend a rogue when he got the better of us. I can give you the personal assurances that our financier, George William Snordwell III, will reimburse the city and private property owners for any and all damages."

"Besides," Combat Wombat was suddenly behind Roland, claws drawn, pointed at the detective's neck, "you wouldn't want things to get ugly here . . . would you?"

Great, Gayle sighed to herself. *Just as things were looking up . . .*

"Knock it off, Combat Wombat," Noctyrne's voice said weakly. The patrolman had returned, escorting her as she walked in a somewhat crooked gait, peeling glass out of her hair with one hand while shaking off the officer's grip on her other one. "It's time to go home."

"Not so fast," said Roland. "I have a load of questions for—"

Enough.

"Detective," Gayle drew herself up to her full height, "we are well within our rights under the Lee Act to operate in this borough and pursue superhuman criminals who pose an active threat the body public. GAP's sensor logs recorded the whole thing—we were attacked and defended ourselves, and might even have apprehended the perpetrator had your men not intervened. Which places you, I might add, in violation of statute nine of the Lee Act, paragraph 6, stating *local law enforcement shall assist if possible, but above all in no way hamper the operations of registered superhero teams operating within their rights.*"

Gayle desperately needed to take a breath, but didn't want to give the Detective a second's pause . . . his mouth kept half-opening at every comma to try and interject. "Now unless you want me to recite the possible penalties for noncompliance, up to and including revocation of your badge and thirty days incarceration, I suggest you let us on our way."

Her chest heaving, Gayle finally stopped, making vain attempts to collect herself.

"Yeah," said Combat Wombat, pulling his claws in and giving Roland a very, very strong pat on the shoulder, "what she said. Now get lost."

Roland shook his head, eyes slightly wider, forehead a little more creased. He looked at Gayle as if for the first time.

"I'm impressed," the detective finally said, holstering his weapon. "What's your power, lady? Super-intelligence?"

Then the most amazing thing happened. Detective Roland smiled.

Gayle blinked. She searched for words, finally settling upon, "Wouldn't you like to know?"

Then, to hide the red blush of embarrassment spreading across her face, she turned away. "Come on, Combat Wombat, Noctyrne. Let's get GAP righted and get the hell out of here. I think I managed to plant a tracer on Buzz. He referred to `the guy we're after,' which suggests he knows something about the perp."

"Unless that's just a lie to cover his rear," said Noctyrne. "For all we know, he's the one responsible for the assault at the club. He's certainly sleazy enough."

"Not his style," said Gayle. "He doesn't have mind control, and doesn't need it. He'd wine and dine them first."

Friendship kept her from adding *as you should know*, she added silently. She probably shouldn't have even said that much. Noctyrne was blushing already, and she was sure George was shifting uncomfortably in his suit.

"Buzz is involved somehow," GAP said as the others helped him rise to his mighty feet. "Let's get on his trail before it grows cold."

Gayle whistled, and the Stallion, operating under autopilot, drove up to meet them. As they piled in, Detective Roland trotted up to the side window.

"I don't think I caught your name," he called to Gayle.

She turned in her seat, touching the brim of her fedora. "Gal Friday," she said, although she wasn't sure he could hear her through the glass. It was just as well. Part of her wanted to blurt out her phone number. Another part wanted to smack him, and a third part wanted to smack herself.

Then the Stallion roared like its namesake, and Roland receded into the blackness behind them.

INTERLUDE

"The doctor's attaché, Ehat, was here," said Thunderbolt, perched atop a skyscraper overlooking Downtown, below which Kevin's place glittered with blue and red sparks of ant-sized police cruisers. "We were too late again."

"But we're getting closer."

"At least Shandon is secure. I saw to that earlier. If we need him, we know where to find him."

"Ehat's beginning to attract attention," said the bald man beside him. "Local law enforcement is on to him."

"Fine, Cerebellum. All the better. If they catch him for us, Mayor Ironheart can extradite—"

"Don't be naïve, Sarah," said Thunderbolt. "They won't catch him. They can't. They're Normals."

"Not just Normals anymore. There were other supers on the scene tonight."

"Who were they?"

"Metahumanics Commission registry has files on the individuals," said Cerebellum. "Herotown ledgers have them registered under the team name `The Friday Knights.' Strictly small time. I'm sure they have no idea what's going on."

"Keep an eye on them," said Thunderbolt. "Or a brain. Or whatever."

"Any chance they can do our work for us?"

"Small timers like them? Doubtful. But if they do, better to play it safe, take some precautions."

"Such as?"

"Talk to the President. Hint at what's at stake, ask for authorization and support."

Sarah frowned, drawing her sweeping silver wings close to her body. "I thought we didn't want to involve him."

"He already knows enough to want to know more. That's our hook. He'll cooperate, if only to learn."

"Don't underestimate him," said Cerebellum. "Captain Omega says that was our biggest mistake years ago, underestimating him when we was just a Senator in the Forum. Look what's happened to the world since."

"You're twisting his words. He didn't mean it like that."

"It doesn't matter anyway," said Thunderbolt. "Once we recover Ehat, President Lee won't be a problem ever again."

Sarah Spenser, aka the Silver Peregrine, was no small woman. Still, turning to Thunderbolt, she needed to look up a full eight inches into his eyes. After a moment she turned away, cast her gaze downward to the insect lights below.

"You scare me a little when you speak like that, Thomas."

"Look around you, Sarah," he said softly. "I mean, really look. The alternative should scare you more."

The trio retreated into the darkness.

Since the Superhuman Question and the current environmental crisis with post-Trinity radioactivity are so related, it makes perfect sense for the State to use a singular policy for dealing with both: one of containment.

—Senator Augustus Lee, proposing the Lee Act before the Forum

GAYLE

"Dammit. Trail's cold. Buzz must have felt the tracer and destroyed it."

"If he wanted to contact us, why make it tough for us to follow?"

Gayle paced the rooftop, trying to fight the twitch in her fingers. She hated standing on top of skyscrapers, and at two dozen stories, this building hardly even qualified. A glance to the horizon showed the Uptown Mesopolopolian skyline reaching high and vanishing amongst the clouds. Gayle didn't like looking up, but it was better than looking down.

Herotown was invisible from here. Skyscrapers blocked all view of those walls and gates which seemed so tall and imposingly real from within. *Not only can't the Normals see us, they can't even see the walls that keep them from seeing us.* Zeppelins floated lazily overhead, ducking in and out of the tallest of Mesopolopolis' structures. The red and blue running lights of the airships winked and blinked at intervals, as if exchanging some juicy secret gossip known only to those who dwelled amongst the clouds.

Gayle closed her eyes, then filled the black canvas of her eyelids with images from her college days. Mesopolopolis University stood proudly in the very heart of Uptown, and Gayle stood even prouder along the banks of the Phoenix River with notebook in hand as joggers and rollerskaters breezed by her, followed by trotting dogs, rolling baby carriages, and their trotting, rolling, or wheezing owners. She would search both dogs and baby faces for resemblance to their adult chaperones, and laugh to no one in particular when she found it. Gayle never walked alongside anyone. Who was there to walk with?

She would curl up beneath an artificial tree in the Model Gardens and study her briefs, watch the crew team slide across the waters of the Phoenix, pick out familiar commuters at the monorail station platform who never realized they were being observed. On daring days she would explore the subway tunnels, and on maudlin days she would stroll slowly through the art museums. Throngs of people always surrounded her, the infamous Mesopolopolian hordes, but they existed only at her sufferance. She could choose isolated individuals and zoom in on them, shutting out all other stimuli to track her quarry's path. Alternately, she could wipe the entire mob from existence, render the bodies invisible and stare at the skyscrapers beyond. The city was hers—it obeyed her will through an unspoken and very secret compact. At least, until graduation.

Now, far from welcoming her with the assurances of a long-lost lover, the City of her college days now six years past seemed to have forgotten her name. The wind whipped her, the jutting buildings turned their backs, and she yearned to tell them it wasn't her fault, that the law had made her return to Herotown upon graduation . . . but all she got in return from her mental pleas was another wave of vertiginous nausea.

"No heat signatures," said GAP, scanning, "but then, Buzz never did leave them. Amazing, given all the hot air he puts out."

Noctyrne made some noise that might have been a grunt of agreement. Her gaze had rested anywhere but on GAP ever since Buzz made his appearance. Gayle could empathize.

You never do get over them, no matter how infuriating they may be. If that were Waley we had met back there, instead of Buzz . . . you might have to institutionalize me.

No, some inner voice told her, *you're stronger than that.* But she didn't feel very strong, not with the nausea of vertigo pulling at her guts every time she took a step across the rooftop.

Craig wandered up and down the slate, pausing every few feet to punch a very unforgiving brick outcropping. "Well, this has been a real productive use of time. What about our supposed case of the hypno-kisser?"

"I don't know," said Gayle. "Buzz made some vague claims about some larger issue he needed to tell us about."

"Then why didn't he stick around?"

Why did they expect Gayle to know? "Oh, Buzz is probably a dead end anyway. Let's go back to tracking the mental emanations."

In her heart of hearts, Gayle didn't know what to believe about Buzz, but anything that got them off this Spirit-forsaken roof seemed worthwhile.

The Stallion drove through the silent streets, headlights sweeping the blackness for clues and finding only a perpetual wall of dark, ever just beyond reach. Yet Mesopolopolis proper, even Downtown, even at this hour, was alive. Cyclists flashed passing signals to one another, pedestrians shuffled back and forth within the cones of light that cradled them all along the sidewalk. A few minutes earlier, Gayle had watched an ambulance race by, with autos rushing to take advantage of the path left by its wake, forming a tail like a Chinese Dragon behind the emergency vehicle.

There was something almost playful about the entire scene, about automobiles in general, jockeying about in their restricted lanes while the rest of the world passed by on cycles or whisked along above on the monorail. Automobiles played out their own little dramas in their tightly confined world, as did the occupants within them. As happened so often, Gayle felt as if she were watching the team from outside the Stallion looking in, one more metal-encased tableau among many.

"Telepathic emanations are notoriously difficult to track," George was explaining. "But we have Georgie Porgie's signature, now. All we need is for him to strike again . . ."

Noctyrne wasn't listening. She was staring at the windowglass. Did she ever wish she had a reflection? Gayle wondered. The wishes of superheroes were always surprisingly simple ones.

"You ok, Gayle?"

"Hrm?" It was Craig. Craig, of all people. Could wombats smell exhaustion?

"You look like a wreck."

That was Craig. Always delicate.

"It's well past midnight. I'm tired"

"Tired as if a grizzly had been chasing you, you mean."

Gayle shrugged. What was she supposed to say? *Yesterday marked my twenty—sixth birthday and I'm single, out of work, a practical charity case?*

"You want to hang out afterwards?" Craig pressed. "I've got a whole cooler full of beers, and I need some excuse to sip 'em slowly. Drinking's no fun when you have a super-metabolism. We could stay up late and play video games, or watch the new *When Animals Maul* video I bought. Come on, it'll be great!"

"That's ok, Craig," Gayle smiled weakly. "You save that video for when you meet the girl of your dreams. You don't deserve anything less for company."

Craig shrugged, unaffected. "Your loss, Big G."

"Say, Gayle," George piped up, saved her from having to return to her own thoughts, "you're the one with the degrees in supercriminology. What might motivate a telepathic criminal to hypnotize women, kiss them, and run?"

Degrees in supercriminology. Honors and citations. For all the good it's done me . . .

"Super powers or no, a sex offender is a sex offender. Feelings of inadequacy, isolation, frustration in areas of life where they don't have control . . . super powers only make it easier to act on one's control fantasies towards others."

"Even just to kiss them?"

Craig shrugged. "Maybe that's all he needs. Maybe he gets off on just that."

"I don't know," said Gayle. "I watched those video tapes. The perpetrator seemed to be searching the crowd pretty intently, as if he was trying to find a very specific target. I think he was looking for something . . . and maybe he ran off after a kiss when he realized he hadn't found it."

"What could he be looking for?" asked George.

"Tongue rings?" Craig suggested.

Gayle was too tired even to punch him.

They drove for another two hours before George reluctantly declared the trail cold. Then it took another hour for them to get back to the gates of Herotown, twenty minutes for the Peace Officers to search them and their vehicle, and thirty more before Gayle stumbled back into her apartment and collapsed onto an unforgivingly stony mattress.

George had offered her the guest room at the Friday Fort, as he always did. Gayle refused. Her 12 by 12, one room apartment may have been cramped, but she had worked what little domestic magic she knew to make it home. An imitation oak desk nestled snugly in the corner, a real find at some tag sale last year, topped with a coffee mug brimming with pencils and pens. Several notebooks lay neatly stacked atop a detailed street map of Mesopolopolis, both Herotown and the city proper. The tattered magazines and food-stained plates were encroaching upon the desk and any other free surfaces in the room, despite Gayle's vigilance. The fight against entropy was always an uphill battle.

In the opposite corner, father's easy chair, brown and fuzzy and smelling of pipe smoke, nestled in like it owned the place. Her father had loved that chair so much that he insisted on taking it with them when the Relocation came. A lifetime's accumulation of furniture, ornaments, dishware, even most of the books, had to be abandoned, but he would be damned if that chair wasn't coming along.

Gayle was only nine at the time, but she remembered very clearly helping him heft the giant mossy thing up to the roof of the automobile and tying it down, while her mother looked on disapprovingly. Gayle's father had always been better with books than with his hands, and sure enough the ropes came undone mere seconds after they "secured" it. The chair began to slide down, and Gayle and her father scrambled first to one side of the auto, then the other, frantically trying to keep it from falling. Her mother had begun to laugh—the only time Gayle had remembered her laughing during the entire year following Trinity.

A picture of the three of them, taken during that year, rested on the bar of the gunmetal gray heating block that obnoxiously took up the third corner of the room. Given how seldom it functioned, Gayle felt comfortable in using it as a shelf for mementos. A small stuffed elephant, and of course, her diplomas from Mesopolopolis University, both undergraduate and graduate work, all rested atop a makeshift bookshelf composed of the first three volumes of *Scoper's Supercriminolgy*, a leather-bound edition of the Mesopolopolis Penal Codes, and, of course, Captain Omega's *Justice for All*.

Packed away under her bed was the complete set of the *Chronicles of Metahumanity*, another inheritance from her father. To open the proud, stiffly-bound tomes and flip through the laminated pages almost seemed sacrilege, but her father had always told her books were meant to be read. Still, despite all his dog-eared volumes, somehow he had kept these in pristine condition, as if recognizing a certain holiness about them. The ceiling of their "shrine," Gayle's twin bed on a trundle frame, folded up into a rather homely looking couch, with the aid of a reversible quilt for a seating spread. Cartoon badgers on one side, and a matronly floral pattern on the other. Gayle never entertained guests—she usually kept the badgers showing.

A small, squat space heater that looked like a miniature garbage can hummed beside Gayle's bed, providing decent warmth. The ugly but useful little thing doubled as a hot plate for cooking and was the only apartment gift she had ever accepted from George.

Gayle had bought the Skovakian fichus all on her own. Her window overlooked an alleyway whose most prominent feature was a seldom-emptied green dumpster, so she preferred to have something more pleasant to look at. The fichus, not content to stay and be the object of Gayle's windowtime gazing, had spread its thin, leafy cords all around the corners of the room, winding them around the doorframe, the lighting fixture, the nonfunctional heating block. Gayle had drawn the line at the bed—had she wanted to sleep in a jungle, she would have moved to Skovakia.

The plant's tendrils added to the claustrophobia, as the desk lay flush against the bed, the bed flush against the heating block, the heating block banged into the easy chair. Gayle never technically needed to touch her feet to the floor if she wanted to move anywhere in the room—she could just hop furniture, all the way to and from the heavy pseudowooden door and its multiple locks. No, the apartment was hardly spacious, but it was cozy. Moreover, it was hers. Without something to claim as her own, Gayle didn't feel entirely human. She almost never felt superhuman . . . except, of course, on Fridays.

It was not until 11:00 the next morning, when she rose with a characteristic aching back and an itchy pull at her costume, coupled with a soft curse for forgetting to undress last night, that she saw the telltale red light on her answering machine. Messages.

Some naive, schoolgirlish part of her heart hoped to hear a message from Detective Roland. Ha. Instead, her landlord's rough, metallic voice made various threats and imprecations if she came up with the rent late again. Gayle had never come up late with the rent. But then, her landlord's cyborg brain never had quite functioned correctly. He could be a very nice man when the kill-protocols weren't dominating his brain, and besides, those servos in his right hand made him absolutely invaluable when it came to fixing leaks and electrical shorts. Gayle was confident she would sort it out with him should the two meet in the hallway, even if she did have to run away for the first few minutes until his combat mode disengaged.

Her apartment lacked a shower, so, after her morning martial arts exercises, she simply threw on her civilian clothes and trudged down the rickety stairs to where the outside world awaited. By daylight, the streets of Herotown looked even bleaker than they did after nightfall. Shadowy outcroppings that hinted at gothic shapes were by day revealed to be little more than bare ledges, barren flagpoles, and torn awnings. Ten year old trucks plied the streets in the early morning, coughing diesel fumes and scattering pigeons that had flown over the gates. Still, life bloomed here, if you knew where to look. Most of the street vendors began setting up shop by eight, so by the time Gayle reached Sentinel Avenue, the full force of the Freakside Market was already winding down. Nevertheless, the multicolored flags flapped in the breeze alongside hanging lanterns, and the shouts of vendors competed with the clatter of bicycle bells, automobile horns, and, today, the sounds of a flute from a very persistent cornerside musician. Fat women with burly arms, sometimes four or more of them, proffered dubious looking fruits and vegetables, while a man with a minotaur head hawked fresh, prime cuts of beef. Who better to know?

"Gayle," purred a young, orange-skinned woman whose eyes looked at least ten years older than 19, which Gayle knew she was. "Here for wamba-melons? I save one for you. Green kind, with hard skin, just like you like."

"Morning's almost over, Cima," Gayle said jovially, "but I'll still take the melon. How much today?"

Cima juggled the melon between her hands. "Normally, 10 cubits. For you, Gayle, 8."

Gayle knew she could get wamba-melons from the Megamart for 5, but bought one from Cima anyway. She smacked it hard against the fire hydrant beside Cima's stand, dug her fingers into the crack of the skin, and pulled it open. Orange, juicy pulp, the color of Cima's skin, oozed out from the inside. Gayle licked it off her fingers and let her gaze wander to the newspaper dispenser, where the front page of the *Mesopolopolis Times* showed through the window.

*Superior Squad Foils Dr. Mellifluous' plans for Freezing Mesopolopolis * * * Skovakian Air Force hits targets in Central Bulravia: General Antikva confident that Victory over Irresponsible Government is Near * * * Shandon Space Murder Trial to Begin Next Week * * * Mayor Ironhold Promises "Tough Response" to Homeless Problem.*

Gayle was tempted to look inside to see if the assault at Kevin's Place made the news at all, but after blowing 8 cubits on the melon, she didn't feel like shelling out another 2 for the paper. Nevertheless, a "tsk" from behind meant Cima had caught her staring.

"Why you read that junk? We have perfect good paper right here. And I no mean the *Guardian*, either."

Of course not. The *Herotown Guardian,* "official" paper for the borough, was owned by Normals and consisted of little more than coupons and updates to the Living Codes.

"I just renewed my subscription to the *Spandex Scene* last month," said Gayle.

It would be nice if the paper actually came to her door every day, instead of every third or fourth, or on some occasions once a month. But that was to be expected. When she wanted news, she turned to the *Times,* just as she had every day since she was old enough to read. True, the *Times* didn't tell you when street carnivals and warehouse dancers were held in Herotown. The *Times* didn't reprint artwork from Supers, or publish their editorials. The *Spandex Scene* always gave her a bit of the lift in the morning, true, but Gayle could hardly call it a newspaper. She read it for the culture, to get the latest powerstunt team scores, or to shake her head in amusement at essays supposedly written by citizens of Superion City who offered bold, nonspecific promises for ending the gated system, and news reporting laced with pro-superhuman rhetoric.

No wonder the Normals don't respect us. I've seen high school gossip sheets with more class.

Still, she had seen Cima and most of the Freakside crowd swear by the paper, gathering in large groups where the best orator would read the articles aloud, almost like some sort of prayer service. Who was Gayle to take that away from them? Cima, in her teens, surely had no recollection of a life before the Relocation. She had most likely dropped out of school, would almost surely never go to university. Herotown was her world, the *Spandex Scene* her *Times.*

Gayle did almost wish for a copy of the *Scene* herself, if only for the Help Wanted pages. Fortunately, the Employment Bureau lay only two streets away from Freakside. Waving goodbye to Cima, Gayle pushed through the already thinning crowds of marketgoers, munching on her wamba-melon and wiping the juices away from her chin with her sleeve. The Normals didn't trust any of the "new fruits" to come out of the lands near Trinity, and Gayle shied away from most of them as well . . . but wamba-mellons were her weakness. Besides, the icy-sweet pulp was filling enough to be breakfast and lunch for the day.

Shandon Space Murder Trial. The headline called her mind back to Buzz's babble the night before. "Something intense is going down between the headlines." Gayle was familiar with the case . . . everyone in the State who ever read a newspaper was. Hell, everyone in every civilized corner of the Earth. News stories hardly got bigger. But what could it possibly have to do with them? And even if she knew, what could she *do* about it, alone and unemployable?

The usual long lines awaited Gayle at the Employment Bureau. A sea of capes, tights, helmets, and battlesuits clogged the office space as a flickering LED terminal dangled from the ceiling, displayed the "Now Serving" numbers. By the time Gayle finished her melon, she had reached the job placements board. Her eyes floated immediately to the top tier:

Courier Needed : Flight or superspeed of at least Class 2 a must. Contact H6531146G

Superteam needs "Strong Man"—already have brainy leader, hotshot kid, and "the girl." Please no battlesuits or other Class C abilities: natural powers only. Contact BB444

Radiation—Invulnerable Man or Woman, Class 3 or higher, needed for work in uranium mines. Good pay, good benefits. TTL9090

New Superteam—The Avenging Revengers—holding auditions. Class 4 powers or under need not apply.

Gayle sighed. What had she been expecting? Oh yes, divine intervention. Well, on to the next tier down—the professional jobs. *Medical technician, inventory supervisor, food services manager.* Nothing Gayle had the qualifications or experience for, despite her graduate degrees. Herotown didn't have many of these jobs, so the competition was fierce. Nothing was worse than going to medical school outside the gates for eight years only to return and find that Herotown only had one functioning medical hospital. The courts were still filled with people who had received their law degrees before the

Relocation—that generation would have to die off before new blood could really enter Legal.

Finally, Gayle's eyes sunk to the third tier: *waitress, custodian, passport clerk*. These jobs were almost as coveted, despite the low salaries. Gayle couldn't conscience taking one of these jobs away from someone who really needed them, who didn't have a guardian angel waiting in the wings like she did. At least, that was what she told herself when she refused to drop her resume in that bin.

Instead, she put it in the waiting pool under tier one, the superhero positions, there to join a pile of its cloned brethren. After every case, she updated it and submitted it again . . . as if that would somehow change the fact that her super-power made her almost completely unemployable.

She remembered how Waley used to laugh at her back when they were teenagers, that infuriating irreverent laugh that only made her want to smack him . . . yet somehow they would always end up kissing.

"Friday. I just don't get it," he would say. "I mean, how does your body `know' it's Friday?"

"What are you talking about?" she would look up, annoyed, from whatever textbook she was studying.

"I mean, Friday is a completely human invented concept," he'd tease at her hair, pulling at the curls until she took a swipe at him. "Is it based on the a solar cycle? I mean, if the same time passed, but humans changed the way they figured days . . . made it like a four day week, or something. Would your powers know?"

"How should I know?"

"What if you crossed the international date line, and then crossed back? Haven't you ever been curious?"

"No."

"I'll tell you what *I'm* curious about." His eyes would flash.

"I know what you're curious about. The answer is no."

But of course, they would end up kissing. And more.

Gayle felt that headache come on again, the headache that always warbled around her temples whenever she thought of the old times with Waley. They had been so young! Not that much older than the children she saw playing in streets outside the

Employment Bureau, although her clothes had never been that filthy or ragged. Two boys, twins, were tossing sparkles from their hands, while another playmate hovered a few feet above, swiping at them with a large stick.

They were playing "heroes and villains." Gayle stared at them sadly, wondering how many of these tykes would actually grow up to be the former, and how many the latter? It was so easy to become a villain . . . all it took was a super power and enough frustration, both of which were abundant commodities in Herotown. By their teens, it wasn't too hard to get a gang together and go terrorizing the neighbors. Most people in Herotown could fight back, though, which meant sooner or later, the gangs would get the idea in their collective head to cross the gates and go pick on the Normals. The Peace Officers would stop some of them, but others would get through to Mesopolopolis and wreak havoc . . . giving the Normals all the more reason to maintain the walls around Herotown. Idiots.

Of those that survived to adulthood, some would reform, some would sell themselves off as mercenaries to other nations, and a few would set out for Superion City—foolishly. Captain Omega had no tolerance for supervillains. Any villain heading there, seeking asylum, would get more lenient treatment from the Normals. Gayle had heard stories that Omega kept a hall of uniforms stripped from such intruders, and left their owners to wander naked on the unshielded surface of the moon outside the colony. Of course, only someone like Cima would really believe any of that.

Besides, Gayle's power made her as ineligible for villainy as it did for herodom. So what was she to do? Well, dry-cleaning, for one. Gayle dropped off her costume at Midge's Cleaners on the corner of Sentinel and Helios ("We Clean Everything from Capes to Drapes"), then walked down Helios to the small park there. The air was getting too cold for many park-goers, except those with fur or heat powers. Gayle sat with her thoughts for an indeterminate amount of time, and then noticed a ruffled copy of the *Spandex Scene* by her feet.

It lay open to the personals section. On a lark—Gayle certainly didn't lack for time—she scanned the columns. After a few moments she found herself wishing for a red pen to correct the spelling mistakes in them.

Looking for sweet, sensitive, honost woman, who won't mind a prehensile tail.

Or, apparently, a bad speller.

Gayle hadn't been on a date since Noctyrne had set her up with the kid brother of her friend Hurricane. Hurricane was a sweet, charming, modest, and naturally, married superhero from the north side of Herotown. Hurricane's kid brother was a punk who went by the name of Tropical Depression. All evening, he had kept creating small winds to blow Gayle's skirt up as she went up or down a staircase. When he called up fog and tried to use it as a cover to feel her up, Gayle had seized him by the lapels thrown him clear across the movie theater. Honestly, she had figured he would have created a wind to cushion his fall, and he did—only breaking one or two minor bones in his leg. Message received.

There's a reason I only date on Friday nights, Gayle thought to herself.

A beep from her cuff-link communicator startled her attentions back to the present. The *Friday Knights* signal. Damned George probably needed another consultation on what lacy underwear to buy for Noctyrne. Gayle hauled herself to her feet, distressed at how much her legs suddenly ached, and caught the trolley down to Guardian Boulevard and the warehouse district.

George would be waiting, along with Noctyrne and Craig the Combat Wombat—her teammates, her friends, her wonderful distraction from the cold air and the unpaid rent and the memories of Waley and the lingering headache that throbbed in the brain of every man, woman, genderneutral and child in Herotown. She didn't have to think about any of it with them—especially not her dismal excuse for a romantic life.

"Gayle!" George broke into a smile as Gayle entered, and she warmed, as if dipped back in water after too long outside the pool.

"You're just in time," said George, gesturing towards the guest room. "Detective Roland is here, all the way from the city proper. He wants to speak with you. Alone."

3

"You've barely touched the steamed peas."

"I'm not hungry," Gayle spoke into her napkin.

What on Earth was she doing? So what if George and Noctyrne were trying on wedding costumes in the Friday Fort, couldn't the two of them had just talked there? No, that wouldn't have been professional. Heaven forbid Gayle ever act unprofessional.

Roland was quick to suggest Bulravian restaurant on the corner of Solitude and Freedom as an alternate meeting place. Given the war abroad, Bulravian restaurants had lost their popularity in mainstream Mesopolopolis, but then, Herotown was the place where the dejected came to roost.

So here they were, talking yet not talking.

"More cilantro?"

"No thank you."

Five more words. Gayle was counting. At this rate, they were averaging about fifty words an hour, Roland's clipped, barking speech towards the waitstaff notwithstanding.

"So, ah," Roland scratched the back of his neck absent-mindedly, "the case."

"Yes," said Gayle, straightening. Why was she slouching? This was Herotown. She was on her turf. But she wasn't in costume. Should that have mattered? Roland was wearing that brown suit. *He* got to hide behind his costume.

But the way the brown in the suit and the brown in his hair brought out that wonderful, warm brown in his eyes . . . Gayle wasn't sure she would want him wearing anything else. Except, well, nothing.

She slapped herself with a mental hand. What was she thinking?

"We've, ah, got some new leads, that I, ah, shared with GAP. As the best criminologist on the team, he felt you were the person I should speak with."

Perhaps, thought Gayle. Perhaps George and Noctyrne were just too busy picking out silverware for the wedding to be bothered. No, that was unfair. Wasn't it?

"Thanks for the courtesy," Gayle spoke to some unseen spot above Roland's right shoulder. "You didn't have to consult with us."

"I want to solve this damned thing," said Roland, stabbing at his peas as if apprehending escaping felons. "I'll do whatever it takes to accomplish that, even if it means calling in—"

"Superhuman freaks?"

Roland's chopstick came to a halt. "I was going to say, expert consultants."

"Oh," Gayle stared self-consciously at the tops of her hands.

More silence. The waiter came by to refill their water, only to veer off when he saw they hadn't touched it.

"So, the case."

"Yes, the case."

Roland cleared his throat, then began laying out the details. The police were treating this "Georgie Porgie" perpetrator as a rogue superhuman, and thus had been cycling through the Metahuman Commission's database for possible suspects. So far, all of the likely candidates had been accounted for with airtight alibis. Besides, none of them matched the physical description of the offender. Roland feared they might be dealing with an unregistered super, or one who didn't register a change in his powers. That alone would make this case a great deal more serious than just kiss-and-run antics. And then there was the matter of the Bulravian accent . . . if this man was some sort of fugitive illegal immigrant, or worse, a spy from that enemy country . . .

"Hold on, Detective. Our perp's behavior sounds pretty out of character for a spy. Don't spies tend to keep hidden?"

"I don't know. Maybe it's a terror tactic. Maybe it's part of a more elaborate plan."

"I suggest we stick to the bare basics. Assume he's working alone, since we have no evidence otherwise."

"Well, that *is* the plan I'm working on," Roland sounded a little defensive and a little disappointed at the same time. "Motive is the sticking point right now. That's what I was hoping you could help me with. Criminology, I know about. But supercriminology?"

Gayle sighed. "Looking for insight into our strange, inhuman minds?"

"I wasn't implying—"

"Of course not. In any event, superhuman psychology varies widely depending on the nature of our powers, in addition to any of the normal developmental baggage that any human being carries around from his or her past. Telepaths, as Georgie Porgie seems to be, can have particularly intense psychological disorders."

Roland nodded, making eye contact, with a kind of genuine interest Gayle seldom saw outside of a college classroom.

"Just like you and I have to learn to shut off the kind of background noise we hear in a restaurant like this," Gayle gestured to the room around her, "telepaths are constantly bombarded with the stray thoughts and emotions from everyone around them. They walk through life as if it every room was a crowded party."

"Then an actual crowded party, like the club where the perp attacked that girl, should have been hell on a telepath's mind."

"On an undisciplined one, yes. Most novice telepaths avoid large crowds, and even experienced ones have to concentrate deeply."

"The perp doesn't look very frazzled on the tape. He looked confused, a little haunted . . . but once he saw that girl, he snapped into focus."

"Maybe she reminded him of someone special in his life," Gayle offered. "Maybe that's his M.O."

"Thought of that. The list of victims has now risen to four, all women who have very little in common except for youth and attractiveness. I would just call him a garden variety pervert, except he doesn't actually *do* anything except kiss them and run."

"He might have a fetish," said Gayle, "although for a telepath, kissing is a rough fetish to have. Physical contact of any kind magnifies a telepath's experience a dozenfold. A kiss brings forth a tremendous rush of thoughts and raw, visceral, undigested feelings. Think of how your very first kiss felt, Detective, and multiply it by a billion."

Roland stared uncomfortably at his plate. "Maybe he's some sort of masochist, or pain junkie who gets off on discomfort."

"Perhaps. But then, why be so selective about his victims? He seemed to hunt pretty hard for that particular girl in the club, passing over a dozen others just as pretty."

"We're missing a piece of the motive. He's definitely looking for something, and so far, he hasn't found it. My fear is what might happen when he does."

Gayle nodded. "Well, you're on the case, and it sounds like you're following all the right procedures."

A pause. The two stared at one another, then returned to their food. Gayle pushed hers around a bit on the plate. "So can I go now?"

Roland blinked. "You're hardly being detained. Is something wrong?"

Some detective. Now he finally notices.

"Well, I would just like to know why I'm here. Just me, in my secret identity, no less, at a restaurant."

"I, ah . . ." Roland stopped, suddenly searching the peas on his plate for an answer. "I, ah—"

"There's no need to apologize." Gayle stabbed a pea through with her chopstick. "The Lee Act gives you every right to access everything about me, right? Name, address, bathing suit size, eyeglass prescription."

The brown rings widened slightly. "I didn't do any of that, Miss Fellman. Not beyond what was relevant to the case."

Gayle's hand held the chopstick up, frozen. "Oh." A pause. "I'm sorry." Another pause.

"We're even then," he mumbled. The next words rolled out awkwardly, as if his mouth was trying to crack a walnut. "I . . . ah . . . asked you here to apologize myself. For last night. The way I treated you and your team. I was . . . a little stressed."

"I see," said Gayle. "Well, I ah . . ."

What should she say? Acknowledge him, acknowledge him!

"Thank you. You're right. I mean, you're stressed . . . I mean . . ."

Oh, that was brilliant.

"There's no need for anything further about it. And I guess, now that we've consulted about the Georgie Porgie case, there's need for any further conversation. I'll just call for the check, put down my money, and be out of your—"

"No!" said Gayle. Then she stopped. What did she even want to say? And what was that damned chopstick still poised between her chest and her mouth for?

"What I meant," she finally took the pea to her lips, "is that you don't have to treat. I can afford to pay my share. And besides, I'm not done eating yet."

Roland nodded. He didn't smile, but his jaw sort of relaxed. It suddenly seemed to Gayle that, wherever Roland's confidence had momentarily fled, it had managed to find its way home. Great. Gayle's was still AWOL.

"So I don't know a thing about you," he said. "Not even your name."

"Gal Friday is fine for now," she said, taking another pea, even though her stomach had moved beyond peaceful protest and was starting to throw molotov cocktails at the rest of her digestive system.

"Fair enough," he said.

Not, it wasn't fair at all. A secret identity was all a superhero really owned. To reveal it was to let someone into the most intimate of places. Of course, the Lee Act allowed such easy violation of that intimacy . . . but Roland hadn't taken advantage . . . .

"There are so many superhero teams out there," said Roland. "Hard to keep track of them all. I didn't know the Friday Knights at all until yesterday."

"There's a reason. We're not exactly what you'd call the first-stringers of the heroic world."

"Surprising," said Roland. "Given how high-profile some of your members are. Your patron, George William Snordwell, is heir to the Snordwell military industrial fortune. Every SWAT team in Mesopolopolis uses equipment his father designed."

"The Peace Officers use that equipment, too," Gayle said, a little more icily than she had wanted. What was wrong with her?

"Yes. I, ah, could see how that might, ah, make your team a little less than popular on this side of the Wall."

Where was he going with this?

"And, ah, Combat Wombat . . . word is he's the nephew of . . . well . . . you know . . ."

"He is," said Gayle. "Look, this is hardly the first time someone's mentioned this fact to me, so if you're trying to make some sort of accusation—"

"No!" said Roland, then checked himself as glances drew his way. "No, I mean," he readjusted his tie, and Gayle couldn't help but take some small pleasure. Then she chided herself. She had led him into that, hadn't she? What if he was just trying to make conversation? Well, he sure had an odd way of doing it.

"You know," Roland started to trace and unclear shape with his hands, "when I was a kid, I actually had an action figure of Twister. Hell, I had action figures of all the Amazing Elite—you know, back in the day when people still bought action figures of Superheroes. But wouldn't you know it, Twister was my favorite."

"He was a lot of people's favorite," said Gayle. "With that kind of legacy, Combat Wombat could have had his pick of any superteam on the planet, until . . . ."

And then, of course, the sentence no one ever had to finish.

"Look, I don't even know what I'm trying to say here," said Roland. "My specialty is looking at clues and drawing conclusions, and right here, right now, every clue leads me to the conclusion that this particular conversation is headed into a flaming pit."

He pulled out his wallet and began sifting through the bills inside.

"Local currency would make it easier on the waiter," Gayle muttered.

Why was she doing this? Instead of stopping him, insisting he say, she was calling attention to all the differences? Well, those differences would come up sooner or later, anyway. Better to air them out now, right?

"I had some money converted before I came," he lay down enough cubits to cover his meal. "You ought to try giving people credit every now and then, Miss Friday," he reached for his hat. "Seeing that you worked with people like GAP and Combat Wombat, I had concluded you were the kind of person who could see past appearances to the redeeming qualities in a person. Maybe I'm not as good a detective as I like to think."

"Wait!" Gayle finally let the word escape. "Wait, please." *I'm being a total jerk today, and I'm not normally like this, honest! Or am I? Is this just the real me coming out?* "Please, sit down, and put the money away."

Missing no beats, Roland scooped up the bills and returned to a sitting position.

"The Friday Knights are a very . . . unique . . . . super team," said Gayle. "But we're the real deal. We fight for truth and justice like anyone else. I'm proud to be a part of them."

"I had assumed you were," said Roland. "While I didn't look up your identity, I did look up your record. Top of your class all through high school, *Summa cum laude* with bronze clusters from the Mesopolopolis University of Criminal Justice, high marks on every evaluation from the Metahuman Commission, spotless criminal record. I would imagine someone like you, Gal Friday, could have her pick of any team she wanted. For you to pick the Friday Knights must mean you saw some value in them."

"Thanks for the flattery," said Gayle, "and please, please pardon how this is going to sound, but . . . you're thinking like a Normal."

"Oh?" Roland looked more amused than offended.

"My record matters a great deal to the Metahuman Commission, but superteams . . . well, they care mainly about super-powers when they recruit. And mine are . . . well . . . let's just say, not terribly compatible with most superheroic agendas."

"Really?" Roland said. "According to your official file, you rate A5—you possess super strength and endurance at the second highest levels possible. I would imagine that's in pretty high demand."

"It is," said Gayle, and suddenly her eyes fell to her plate once more. "But there are . . . other factors involved. Factors that, forgive me, I'd rather not discuss right now."

"All right," said Roland, running a frustrated hand through his hair. Gayle looked up to watch the follicles part. At rest, his hair looked sculpted, solid, proud. But parted, she saw the jagged edges, the speckles, the wear and tear.

"Let's try a lighter topic," Gayle offered. "How about . . ."

Well, how about what? She didn't follow any sports except the local powerstunt games, the news was never an uplifting subject . . . what did that leave except shop talk? No, Gayle went to restaurants to *escape* from her job, and, when she thought about it for a moment, she figured Roland might, too.

"How about dry cleaning," Gayle finally spat out. "I have a pile of dry cleaning currently waiting for me to pick it up." What? What on Earth was she saying?

For the first time since they had met today, a smile spread across Roland's face. The smile widened, then revealed slightly yellowed teeth, which parted to admit a full laugh.

"What?" said Gayle. "I don't hear you suggesting anything better."

"No, no, it's not that," Roland shook his head.

"No? Then what is it?"

"I'm just . . . I'm just . . ." He fought to bring his face back into composure, but his eyes . . . those lovely brown eyes . . . were regarding her as if he had just seen a stone gargoyle speak.

"I just didn't, well, expect—"

"Expect what?"

"That you'd have, well . . . you know . . ." Roland's hands came up, again trying to trace some shape in the air for illustration. "That you'd have . . . ."

Something in Gayle began to burn. "That I'd have dry cleaning today? Or that I'd have dry cleaning, period?"

"Now wait just a moment," Roland began, but she saw it in his eyes. Those damnable brown eyes which she suddenly wanted to pierce with hot pokers.

"You didn't expect that I'd have dry cleaning at all," said Gayle, "right? Or shopping, or bad lunch dates?"

Gayle drew herself up. "Why the hell not?"

Roland opened his mouth to speak, a small giblet of saliva dripping from his lower lip, but Gayle raised her hand. "No, no, don't tell me. I'm a super hero. I'm not supposed to have a real life, right? When

I'm not off fighting the forces of evil, I'm supposed to just get packed up back into a box in my secret cave until I'm needed again, is that it?"

"Now see here, hold on—"

"No," Gayle threw her napkin to the table, "I'm sick of holding. I'm sick of holding myself tall and proud even when I feel like ripe nuclear waste. I'm sick of holding myself to a higher standard, having to be extra virtuous, extra smart, extra noble, as if I were some super-powered nun, because that's what a heroine does. I'm sick of putting my life on permanent hold—dating, friendships, hobbies, any of those little pleasures that make you *real*—because that's what's expected of me, and then wondering why the government and the newspapers and everyone outside the Wall thinks of me as something inhuman. Including, apparently, you, Detective. Good luck on your case, and good day."

Gayle took stood to leave, reaching into her purse for money.

"Stop right there," Roland called out, and for a moment, Gayle felt like a criminal on the run. He was using his "police voice," and, despite every rational thought in her mind, she froze in place nonetheless.

"You think I don't understand any of that?" Roland rose. "You don't think that, as a police officer, people expect me to be something larger than what I am, too? Every day, every person I meet expects either service and protection, or a fight. Nine out of every ten conversations, I'm either grilling someone or telling them everything's going to be ok. No one ever asks *me* questions, and if I waited until some mook came along to tell me everything was going to be ok, I'd never get out of bed in the morning."

"Then what—"

"No, you had your chance, Gal Friday. This is my turn. You've taken every opportunity here to remind me of how bad you have things here in Herotown. You think a hop over the Wall would solve all your problems? There's splen on the other side of that Wall, too, and I wade ankle deep in it every night. We've got homelessness, poverty, gamblers and thieves and murderers and every kind of scum you can imagine. But the difference is, us Normals have to face all of that without super strength, without hyper speed, without bulletproof skin. I've been working ten years on the force, and every night in my one bedroom apartment, I try and talk myself to sleep, talk myself into believing all the little cases and arrests and cats out of trees I've accomplished make one bit of difference. If someone like you wants to make a difference, all she has to do is just pick a beached ship out of the sea, or blow super-breath on a blazing fire."

"It's not that easy at all!"

"Like hell! As you reminded me last night, you and I have the same damned responsibilities. The difference between us is, yours actually *mean* something, because you've got power."

"The difference between us," Gayle hissed, "is that you chose yours. I was cursed with mine."

"Oh, really?"

"Yes, really. As in literally, cursed. When I was seven years old, my father took me to a carnival, and, when I figured out how the magician was really making those rabbits disappear with mirrors and pulleys, I couldn't keep my damned mouth shut and announced it to everyone in the audience. Just my luck, his assistant was a real live Gypsy sorceress, and she put a curse on me. That's what the `A' means in Class A-5V, `A' as in `Alteration', as in, not from birth, as in, too bad, poor thing, what an awful twist of fate, glad it didn't happen to me.

"So thanks to her, I get super powers one and only one day a week, and that's Friday. Friday! That's the `V', for *variant*, as in, only works sometimes. In the Big Leagues, Detective, no one wants to hire a heroine who's only good one day a week. Since most crime happens at night, that leaves about five hours, maybe one or two more in the winter, until midnight, when I become just an ordinary woman again. Well, ordinary, unless you ask the Metahumanics Commission, which classified me as Super and relocated my family and I here. But hey, I've made something of a life here in Herotown, and on good days I even enjoy it, so don't you dare think I'm asking for your pity . . . and don't you dare tell me what my advantages are, because the way I see it, I got the raw end of both deals."

Gayle stood with all eyes in the restaurant fixated on her. Roland stood three feet away the entire time, resolute against her voice, never breaking eye contact. His jaw muscles did not tighten in that way most men's did when argued with, always primed for their chance to make rebuttal. He just stood there, taking in her words.

"I'm done," she added, and then turned to the assembled restaurant patrons. "I'm done," she said again. "One night only, thank you for coming."

"I'm sorry I brought you here," Roland said, actually sounding apologetic. "I suppose we're both better at our jobs than we are at being real people, yes?"

He turned to go, and Gayle watched him pass beyond the hostess' station, out the door, into the streets of Herotown beyond. Some small voice inside her screamed to run after, to fling herself at his feet, to genuflect and blubber apologies. Another, louder voice told her to chase him down and beat him unconscious. She did neither. She reached into her wallet, laid down her money on the table, along with a generous gratuity for the waiter. Gratuity? Hell, he should be paying *her* for the show. But no, can't be impolite. That would be unheroic.

Wasn't it also unheroic to scream her life's problems out to the detective? It's not like they were his fault, after all. *Idiot! Idiot! It's not too late, run out, you can catch him.*

Gayle put one foot forward, then another, then finally propelled herself out the door and started to break into a run. She got three entire steps off the curb before a hand grabbed her from behind and slapped a rag against her mouth and nose. Surprised, she immediately and instinctively inhaled. By the time she recognized the scent of chloroform, her consciousness was already fleeing. Gayle managed one good wriggle against the grip that had now ensconced her waist and shoulders as well, then slumped forward.

"The Fusion Drive is an admirable invention in its potential to propel humanity to the stars, where its eyes have always been cast. Before we migrate out there, however, should we not cast those eyes into the mirror, and ask whether we are merely spreading the diseases of our immorality out to where they will infect other worlds?"

—Captain Omega, in an interview with the *Mesopolopolis Times*

TENZIN

"Without the sensor logs from the space mission, we have no case."

Gordon Holloway, Esquire thundered through the Mesopolopolis Attorney General's office in the Federal District, scattering interns and aides like mosquitoes—they whirled out of the range of his rage, only to sidle back towards him, eager for sustenance. Gordon himself certainly lacked no sustenance. The man's 240 lb frame seemed ready to burst from his business suit by sheer force of anger alone.

"Where are those damned computer geeks? Haven't they recovered any of the data yet? What do we pay them for?"

"They've been working for weeks," Tenzin Myata, Holloway's protégé, said softly. The slender, thin-armed man with a finely shaven head had long ago learned that speaking softly around Holloway tended to remind the larger man of his own volume.

"I fear the data corruption is quite severe."

"Severe." Holloway's voice, to Tenzin's regret, did not lower. "Too severe for just random electrical disruption, right? Severe enough to have been the result of manual tampering?"

This conversation was one Tenzin had taken part in a dozen times. Dutifully reprising his role, he replied, "For every expert we bring in to say that, the defense can bring in one to counter. The average juror lacks the knowledge to discern."

"Then that leaves us with Criminal Negligence. Bah. Barely worth the cost of bussing him across the city."

Bah indeed, Tenzin sighed. Criminal Negligence didn't make headlines like Murder did. A conviction on Criminal Negligence would not propel Holloway into the AG's seat. Attorney General Halbert's extended bout with the Orange Sickness was the only reason Holloway was arguing the high profile "Neville Shandon Space Murder Case" to begin with. This was his chance, Tenzin knew too well. If Holloway rose, his gravity would pull Tenzin along with him, and if Holloway failed, and needed someone to blame . . . well, Tenzin was a man of duty, and duty sometimes demanded a little martyrdom.

How fortunate, then, that Tenzin brought good news.

"I finally made contact with Doctor Michelis."

"The Lieutenant's wife?" said Holloway. "About damned time. Where was she all along?"

"Humanitarian League mission in Bulravia. Tending to victims of the war with Skovakia."

"Her husband dies ten billion miles away in space, and she's too busy tending the lepers to help nail his killer? And Bulravians, no less? After all those bastards did? Maybe if the Humanitarian League didn't hug and coddle and patch them all up, they'd get the hint and play nice with the rest of the world."

Tenzin remained expectantly silent. As predicted, Holloway's steam passed.

"All right," the Assistant Attorney General finally breathed, "well, better late than never. Did she have a copy of the transmission he sent her?"

"Yes."

Holloway shivered with compressed energy. "Well?" he finally ejaculated.

Tenzin allowed himself a thin, controlled smile. "She's released it. I have the text right here."

"Damned Virtual Privacy Act. We could have had this weeks ago if only mission control wasn't prohibited from opening the personal communiqués of Normals, or keeping any copies. So what *was* Lieutenant Michelis' last letter to his wife? Please tell me it's not just some damned grocery list?"

"No," said Tenzin, handing his boss a small datapad. "Something far more interesting."

Holloway's eyes bounded up and down the screen like ricocheting bullets. Finally, his lips stretched into a smile, like ground swelling and cracking during an earthquake.

"Well, I'll be a cloned sheep. Tenzin, this is exactly what we need."

Tenzin's head bowed slightly, silently.

"Bulravia's internet connections have been down ever since the war began," Holloway fondled the datapad, turning it over and over. "You had to have physically taken this from the war zone. How on Earth did you manage that?"

"Via a useful agent," was Tenzin's reply.

Tenzin couldn't very well say "from a superhuman freelancer operating illegally outside the Herotowns, financed with money from the State." None of the books would say that either. Holloway may have been a blowhard, but he knew well enough to pick up on cues.

Besides, the Attorney General's knowing grunt indicated that he understood when a lesser evil was necessary for a greater good. Tenzin himself didn't believe in good and evil—Western concepts that they were—only balance and imbalance. The deaths of Lieutenants Michelis and Al-Awadi during Earth's most high profile space mission in years had caused a grave imbalance among the population, and Holloway, as ungainly as he seemed, was just the man to restore the balance.

Tenzin hoped he wasn't going to ask to subpoena Dr. Michelis. She'd been out of contact ever since Tenzin's agent got her to sign the release.

But no, Holloway was too focused on the pad, caressing it with his thick, stubby fingers. It was all he needed.

He licked his lips. "Shandon's mine."

It was most likely the attempts to officially sponsor and market powerstunt competitions to the masses that, ironically, led to the sport's fall in popularity— they began and ended as games of the street, and the finest competitors preferred elite standing in the eyes of their neighborhood to adoration by faceless masses across the State . . .

—From the *Chronicles of Metahumanity*

GAYLE

Gayle was 17 years old, standing proud but shaky on gangly legs. Her hands moved into her pockets as she stepped into the wind blowing across the harbor and into Desperation Flats. Steam rose from vents along the sidewalk, sending plumes of cabbage-smelling smoke into Gayle's path. Today, she didn't mind.

"Waley!" she called out into a small mob of teenagers huddled around the rusted skeleton of a dump truck. One, a runty boy who looked barely postpubescent, was balancing on one finger atop a smokestack on the cab. He, or one of his friends, evidently possessed some sort of gravity nullifying power. Whoever it was, they weren't very competent with it. The runt tottered like a reed in the wind, first this way, then the next. With each near fall, the crowd jeered and "oooh-ed." Some of the girls clung more tightly to the jackets of their boyfriends.

"Cu'mon, Widge," one of the boys below called. "This is kid stuff. Yu'never gonna make the cut next week if yu can't even do the spin trick."

"I can do it," Widge protested from his precarious position. "I can do it easy, just you see."

71

A chant of "Widge! Widge! Widge!" began to rise from the crowd. Gayle, who had been drawing near, brought her pace to a halt. She had been scanning the crowd for Waley, but the spectacle atop the truck had a way of demanding her attention.

"Aw, anyone c'n do that," another boy called, and Gayle's nose caught a burst of ozone. "Try this!"

A small fireball launched from the crowd, drawing jeers from some and laughter from others. A white flash of panic leapt across Widge's face as he twisted to avoid the tiny burning projectile. His body flew off the smokestack, as if flicked by an invisible finger and thumb, tumbling towards the crowd below.

Despite herself, Gayle cried out.

A sea of arms awaited Widge, and he landed in the human net, cursing all the way.

"Geebus, Widge," someone said. "Yu gonna lose us the tourney for sure."

"No fair! Mel was jerking me!"

"That wan't jerking. You want to see jerking? I'll show you—"

"Hey, cut it, guys. Cut it now!"

Gayle recognized Waley's voice immediately. She snapped her head around to see him dislodge from the crowd, purple-and-red speckled overcoat draped around his thin, wiry shoulders like some Candyland version of Count Dracula. She could never help but chuckling at that outfit, yet "the mantle," as he called it, commanded respect from the gang. They parted to allow him through.

"Mel's right, y'know," said Waley, voice calm and sing-songy. "Widge, if you wanna be on the team, you gotta practice."

"I do!"

"Yeah," said Mel, "in between seein' that honey of yours."

Ooohs bubbled up from the crowd. Gayle sighed. How juvenile.

"Don't yu be knockin' Rissa, Melvin!" Widge feinted a punch, driving the other boy back. "Yu just jealous!"

More ooohs.

"Enough," Waley's voice cracked like a whip. "Widge, you know the rules. For this week, everything takes a backseat. That means *everything*," he pointed unceremoniously to Widge's crotch.

"And you, Mel," he turned. "Remember, we're a team. We ride one another when we need to, but when the chips are down—"

"I know, I know," Mel sighed heavily. "I'm behind yus. Behind all yus." He grimaced as he turned to Widge. "Even yu."

Widge stared at the ground self-consciously, grunting his acceptance.

"All right," Waley clapped once, a devilish smile spreading across his face. "Let's get back to it."

Oh, no he wasn't. Not now. Not today.

Gayle bounded over to Waley. "Why don't you get back in a moment. I have something to tell you."

The oooohs returned from the crowd.

A frown smeared across Waley's face for just a moment. Then he flung an arm around Gayle's shoulders, pulled her close, and kissed her deeply, almost savagely, before the crowd. Gayle's heart raced, her body shimmered, even as she pushed him away. The crowd laughed as they watched him fall back.

"I'm borrowing your leader," said Gayle.

"Oh, so we gotta double standard, eh?" one of the boys called.

"Shut up," Melvin punched him in the arm. "That's Waley. He's different."

"He oughta get himself a *real* girl." One of the skanky little ponytailed girls shook herself brazenly, eyes glowing green with whatever power it was she possessed. Gayle didn't know, and didn't care. Not today.

"I'll be back in five," said Waley, throwing up two fingers on one hand and three on the other.

Laughter, mixed with hisses and jeers. Gayle's armor stopped most of it. She knew she wasn't well liked. But after next week, none of it was going to matter.

"Sorry to interrupt," Gayle said as, arm-in-arm with Waley, the two walked away down the alley.

"Naw, 'sokay," said Waley. "They're good guys. Jerks sometimes, but good guys. We might really have a chance this year at the finals."

"Not if your stunters get themselves killed first."

"Who, Widge?"

"Yes, Widge. That fall could have killed him."

"Naw. We caught him."

"Only because he fell towards you. What if he had fallen backwards, off the other side of the truck?"

"It's a good thing he didn't."

Gayle sighed. Even Waley's being Waley wasn't going to bring her down today.

"I got a letter this afternoon," said Gayle. "Postal wagon brought it special delivery, from beyond the Wall."

Waley grunted the same way he did every time she mentioned anything in the world beyond the Wall. Well, this time would be different.

"It was from the University," she said. "The *real* university, Waley. The University of Mesopolopolis."

She paused, knees knocking, resisting the urge to dislodge from his arm begin skipping.

Waley cocked his head. "Yes?"

Gayle could contain herself no longer. "I've been accepted!" she shrieked, breaking loose and leaping up in the air. "Waley, Waley, they accepted me! They accept fewer than thirty students a year from Herotown, and they accepted me!"

A thin smile forced its way across Waley's face. "That's great, Gayle. I'm happy for you."

She threw out her arms, seized his shoulders, brought her forehead up to his. "Damned straight you are. Waley, this is what we've waited for our whole lives. A chance to get out of this dump. A chance to make something of ourselves."

She twisted her head to kiss him, but his lips only parted lazily, passively receiving her. The difference from his kiss minutes earlier was so marked that it hurt.

She pulled back a few inches.

"Well?"

"Well what?"

"Well? Isn't this the part where you grab me, sweep me up in the air, twirl me around a few times and tell me you're happy too?"

"I told you I was happy."

"Oh please," Gayle felt a small elevator begin to sink in her stomach. "Can't you ever take anything seriously?"

"Believe me, I take it seriously, Gayle. I've only been hearing about this university quest of yours every day for the past year. It's as serious to me as any other chronic condition."

"Oh, *you*," Gayle pushed off from his shoulders. "You're not in front of your friends, you know. You don't have to put on the act."

"That's not an act," said Waley. "This," he jumped up in the air, ten feet, and hung there, hung as if suspended by wires, then somersaulted several times in place before returning to land on the point of his toes, "is an act. Ta daaa!"

"Ladies and gentlemen," he called out to no one in particular, "the amazing Wayfarer!" Waley bowed deeply, then sighed at Gayle's disapproving gaze.

"I remember," he said, "when that would make you laugh."

"Waley, we were ten years old then."

"Maybe I still am," he cocked an eyebrow.

"Waley," Gayle fought hard, so very hard, to hold on to that warmth she had been nestling inside her. She felt it slipping away like soap grasped in a shower. "Can you please, please, stay with me here for a moment? Waley, I've been accepted into Mesopolopolis University."

"I know," he nodded. "I heard you. Mel's firecrackers haven't made me deaf yet."

"Waley, everything's going to change now. For the better. I'm going beyond the Wall, Waley, can you imagine that?"

"Yes," Waley's voice grated.

"It'll be so romantic," she ran towards him, took his arms in hers. She felt them sag limply, and clung all the tighter. "You can get day passes, come visit me. We can take walks along the water—the *real* Phoenix River, Waley, not our irradiated little bays here in Herotown. We can dine at real restaurants, go to shows . . ."

Her eyebrow arched wickedly. "You can get a night pass and stay over in my dorm room."

Waley hung limply in her grasp.

"Well?" she asked. "This is a conversation, you know. That means both of us speak."

Waley shrugged, his eyes resting everywhere but on her. "I said I was happy for you. Twice. This makes three. You could just record my voice and play it back if you want more."

"Ooh!" she pushed him aside. "Why are you being such an unremitting jerk lately?"

"Look, you know about the powerstunt tournament this weekend," said Waley.

"How could I not," said Gayle. "Talk about chronic conditions."

"We've been practicing like madmen all week, if you care. We really have a chance to make the finals on Sunday."

"Sunday?" Gayle suddenly felt an invisible blow knock her upside the stomach. "Sunday, Waley?"

"That's what I said."

"Waley," her eyes widened, her pitch rose, her posture sank, "Sunday's graduation day. You know that."

"I told you I wasn't going to graduation," he said. "You know I'm not into all that school stuff. I learned what they tossed me, I earned my diploma. They're give it to me whether I'm physically present to take it from some fatass teacher's hands or not."

"But *I'll* be there," said Gayle. "I'm giving the Valedictory speech. You have to come!"

"I've heard you practice it. It's a good speech. I told you that."

"Waley, what is *wrong* with you?" she felt the tears, damn them, damn them, forcing their way out her eyes. "For months now, all year, you've been acting colder and colder to me. Waley, this is me! Gayle! The girl you played heroes and villains with in your aunt's backyard, for heaven's sake!"

"Used to, Gayle," Waley finally found her eyes, as well as the volume in his voice. "Used to. Key words. The girl who *used to* race down Triumph Avenue with me on rocket scooters,. The girl who *used to* keep score at our powerstunt matches, who *used to* tell me our friendship was the most important thing to her on the planet."

"It is," Gayle cried out, grasping at him again. "Spirit Above, Waley, why do you think I'm so upset? You're the most important person in the world to me. That's why I want you there with me on Sunday, and with me all through college, and after that."

"Not with you, Gayle," said Waley, again hanging limp in her hold. That felt worse to Gayle, somehow, than if he had pulled away. "I'd be in the audience on Sunday. I'd be an unwelcome guest at your college."

"That's not true!" Gayle sobbed. "Waley, you know that's not true! Nothing could be farther from truth!"

"Gayle," Waley wound his face tightly, but didn't cry. Why, why, why didn't he? Was his super power to be immune from emotion? "Things have changed. We're not powerstunt partners these days, Gayle, we're study partners. We don't talk about movies or games, we talk about the future, and politics, and how we're somehow going to join superhero teams and save the world."

"Well?" Gayle looked up at him through a haze of saline and mucous, "aren't we?"

"Get real, Gayle," said Waley.

"Oh, and you live in reality?" she snorted.

"Look, stop crying," he reached out to smooth her hair, but she jerked her head away from him. "Gayle, calm down. I'll try to make graduation. No promises, but—"

"No promises," Gayle grit her teeth. "All great superheroes have a catchphrase, Waley. Captain Omega's is `For Justice and Peace!' Yours should be `No Promises."

"That's unfair."

"No, Waley! What's unfair is missing the most important day of our life for some stupid powerstunt rally."

"Our life? No. *Your* life, Gayle. Graduation is important to you. This is important to me. Sunday isn't just a powerstunt rally, or even just a game. It's the *tournament.* Once a year."

"My graduation is once in a lifetime!"

"Ohhh!" He finally did push her away now. "There's no talking to you, is there? It isn't even really my choice. I'm the captain, I can't be absent. They need me."

"*I* need you!" Gayle screamed, hating herself for screaming, hating Waley for refusing to. Fighting to keep her voice in check, fighting a losing battle against the tears she was wiping off her face with her sleeve, she continued. "You've been disappearing there every weekend for the past two months."

"I'm a super. Supers do super things, Gayle. They don't sit around and study."

"But you don't even go out and save the world. You just put your life at risk in stupid stunts designed to impress stupid people!"

"So you think I'm stupid now? Because I'm not in some University run by Normals, for Normals?"

"Stop it!" Gayle stamped her foot.

"Why the hell save the world?" Waley threw up its arms. "The world doesn't care splen for us. We have these powers, so let's have some fun. You used to understand that."

Gayle stormed towards him. "Why . . . are . . . you . . . . so . . . cruel?"

"Why are you so deluded?" Waley leapt up, leapt high in the air and hung there, out of her reach, as she stretched and jumped futility. Once, her fingertips brushed the bottom of his shoe. He rose higher.

"Open your eyes, Gayle! When you see what's important, I'll be waiting. Or maybe I won't be."

Gayle shouted, cursed, jumped up again and again, reaching from him. Out of breath, she finally collapsed to her knees, sobbing, pounding the pavement. Waley began to shudder, shake, double over into something that might have been tears, but Gayle would never know. He leapt onto a nearby windowsill, then jumped off into the air again, bounded back towards his friends, out of sight.

As she remembered events, she would pick herself up, eventually, look for Waley and his crowd, not find them, and begin the long walk home, not yet realizing that this was the last time she would ever see Waley's face. On Monday, the day after both graduation and the powerstunt game, she would be cradling his one sentence departure note, soaking the paper damp with her sweat, eyes so tear-filled that even the simple words *I'm leaving this lousy hellhole—cheers and beers to you in your great new life* would cease to be legible. But somehow, this time around, the note was in her hands already, and the pavement was turning swiftly to quicksand, into which she began to sink.

Gayle shocked herself back to clarity, began to flail her arms, looking for some sort of handhold, but everything she grasped melted away. Some terrible force was pulling her downward, tugging at her ankles and knees and waist, pulling her beneath the liquid sidewalk.

She cried out Waley's name, waved her arms, begged for help from anyone in hearing distance. No one came.

As she sunk down to her neck, she saw George and Noctyrne appear around the corner, in their meticulously arranged medieval wedding clothes, radiant and confident and so fulfilled. She saw a procession pass behind them, Craig and all her old classmates from the University and Detective Roland, all marching right within easy reach of her. But none of them heeded her calls, none of them even registered her existence. So she sank. And sank. And sank.

"Help me, please! Please!"

"Open your eyes, Gayle," Waley's voice echoed in her mind. Then the quicksand covered her mouth, tasting like detergent-treated cloth . . .

. . . . Gayle suddenly awoke to find a rag between her teeth. She stifled her cry of surprise halfway through, but it was too late. Footsteps sounded from somewhere behind her. Instinctively, she tried to bring her arms to bear, only to find them tied behind her. Legs as well. She twisted futilely, trying to turn around in her chair. Yes, she was seated, and someone was coming from behind . . . .

"Wakey wakey, eggs and bakey."

Gayle knew that voice.

"Bzz?" she murmured through the gag.

"The one and only," Buzz's voice circled from around from behind her. She heard the footsteps come by her right side. She struggled, craned, then felt a painful flick of fingers against her ear. She flung herself uselessly to the right, and Buzz laughed.

"Now, now, G.F, this isn't what you think. I'm sorry to disappoint, but drink as you will, you're not getting any Buzz tonight."

Gayle growled. Squirming, she managed to bang her arms against her waist. No utility belt. Pockets probably emptied as well. Not that she didn't keep equipment in more secure locations, but accessing it would take a bit of doing . . .

"Please forgive my manners," he said, still infuriatingly outside her range of sight, "but, given the terms on which we last parted, I had to make sure I was safe from your trademark rages until you heard me out."

Gayle blew angry breath from her nose.

"Ok, as a gesture of good faith, I'm cutting loose the gag."

Gayle felt a swift pull behind her ears, and the gag fell down. She spat it forcefully from her mouth.

"Buzz!" she cried out. "When I get loose from here, you're going to wish you had never crawled out of whatever sewer you—"

Gayle's voice trailed off as Buzz came into view. He did not look his usual dapper, slick self. A green, viscous ooze covered his black coat, torn in parts to reveal bright red gashes across his torso. Cracks crisscrossed his sunglasses, which did not obscure enough of his face to prevent Gayle from seeing the purple puff of two blackened eyes. One of Buzz's legs dragged limply behind him as he walked, as if sprained or broken.

"The sewer would be preferable, Gal Friday," Buzz coughed violently, "to where I've been."

Gayle wanted to spit. She wanted to sneer. She wanted to spout some imprecation. But her words unexpectedly crumbled in on themselves.

"Buzz?" she whispered, "what happened?"

"It'll take too long to explain." He hobbled out of the range of the dim light, to return, heralded by the sound of scraping metal, with a folding chair. He sat down, a challenging act by the look on his face.

Gayle wanted to reach out, inspect the wounds, offer him aid. Then she remembered he had her tied to a chair. As if seizing upon a misplaced pair of reading glasses, Gayle found her anger again.

"Who did you piss off this time, Buzz?"

"I wish I knew," he laughed, only his trademark cackle ended in a wheeze. Broken rib? Pierced lung? "I was just doing a job."

"For who? The automobile crash test association?" She began wriggling her wrists, twisting, trying to find a flaw in her bonds.

"Maybe. Could be, for all I know." Buzz shrugged, and even that act brought a grimace. "This is the kind of work where you don't ask questions of your employers, if you know what I mean."

"For Spirit's sake, Buzz . . ." said Gayle. "So what do you want from me?"

"I dunno," Buzz craned his neck back to look at some distant point in the blackness above their heads, "maybe a soft, feminine shoulder to lean my wounded head on?"

"I'd sooner break it, Buzz."

"Same old Gayle," he smiled, and Gayle saw several of those expensive pearly whites missing. "In all the months I was a part of the team, you'd never, ever flirt with me. That's what made teasing you so fun."

"I don't know," said Gayle. "Your fun never included tying me up before." Her hands kept twisting, still without success. Her right index finger housed a fake nail with a depressible razorblade, if only she could find the proper angle to use it.

"Well, desperate times and all . . ."

"Desperate? What do you know about desperate, Buzz? While some of us are scraping pennies, you're out there pulling lucrative contracts from people whose names you don't even know. Do they have you tripping old ladies and stealing their handbags?"

That's it, Gayle told herself. *Keep him talking.* She had worked one of the bonds around and over her right thumb. It was a start.

"Shame on you, Gayle," Buzz coughed, a sound like a gunshot inside a tin can. *No! Don't pay attention! Every time you stop and think about his injuries, you stop trying to free yourself!*

"I've never turned to Villainy," said Buzz. "You know the Man don't fly that way, and never will."

"Not knowingly."

"I don't take jobs that require murder or theft . . . well, not from anyone who doesn't have it coming, anyway. I'm strictly a sabotage, undercover, spy stuff kinda guy. That's the stuff that the ladies like."

Gayle rolled her eyes. "I'm positively swooning." *Two more fingers free!* "So did someone finally catch up with the Man and give him what he deserved?"

"Guess so," said Buzz, "but damn if I know why. This was a courier job. A simple pickup and drop-off."

"Really?" Gayle arched an eyebrow.

"Well," Buzz grinned, "convince someone to sign it away, pick it up out of her hands, and drop it off into someone else's hands."

"Ah." Gayle struggled to keep her face impassive as she felt her right hand slip loose. "So what went wrong?"

"Mission accomplished just fine. But someone apparently didn't approve. Someone who hires people with big muscles and bigger guns."

"Buzz—believe me when I say I'm sorry you got what was finally coming to you. But Buzz, you got what was finally coming to you. I still don't see why you need me all tied up here."

But not for much longer. She was already using her razor nail to cut. Ten seconds, maybe fifteen, and—

"You're not my prisoner, Gayle."

"Oh really? That's a relief. The ropes had me fooled for a minute."

"Like I said, this is only a temporary thing—"

"Extremely temporary," said Gayle, and with that, swung her newly freed arms up and back. The shift in her weight caused her to topple backwards, but that was her intention all along. Buzz was already beginning to blur, to rush forward to catch her, but Gayle had calculated the time. Falling into a handstand, she swung her legs, tied to the chair as they were, up into the air, at the precise moment connect with Buzz's oncoming body.

The satisfying smack should have filled her with triumph, but Buzz's cry of pain only made her wince. Gayle let the chair smash down against the floor, jarring its legs loose from the frame. Then she rolled out of her arch throwing her arms forward to un-do the remaining bonds.

Injured as he was, she didn't expect Buzz to recover so quickly. But a sudden grip around her upper arms told her she was wrong.

"Gayle, stop it!" he hissed into her ear, and, at this proximity, she could smell the sickening rot of infected wounds.

Head butt him! said the voice in her mind.

Gayle tried. She really tried. But the muscles wouldn't respond. She couldn't. She just couldn't. Not to any man this injured, let alone one she knew. Even if it was Buzz. Damn it! She was certain Captain Omega never had this problem.

"If you think I'm going to just sit here and be your listening post—"

"I didn't bring you here as a listening post!" Buzz cried out, and at that moment, a crash sounded from above, accompanied by tearing metal. The one light in the room flickered madly.

Buzz gazed up at the ceiling. Gayle craned her neck to follow, and saw fear wash over her captor's face.

"To be honest," said Buzz, "I never did give those goons the shake. I'm afraid, Gayle, that I brought you here to protect me."

2

"Who, how many, what powers or weapons?"

"No idea, no idea, and no bleeding idea," said Buzz as he worked to help Gayle untie herself from the remaining bonds.

"Splen," said Gayle. "You do realize that, against Supers, I'm probably not the best person to have for protection."

"You were the easiest to kidnap," said Buzz, panting. "Besides, this wasn't exactly my most well thought-out plan."

"You should have waited until tomorrow," said Gayle. "That's Friday."

She glanced around the room. "So we're in an underground cellar beneath a factory on Titanium Ave?"

"Yep."

"And the only way in or out is the staircase you've blocked off?"

"Far as I know."

"Brilliant. All right, where's my utility belt?"

"Here," Buzz handed it to her. "The stuff from your pockets is on that desk, he pointed with his good arm."

"The stuff you found, anyway."

Gayle snapped the belt into place, suddenly feeling the kind of security she got from pulling a shade down when she was dressing. Suddenly, no more nakedness. She knew it made no sense, and didn't care.

If only her costume proper wasn't still at the dry cleaners! Inside the folds of her trenchcoat she kept stun-guns, gas-grenades, expanding bolo-nets, and all other manner of gadgetry to help turn the tide of a super battle. Her "off-duty" kit consisted of nothing more than a boomerang, a couple of chemical vials, a single sonic charge, and of course, her cuff-link comm device. She tapped the Friday Knights signal, only to be rewarded with a disappointing error beep.

"We're being jammed," said Gayle. "No chance for a cavalry rescue."

"Naturally," Buzz sighed.

"Well, your super-speed still seems to work," Gayle said hurriedly as the sound of footsteps began pounding towards them. "That gives us something."

"I'm afraid," Buzz coughed a rattling wheeze, "the Man might be starting to check out on us—"

"Then go hide," said Gayle, "get out of the way, before—"

The barricade around the staircase, as well as good portions of the walls on either side, exploded in a shower of concrete and pseudowood, spraying a blizzard of insulation in Gayle's direction. Her arm shielded her eyes, but the dust and powder invaded her lungs, sending her into hacking fits to match Buzz's.

Shapes began to move and shimmer in the haze, and Gayle's instincts told her to duck just before a fist came flying in her direction. Taking advantage of her momentum, she kicked out as she fell, and her boot connected with a hard, metallic surface.

"Ow!" she cried out as she recovered into a crouch. Whoever this was, he or she was either partially invulnerable or wearing armor. Wonderful.

She heard Buzz cry out from somewhere behind her, but she didn't dare crane her neck to look—one of the shapes was finally coalescing into a bulky human form. The invader boasted football player physique, topped by a tiny head with infant-sized red night-vision goggles over its eyes. Two meaty arms bore an assault rifle as easily if it were a plastic squirt gun, sweeping the cloudy air with its laser sight.

Knowing she was most emphatically *not* faster than a speeding bullet, Gayle flung herself out of the way of the red line and scrambled around to the man's back. He turned slowly, trying to follow her. Good. He was as sluggish and ungainly as he looked. That might, *might*, give her an advantage.

Even "invulnerable" Supers weren't invulnerable everywhere. Most had some sort of weak spot, and orifices were always a good place to start. Gayle popped open a pouch on her utility belt, produced a thin chemical vial, and, with a fluid motion, leapt up and hurled its contents at the tiny target of the man's ear. Most of the contents splashed uselessly around his cheek and shoulder, but a little of it managed its way into the ear canal . . . and a little was all Gayle needed.

Immediately, he doubled over, raising a hand to his ear and dropping the rifle in his other one with a clatter. The inner ear was the center of balance, and enough T-192 (one of those lovely radioactive byproducts of Trinity) splashed inside would bring immediate nausea and unbalance. Gayle took good advantage of that unbalance to hurl herself at the man's knees, using her judo to flip him over and onto the ground. He fell over her with a satisfying crash.

Now where was that rifle? Not that Gayle had ever, would ever, fire a gun, but these thugs couldn't know that. Maybe she could threaten, posture, bluff—

Get punched.

At least, that was her last coherent thought as the impact caught her from behind, sending her hurling across the room until a desk rudely arrested her flight. Pain splintered through her ribs and shoulders, as Gayle fell back to the ground, and the room spun as she struggled to get her bearings.

Another muscleman was approaching, this one taller and lankier but still an excellent poster-boy for steroid treatments. He wore the same goggles and carried the same weapon. Professionals, thought Gayle, amidst bursts of pain from her aching bones. Well, so was she. Sort of.

Gayle reached into her belt again, pulled out the boomerang, and flung it at her attacker. He easily ducked out of the way, raising his weapon to train it on Gayle. The red light fixed itself on her forehead, and his finger moved to the trigger.

Then the boomerang, on its return trip, clocked him in the back of the head.

The impact didn't seem to hurt him, but it did get his attention, and Gayle forced her screaming limbs to bring her to her feet, to make use of the distraction, and run out of the way just as the man fired off a round. The gunfire blew the already beleaguered desk into splinters.

Suddenly, Gayle heard Buzz's voice.

"You . . . don't . . . mess . . . with the Man," he growled, raining a series of hyperspeed punches upon yet a third intruder—or was it the first one, that Gayle had downed with the T-192? The hulking thug waved its fists futility at the blur that was his opponent, but Buzz avoided every blow, landing a dozen of his own per second. Unfortunately, their effect seemed negligible.

We're barely keeping ourselves alive, Gayle thought dismally. *We need some way to go on the offense.*

She heard the telltale clack of a rifle being cocked behind her. Lanky Man had found her again. Wait, maybe that was the answer. She darted into his line of fire, waved her arms, and prayed her reflexes were as good as she thought they were.

A second before he fired, she ducked. The bullets sailed over her head to impact against the skin of Buzz's opponent.

Hulking Man screamed and doubled over. Gayle didn't see any blood, but that was definitely pain in his voice. All right, so they were invulnerable, but not completely.

Buzz, taking advantage of his foe's fall, zoomed over to Gayle's "dancing partner" and swiped the rifle from his hands between eyeblinks.

"I hope this hurts you more than it hurts hurt me," he grumbled through a mouthful of blood, and unloaded a full clip into the Lanky Man. More screams. No blood. Buzz fired until the clip expended itself, issuing nothing but angry clacking sounds.

They had the attackers off balance. Ok, so now what?

Gayle barely had time to register that fact before a third man emerged from the shadows, rifle in hand, and clubbed Buzz violently over the head with it. At full strength, Buzz should have seen that coming like a fly sees a newspaper, and dodged it just as easily. But Buzz had practically been on death's door before this fight even began, and the rifle took him down.

What could Gayle do? They had night-vision goggles, which meant her smoke capsules would be useless. But there ears were vulnerable, she had seen that already. Steeling herself, she unlatched the sonic charge from her belt, the last weapon she had remaining, and hurled it to the ground.

Every fire alarm on Earth, every whistling tea kettle, every high pitched child's whine, if squeezed into one piercing noise, might have approximated the sound of Gayle's sonic charge. George had designed it for maximum non-lethal punishment, enough to flatten an entire mob of opponents through the sheer power of sound. Gayle had hoped her preparedness would save her from at least some of its effect. She had hoped wrong.

Her world exploded into pain and pulsing, and the room spun and danced as she felt her knees give out beneath her. Dim swathes of vision seemed to betray images of the attackers falling as well, and Gayle almost took some satisfaction in that, before thought fled entirely, erased by a smear of white pain. Then, just as she thought her heart and lungs and brain would all burst at once, the noise ceased.

Gayle's hands shook as they plied the ground. Her knees bucked and refused to let her rise. She felt as if she were plastered to a spinning piece of driftwood being tossed around a roiling ocean. A thin stream of vomit issued from between her lips.

Some indeterminate amount of time later, Gayle's vision managed to refocus enough to see the three invaders slowly stagger to their feet, lurching this way and that, leaning on one another for support only to fall down again in a heap of limbs. Gayle would have found it comical were she herself able to make any motions at all. This would be the perfect time to escape. *Someone tell it to my body.*

Finally, the thugs rose to a shaky footing. One of them had managed to relocate his rifle, and swept the room. The sight fell first on Buzz, still unconscious, then arced around the room until it found Gayle.

Get up! Get up! Get up!

It was no good. Gayle's brain fired messages, but the phones in her limbs remained off the hook.

If only it were Friday, Gayle spent what were probably her last moments of thought bemoaning. *One more day. Probably less than eight hours by now. Eight bloody hours, and I could have licked these guys with one hand.*

The thug trained the weapon, steadied himself, and fired.

Nothing happened.

Ha! Gayle thought in triumph. *That must have been the empty rifle!*

Triumph lasted for about fifteen seconds until the man reloaded. Steady. Aim.

Gayle refused to close her eyes. She would watch this coming. She owed her father, her team, herself, that much. She heard the faintest of pops, which, with her hearing undamaged by the sonic charge, probably would have sounded like the thunder of a gunshot.

Gayle didn't feel anything. Was that how death worked?

She continued to look at the thug. He was beginning to stagger. Was he still dizzy from the sonic charge? No. He was clutching at his arm, as if it were being stung by bees.

No, not bees. Gunshots.

With supreme effort, Gayle craned her next to see Detective Roland crouched in the hole in the wall, pistol trained on Gayle's assailant. The "pops" continued. Four. Five. Six. Then they stopped.

Gayle still couldn't hear his voice, but the motions of Roland's mouth were most definitely curses as he realized what little effect his weapon had on them. All three thugs staggered slowly towards him, and he darted away from their ungraceful charge, out into the room.

No! Gayle tried to cry out, although she couldn't hear own words. He had just trapped himself in the room with them.

Roland reached down to his ankle, pulled another gun from the holster there, and emptied another clip into the thugs, with similar lack of effect. He circled and backpedaled the whole time, moving closer to Gayle.

By now Gayle was able to draw herself up onto her elbows, but maintaining this posture took all the strength she had. Roland turned to her, said something, but she couldn't hear it. She felt as if she had just come home from a rock concert.

"Go away!" she shouted.

He bent down, weapon still trained on the oncoming thugs.

His lips mouthed some words of encouragement, but the sweat on his brow betrayed his fear.

So now her last sight would be Roland's face. Terribly, tragically romantic.

"Chivalrous of you to come find me," she shouted, "but stupid as hell, Detective. Now we're just going to die together."

Roland said something, but she shook her head and pointed to her ear. He got the message, and bent in close, calling at what must have been the top of his lungs, but to her sounded like a mouse squeak.

"I may be a romantic at heart, sister," he told her, "but I'm not stupid. I didn't come back for you alone."

Gayle blinked. What did he mean?

Then, as the thugs suddenly fell like bowling pins beneath the impact of a blurring brown shape, she understood.

Combat Wombat's "Yeeeeeeehhhhhaaaw!" sounded loudly enough for even Gayle to hear it. Claws flailing, teeth gnashing, Craig lit into the thugs in a blur of fake fur, tearing gashes into their clothing and slicing one of their rifles clean in two.

Noctyrne was next into the breach, gliding gracefully through the lingering remains of the dust cloud to land atop one of the thug's back. She boxed his ears, and then, twisting her head, dove in and sunk her fangs deep into his neck. The larger man shivered for a moment, then collapsed beneath her. She tossed back her head of raven hair, mouth all bloodied, and screeched to the night.

Combat Wombat flung his own "dance partner" into a wall, then proceeded to try and strangle him with his own nightvision goggles.

"Easy!" a reverberating voice boomed as GAP thundered into the room. "Zero body count, people! We're heroes, remember that."

"Relax," said Noctyrne, or at least, that's what Gayle imagined she was saying. She had seen Naomi's hurried explanations before, and could extrapolate the usual defense—she was only taking enough blood to incapacitate her opponent, not kill him.

GAP swung a mighty metal fist to fell thug number two in one blow, and Craig finally brought down his own man with a couple of trademark Wombat Head-Butts.

Noctyrne elegantly wiped her mouth clean with a handkerchief, then rushed over to where Roland was tending to Gayle. She offered some inaudible words of comfort and concern, and stroked Gayle's hair lovingly. Gayle didn't care about the specific content. Her friends were here. She was safe. She could have died happily. Except now, she didn't need to.

3

"Can you hear me now?"

"Ow. Sort of. Yes."

"How do you feel?"

"Like all the aspirin in the world wouldn't make a dent in my headache," Gayle rubbed at her neck. Noctyrne was working out the knots in Gayle's shoulders while GAP used his scanners to check her vital signs for the nth time.

"No permanent damage," he said, "although those ribs are gonna be sore tomorrow. You're lucky Gayle. Hell, we're lucky too."

"If that lovely Detective friend of yours hadn't found us," Noctyrne's voice warbled, "well, I don't even want to think."

Roland, across the room, pretended he didn't hear. He and Combat Wombat were interrogating their new captives, although Gayle couldn't seem to figure out who was playing "good cop" and "bad cop," or whether there was even a "good cop" at all. She sighed. Men.

George wasn't like that, of course. George hadn't taken his scanners off her since the moment the last thug fell. He wouldn't leave until he was positively certain she was all right. She almost wanted to stay, to be under that care indefinitely . . .

Waley would have called that weak. Well, Waley wasn't here.

Buzz sat curled up in the corner, nursing a cup of tea that George had reluctantly produced from within his GAP suit. Noctyrne had wanted to deny him even that. How could a woman who was so caring to her and George be so ruthless to Buzz?

The Gayle thought of Waley again. She could almost, almost understand.

"If it makes you feel any better," said GAP as he saw Gayle rubbing her aching temples, "the sound of that sonic charge was what helped us find you. Roland saw you being taken away, but Buzz moved too fast for him to track. He came to us, and Noctyrne tried to sniff out your trail . . . but Buzz knows a few tricks."

"Tricks?" said Buzz. "This isn't tricks, this is the Man's natural style. If I didn't want to be found, you wouldn't have found me. In fact, you didn't until that sonic charge of hers probably sent half the dogs aboveground into barking fits."

"We traced the sound," said GAP, "and found you here, with your mysterious company," he chucked a metal thumb at the captives.

"They're not talking," Roland sighed as he returned to the mass of heroes. "Frankly, I'm not sure they even have anything to talk about. All the evidence indicates they're hired muscle, probably contracted electronically by unseen parties."

"Sounds like some people we know," Noctyrne looked daggers at Buzz.

The wounded Super shrugged. "Hey, not all of us had the good judgment to decide to marry rich. Some people have to earn their money the old fashioned way."

Noctyrne surged, about to leap, but Gayle caught her by the arm. "Don't let him get to you," she said firmly, and Noctyrne hissed and turned away.

"So what *is* your story this time, Buzz?" asked GAP. "According to Gayle, you're the reason she's in this mess. Any explanation before we haul you off to jail?"

"On what charge, former boss-man?" Buzz grinned his shattered-teeth grin. "Check out all my permits—I was operating all legal in the City. Courier work's not against any law I know."

"But kidnapping is," said Roland. "So if you want any chance of keeping that playboy ass of yours out of prison, you'd better tell us the whole story behind this."

Buzz chuckled uneasily. "As I told our intrepid Gal Friday, I was just doing a job."

"For who?" GAP demanded.

"For the eightieth time, I don't know."

"What was the job?"

"High class splen," said Buzz. "Spy stuff, the real deal. Sneak behind the battle lines in Bulravia, persuade some gorgeous and mysterious Doctor to release a datapad, and get it back to Mesopolopolis. A few tangos with Bulravian ladies added at no extra charge."

"What was on the datapad?" Roland pressed.

"Your mom's little black book," he grinned. Roland grunted, unimpressed.

"Buzz," said Gayle, "you endangered my life, and my friends' lives—who used to be your friends too, as I recall—as well your own. You owe us an explanation. Besides, weren't you trying to tell it to us anyway back at the nightclub?"

Buzz sighed. "I never could resist the charms of a beautiful lady. Ok, the datapad had some sort of communication log on it. Sensor data of some sort, from, get this, the Europa Mission. That's right, the *Santa Maria*, the one Neville Shandon commanded. Frankly, I didn't understand three quarters of all that science splen. The Man had better things to do in school than hit the books, if you know what I mean."

Noctyrne growled. Everyone else ignored him.

"Something's up with that mission. Something big. That's what I was trying to tell you when I ran into you at that nightclub. I knew I was being tailed from the moment I got the goods, but the Man was too swift for the goons. I made the delivery, got my cash, and then decided to let them catch up to me."

"I suppose," Gayle said dryly, "that you decided to `let them' beat you within an inch of your life as well."

"Is it my fault they don't know anything about style? I told them they were too late, but they didn't seem to care. They searched me . . . a little more thoroughly than politeness dictates. Now they still seem to think I have a copy."

Gayle frowned. "Do you?"

Buzz smirked. "Hey, do I ever mix business and pleasure?"

"Yes," said all the Friday Knights as one.

"Ok, ok, so maybe I kept a memento. You know, to remind me of those luscious, languid, Bulravian nights—"

"And probably also figuring," said Gayle, "that if your employer was willing to pay for the goods, someone else might be willing to pay for copies as well."

"You are just too good," Buzz bowed his head. "Remind me again why we never hooked up?"

"Because you're a slimeball," said Noctyrne.

"That never stopped *you*, dear."

Again she lunged. This time it took both Gayle and GAP to hold her back.

"They're not talking," Combat Wombat stalked back. "I say we make necklaces out of their intestines, and make Buzz wear 'em as jewelry on his next date."

"Stand down," said GAP. "Look, in the final analysis, this isn't even our case to investigate. We need to find Georgie Porgie—"

"It's the *same case*," Buzz coughed. "I know the guy you're after. I was following him myself when I ran into you. He worked with the lady doctor. Mondo weird dude. Back in Bulravia he kept himself all locked up in his room, talking to himself. Somehow he followed me back overseas, and I was trailing him to figure out just how he did it. Where he is now, I don't know."

"We don't know where he is," said GAP, "but we know where he's headed."

"Really?" said Gayle. "Where? How?"

Noctyrne spoke. "When GAP and I were out shopping for . . ." She tossed an uneasy glance at all the outsiders in the room. "Er, I mean, when we were out in Mesopolopolis today, we caught another report of an attack. This time, we got to the scene soon enough for me to get a scent."

"You're a regular bloodhound, sweetie," said GAP.

"Oh please," Buzz made gagging noises. "Why not just assign her to a Bloodhound Gang, then?"

All the Supers in the room tensed.

"That's not funny, Buzz," Gayle finally said.

"Actually, we have the Detective to thank for keeping the Bloodhounds off the Georgie Porgie case to begin with."

"What do you mean, GAP?"

GAP turned to look at Roland, who was trying to look anywhere but at the heroes. Was this some kind of modesty?

"When the Detective called us to tell us about your abduction, we had just finished investigating a brand-new Georgie Porgie assault. When the police on the scene found out a superhuman was the suspect, and that Noctyrne had a confirmed scent, they were all ready to enforce the Lee Act and turn over the smell engrams to the Peace Officers."

Again, an unseen ripple of tension ran through the bodies of the Supers present. Peace Officer Bloodhound Gangs employed the most efficient and lethal technology for one and only one purpose— tracking down rogue superhumans. The Lee Act allowed Bloodhound Gangs full authority to act as judge, jury, and, too often, executioners. Once a Bloodhound Gang was authorized, there could be no appeal, no commuting of sentence, and no transfer to a court of due process. Better to be caught by the police, or even other Supers, than a Bloodhound Gang.

"When Roland called, he used his authority as Detective on that case to keep the Peace Officers out. He deputized the Friday Knights, Gayle. Responsibility for solving this case now officially rests on our shoulders."

"You don't know what you're in for," Buzz was saying, but Gayle didn't hear. She was looking at Roland, as if for the first time. The murk of the basement cell occluded the features of his face slightly, and insulation blanketed his brown hair and suit. His normally defiant posture looked sunken, almost self-conscious. Yet, for all of this, he never looked more beautiful to Gayle than at this moment. If her own personal sense of decorum would have permitted it, she would have flung her arms around him right then and there.

Instead, she searched with her eyes, eventually drawing his gaze to her own.

"Thank you," she said, in a voice that shouldered a lifetime of emotion.

Roland smiled uneasily, as much a prisoner of himself as she.

Religion may be the opiate of the masses, but after Trinity, who the hell didn't need to get high?

—Ella Ducharme, former State Poet Laureate

MARLA

Marla Arliss steeled herself at the doors, expecting chanting, cross-burnings, maybe even a blood sacrifice or two. But when the ornate oak portals (real oak, not pseudowood) bearing the golden DNA helix of the Church of Humanity parted, they revealed what looked, to all of Marla's reasoning, to be a particularly festive and egalitarian dinner party. Distinguished-looking middle-aged men wearing blazers and women in Sunday dresses mingled nonchalantly with jeans and tee-shirt clad twentysomethings, circling a snack table loaded with crisp carrots and celery, plump shrimp, a shining crystal bowl overflowing with banana chips, and ivory decanters filled with fruit juices of all colors.

Across the room, other parishioners lounged on plush sofas, some chattering peaceably and others laughing violent, hearty belly-laughs. Most were smiling, and the few that weren't soon found one of the white-garbed Church Stewards at their side, who would congenially take the awkward or discontented individual the elbow and lead him or her to another part of the room, introduce them to the cluster of people there, and subtly slip back into the shadows, hoping the wallflower-in-question would bloom better in new soil.

Marla floated but stayed close to Aylia as her friend dragged her in concentric circuits around the room. Aylia seemed to know everyone. Aylia chatted merrily about automobiles with this man, politics with that one, this article in that newspaper with a cluster of women who would have looked perfectly at home hovering around an office water cooler, avoiding whatever work they were supposed to be doing. Marla never tended to leave her desk at work, and thus felt ill suited to participate.

She didn't even know entirely why she came. Her mother was a Pan-Transcendentalist who didn't believe in Churches at all, and her father, though a Keeper of the Spirit, barely even went to Church on Sundays, let alone a Thursday like this. Of course, Marla hadn't seen any of her family in over two years. Maybe that was part of the reason she came. Yet four walls of her apartment had really never seemed bare until yesterday, until that conversation with Thunderbolt (Conversation? More like an assault!) that had made her feel so very, very small and undefended. Weren't superheroes supposed to protect you? Who protected you from *them*?

Maybe Marla needed to know that some higher power existed, something greater than those impossibly tall, powerful, and beautiful creatures who lived on the moon and glared contemptuously down upon her every day. Aylia probably just figured that weeks of proselytizing had finally paid off. For all Marla knew, it had.

So she wandered like a specter through the mill of happy faces, and eventually, through the slow currents of social drift, she somehow found herself embroiled in a conversation about last year's highly publicized Bulravian espionage trial with a trio of paralegals from a private firm. Before Marla knew it, she was explaining the subtleties of due process to them while munching on bits of dried salmon topped with wamba melon. Somewhere around a heated debate about the precedents set by Mesopolopolis vs. The Tremendous Trio, the chime sounded for worship, and the Stewards began removing the refreshments and ushering the congregants into the sanctuary.

Marla found Aylia's arm and held it subtly as they shuffled into the domed hall. Marla had actually been on the verge of relaxation until now, and once again, half expected some sort of eerie Druidic rite was now to be unveiled. But the sanctuary was not frightening in the slightest. The curved walls were not hung, as Marla had feared, with inverted pentagrams or the skeletons of Supers. Instead, the East wall bore a veritable montage of humanity's achievements—images of cave dwellers pounding out the first wheel, of clipper ships sailing the uncharted seas, of the rickety first airplane, superimposed over a photo of the jet first that broke the sound barrier. White-clad scientists curing diseases were immortalized atop the moon and Mars landings, and the first cold fusion engine. Triumph after triumph. Despite herself, Marla felt the welling of pride and inspiration inside her. If the sermon grew boring or uncomfortable, she suspected she would have no problem just gazing at this wall for hours.

No images of science hung on the West wall—instead, it bore images of families, families from all corners of the globe, all skin tones, all cultures, all modes of dress. Men, women, children, grandparents, cousins, life partners, flanked by yapping dogs and steadfast yaks, bleating sheep and timid mice. All of their eyes, human and animal alike, seemed to radiate a message of friendship, of acceptance. Marla suddenly began to miss her parents.

The rear wall bore religions totems and icons from all over the world, whatever ankh or star or trapezoid humans picked to symbolize that which could not be symbolized. The dome itself tapered off into a giant circular glass window to the night stars above, and behind the modest altar at the front of the chamber hung the golden DNA helix of the Church.

White curtains parted from behind the helix, and "shushes" filled the room as Deacon Allbright emerged.

"Good evening, brothers and sisters," he spoke, and Marla immediately knew why this man decided to be a preacher. His voice echoed with a warm pound that snapped all around him to attention. His sloped forehead looked ready to burst into beads of sweat at any moment, and his black eyes already shined with the crackle of energy. But his posture remained relaxed, his smile jovial, his large black hands spread wide to embrace the congregation.

"I say to you again, good evening," he took to the podium. "It fills me with joy to see so many of you here. In this marvelous modern age of ours, sad, lonely souls sit at computer keyboards, hitting buttons that register little lights on someone else's monitor a thousand miles away, and call that communication. They call that connection. How sad and tragic, sad and tragic my brothers and sisters, that we have come to this juncture."

"Connection is here," he pounded his chest, "and here," he flung his arms out to the masses, "here and here," he repeated the gesture, "with the sound of voices, the touch of flesh, the sight of smiles. Nature intended us to join with one another, and nature smiles upon us as we do, as she is smiling upon us now, brothers and sisters, say amen!"

"Amen," the crowd hummed as one. Marla allowed herself a small smile.

"Connection is holding the hand of your husband or wife, your girlfriend or boyfriend, your life partner, your best friend, your child, pressing your warmth to theirs, feeling their heartbeat, feeling their warmth, feeling the common bonds that unite us all. Male, female, black, white, yellow, red, tall, short, large, small—we are one, brothers and sisters, say amen!"

"Amen."

"We are one and we are many, we are many and we are one, we are together and we are never, ever alone as long as we remember our interconnectedness."

Marla liked how the Deacon pronounced every single consonant in "interconnectedness." As the sermon continued for the next few minutes, she began to look forward to each time he said that word, and was not disappointed, as it returned to his speech every few seconds.

"Now, interconnectedness," he began yet again, and his posture began to shift, his shoulders to arch—he was evidently getting to the meat of the sermon—"does not mean, I say again, does not mean, unity against a common foe. For that is the danger, the danger I say, brothers and sisters, of realizing our power as a group, our power as an interconnected group. We are one, we are one, but that one is a one of light, a one of charity, a one of beauty, a one of mercy. That one is not a one of hatred, cannot be a one of hatred."

"Amen," said the mass.

"There is joy, yes joy, in our interconnectedness, the jumping joy of knowing we are not alone, and this joy brings power. But power is like a drug, I say to you, a temptation, and we must resist temptation. One man or woman alone may be tempted, one man or woman alone is weak and fallible, for this too is that nature of our humanity, say amen."

"Amen." Marla surprised herself by joining in on that one.

"But humanity is not one man or woman, is never one man or woman. Humanity is interconnectedness, all of us together, amen, and together we are strong, we have power, we can overcome temptation. But we have to consciously make that choice. We have to consciously make that choice, as one, or we despoil all that is good and noble in our species, all that this holy Church has gathered here to worship today."

With that, Deacon Allbright launched into a blazing condemnation of last week's beating of a Mesopolopolis University student, a Super on a scholarship program. The perpetrators still had not been caught, and fingers were starting to point towards worshipers of the Church. The Deacon's eyes exploded with a passion that seized Marla by the arteries, frightening and inspiring her at the same time. Spittle flew from his thick pink lips as he called upon what was best in them, what was noblest, what made them humans and not beasts, to speak out against such acts of cruelty.

"Abominations," had become the new word Marla looked forward too, every consonant a piledriver. "These acts are a-bo-min-a-tions," he pounded the podium, "discrediting everything we stand for as a species, every advance we have made, every embrace of our children. We are human when we laugh, when we kiss, when we raise a sister from poverty and shoulder a brother with his chores."

"We are not human," the Deacon pounded again, "when we rain blows upon one another, or any other creature, be it dog or cat or Super, amen!"

"Amen!"

"Supers may not be like us, they may not be inheritors of Nature's gift, they may not be the chosen of her bounty, but so long as Mother Earth tolerates their presence on her soil, we must look to our Mother, amen, we must not disobey her loving commands, amen, we must treat her guests as our guests, amen."

"Amen!"

"Our humanity is our strength, our guiding light, that which sets us apart from the beasts and the fish and the trees and the Supers. A lion which kills does so because of what he is, a Super who kills does so because of what he is, but a human who kills is an abomination, an abomination, and the Church does not smile upon abominations. Nature does not smile upon abominations. When the reckoning comes, all abominations will be wiped from the surface of this beautiful planet, so brothers and sisters, we cannot throw away our inheritance for transitory pleasures, amen!"

"Amen!"

"For the sister who hides behind our doctrine, who claims the Church says we are better than the Supers, I say to that brother, I say, Sister, Sister of my flesh and blood and DNA, have you truly *read* our scriptures, sister, have you truly read them?"

Albright's eyes stared directly at Marla, and feelings of guilt and embarrassment welled up against her will. Aylia had lent her the Church books weeks ago, but Marla had only given them a cursory glance. But Allbright couldn't possibly know, could he?

"Sister, I say," he continued, still staring, for all Marla could tell, directly at her, "have you *read* our scriptures, have you truly read the words, and the words behind the words, which is the Word itself, amen?"

"Amen!"

Marla joined in on that one, as he was still looking at her. Prickly heat flashed up her cheeks, and her heart began to beat faster.

"The Word says we are better than the Supers because we are Human, and to be human is to be light, to be One, to be One in light, interconnected with light, interconnected with one another. To be Human is to be just and noble, to protect and shelter and guide, amen!"

"Amen," said Marla.

"To be human not to beat, not to murder, not to deliver violence unless no other option remains, amen!"

"Amen," said Marla.

"That university student was no super villain, was no Twister, was no abomination, save for his inalterable nature. He had no choice in what he was. We have a choice, brothers and sisters, a choice to eschew abomination, amen!"

"Amen," said Marla.

"We cannot, cannot allow ourselves to fall into the pit of abomination, and then justify it with the holy Word, for that is abomination upon abomination, is it not, brothers and sisters?"

"Amen," said Marla.

"We must defend the weak, raise up the low, heal the sick, for in doing so, we affirm our humanity, and affirm our distance from that which is not human. We affirm our rightness and our distance, our distance and our rightness, our light and our interconnection. And can I get an amen?"

"Amen."

"And I say, can I get an amen?"

"Amen!"

"And I say, can I get an a-men?"

"Amen!" Marla found herself shouting.

Then her pocket-phone rang.

Allbright went on preaching, his eyes mercifully turning away from her, as the flush in her cheeks raged like an inferno. She muttered apologies as she awkwardly rose to her feet, knees shaking, and climbed over congregants, out of the pew, into the aisle and out the door. Her fingers twitched uncontrollably, and she dropped the phone upon the ground before she could answer it.

The ring dutifully persisted until she brought it back up to her ear and pressed TALK. Her secretary was saying something, but Marla couldn't hear her, couldn't hear her at all over the words in the sanctuary beyond.

2

Marla Arliss didn't stop for a shower. Hair falling in ragged strands, stomach rumbling, eyes itching, Marla tugged at her now-wrinkled churchgoing dress as the prison guard admitted her into Neville Shandon's cell at the Penal Dome.

With a savage motion, Marla turned on the light, flooding the room and sending Shandon's sleeping form into small convulsions.

"Good morning," she said, with a little more sneer than she had intended, but not nearly as much as she wanted. "Yes, I know it's 1:00 AM, but time isn't exactly a commodity we have in large supply. The trial starts in three days, remember? Gordon Holloway is at this moment preparing to convince a jury to have you electrocuted, and the prosecution just received a communiqué today . . ."

She glanced at her watch. "Excuse me, *yesterday*," she looked back to him, "that might just grant him his wish."

Marla produced a datapad from her handbag and shoved it into Shandon's shivering hands.

Shandon blinked laconically, gave his sleepy head a few short shakes, then focused on the screen. The color which had just been returning to his cheeks suddenly fled. He let the pad drop to his cot.

"Yes," said Marla, "I thought that would disturb you. It sure as hell disturbed me. Why didn't you tell me about this?"

Shandon's fingers began a sequence of clenches and unclenches.

Marla took a deep breath, re-centering herself. In through the nose, out through the mouth. All right. Focus had returned.

"How did they get this?" he croaked. "The logs—"

103

"Oh, the logs on your ship were erased, Commander. But Lieutenant Michelis sent a message to his wife during the mission. A message chock full of details, a message Holloway somehow got his hands on."

Pain lanced across Shandon's face.

"The drilling operation was hardly routine, was it?" Marla pressed, pointing to the datapad. "You detected some anomalous electrical readings during the operation. You took samples and began analyzing them."

Air hissed from between Shandon's lips.

"Why wasn't this in the logs, Commander? Why didn't any of the samples make it back to Earth?"

Shandon grimaced as if swallowing some unpleasant liquid.

"Look at me!"

Shandon's gaze crept back towards her general direction.

"This looks very bad, Commander. This looks like Michelis and Al—Awadi made a find, which, under the Goltsov Act, would entitle them to stake in any potential profits from its exploitation. Now they're dead, and you suppressed evidence of their claim. This is starting to smell a hell of a lot like motive, Shandon. What the hell is going on here?"

"Please don't use that evidence in court," Shandon said, his voice little more than a papery scratch.

"Ah. You can speak. This is progress."

"Please don't use that evidence in court," he repeated. "There's got to be some way to keep it off the table. The Virtual Privacy Act—"

"Michelis' wife signed it over to one of Holloway's agents, Commander. It's now State's evidence." Marla allowed herself to soften. "Look, I know you're afraid, but this is when we start working together. This is when you tell me everything that happened, and I try my best to make sure that—"

"No!" Shandon cried out, hurling himself up from the cot with such violence that Marla stepped back in fear. Should she call the guard?

"No," Shandon repeated, chest heaving, open palms raised in the air. "Please. I'll plead guilty. I'll plead guilty to murder, to mass-murder, to conspiracy, anything they want. Just please don't let that data go public."

Marla blinked. "I . . . I don't understand."

"No, you don't, and I pray that no one ever does. No one will, if you just wipe out that email, and any traces of it."

"I can't do that," said Marla. "For one, it's evidence. I'd be disbarred, then jailed. For another, this is only a copy. Holloway's office sent it to me because the law requires they share evidence. I told you, it belongs to the State now."

Shandon's body began a slow deflation. He staggered backwards, nearly tripping as the back of his legs hit the cot. A small, animal noise issued from him, sounding almost like "no," cut off by small sobs.

Marla felt like a mother who had just disciplined her two year old too harshly. She drew cautiously nearer.

"Commander," she began, "we'll get through this. I can at least save your life, if not your freedom . . . but you have to work with me."

"It's not *my* like I'm afraid for," Shandon hissed, and neither soft reassurances or stern reprimands could elicit anything for from him.

Marla left the cell more confused than ever. She paced the corridors of the prison, this house of murderers and rapists and thieves, people she spent her life defending and helping to make excuses for. Even at 1:00 AM, sounds rose everywhere—clanging of guards' boots of the metal floors, beeping of monitor lights, the low hum of generators—but all Marla could hear was Deacon Allbright's voice.

With every cell block she passed, with every thought of the criminals within, she heard his voice. "We cannot, cannot allow ourselves to fall into the pit of abomination."

"We affirm our rightness and our distance, our distance and our rightness, our light and our interconnection."

Interconnection. There was a laugh. Marla lived alone. She spoke with no one but her clients, her secretary, judges, and occasional friends like Aylia. Where was her connection? Certainly not with Neville Shandon.

"We must defend the weak, raise up the low, heal the sick, for in doing so, we affirm our humanity, and affirm our distance from that which is not human."

She was trying to defend Shandon, she was! But what if he was guilty, what if he was an "abomination," what about her responsibility to the rest of humanity?

Something still didn't add up. If he was guilty, if he admitted he was guilty, then why suppress the evidence? Whom was he afraid for? Whom was he trying to protect, and was it or was it not Marla's duty to aid in that protection?

"We affirm our rightness and our distance, our distance and our rightness, our light and our interconnection. And can I get an amen?"

"Amen," Marla muttered as she left the Penal Dome and stepped out into the cold, biting, lonely night outside.

"Let me be clear: we do not depend, nor have we ever depended, on Superhumans for our city's policing. The resources of the Superior Squad, as well as any hired privateers from the Herotowns, exist to supplement our own ample police forces . . . to ease their burden and assist them. So long as I hold office, no law enforcement jobs will ever be lost to Superhuman contractors. If anything, said contractors will be employed to increase the quality of the job for existing law enforcement personnel."

—Mayor Claudius Ironheart, election speech

GAYLE

The Stallion careened through the streets of Uptown Mesopolopolis, its inhabitants now duly authorized to remain among Normals for however long it took to apprehend their quarry.

Inside, each of the Friday Knights found a task to occupy themselves. GAP drove the van while Noctyrne, tiny waist twisted around the open window, extended her lithe body out the aperture, the wind billowing her hair behind her. She sniffed the air, narrowed her crimson eyes, and periodically hollered out driving directions. Combat Wombat busied himself at his laptop computer, alongside Gayle and Roland, who, together in the back seat, took on the detective work.

"If you plot the assaults," Gayle was pointing eagerly to the map she held in her hand, "you can see a directional pattern beginning to form. Each attack moves him North and West."

"He's moving away from residential zones," Roland's finger pointed to the map while his eyes never left Gayle's, "towards the city limits. Nothing much there except industry, then the Penal Dome, and then the ocean."

"That makes no sense," said Gayle. "He's moving away from areas with the greatest concentration of his potential targets."

107

"Maybe he's trying to get back to Bulravia?"

"Wrong ocean. Wrong direction."

"Maybe some part of him doesn't want to be assaulting people?" said Roland. "Maybe he's a newly developed Super, coming to terms with what he's become."

"That might make sense. Especially given that he seems to be from Bulravia."

In the State, no such thing as a "newly developed Super" existed anymore. The Metahumanics Commission's screening standards had improved dramatically in the past decade. Their scientists could now tell, *in utero*, whether an individual had the genetic potential for superhuman abilities, if exposed to the right circumstances (like a gypsy curse, for example, but more likely, post-Trinity radiation). As per the Lee Act, upon birth, that child, as well as his or her family if they wished, had to be relocated to a Herotown.

Of course, if the M.C. could detect genetic potential in a mass of barely differentiated cells, the possibility that an adult super, even an immigrant, could escape detection for this long seemed very strange.

"If he really is from Bulravia," Gayle wondered aloud, "he must have somehow sneaked past the M.C.'s monitors at customs."

"I find that hard to believe," said Roland. "This man's not stealthy. *Everyone* sees him at the site of these assaults."

"But somehow no one can catch him. He just uses his mind mojo. Maybe his powers are strong enough to fool even Peace Officers."

Despite herself, Gayle felt a tiny bit of hope at that.

"Sssh!" said Combat Wombat, fingers pounding the tiny keyboard in his lap. "If you want me to crack the encryption on this data-disk, you're gonna have to keep it down. The wizard needs silence for his magic!"

Roland regarded Combat Wombat, as he had been doing all evening, as if Craig had suddenly sprouted wings and antennae. Gayle had already explained Craig's computer aptitude to Roland:

"During all the years he was ostracized thanks to Twister, barred from joining any super teams, do you think he just sat around and built sandcastles?"

"Well, sat around and smashed them, perhaps—"

"And you claim to have detective skills," Gayle had smiled wryly. "Combat Wombat is a computer master. What GAP can do with engineering and circuit boards, Wombat can do with data streams and operating systems. If anyone can break the code on Buzz's data-disk and find out just what it holds that's worth so much money and blood, Wombat can."

"Only," Craig had growled, displaying that unerring animal hearing in picking up their conversation across the room, "if you're quiet and let me work."

An hour later, on the road, he was still working, which meant whoever encrypted the data was good. Then again, Buzz had boasted that "The Man" only worked for the top clients.

Right now, of course, "The Man" was in traction at a hospital in Herotown, admitted under an anonymous name and guarded by the very best rent-a-thugs that George's private fortune could hire. In exchange, he had given the Friday Knights the copy he had made of the data as a "project" to investigate. After so long without a mission, the team was now tackling two at once. Gayle had to admit to a certain thrill.

Of course, Fridays always brought with them a certain thrill. Despite last night's ordeal, Gayle had set her alarm clock for dawn. She had to experience the whole day, drink in every second, of a life that suddenly leapt from mundane, even oppressive, to extraordinary, all with the tick of a clock hand.

She woke up to snowfall, a genuine one this time, that caked the ground below in a rich layer of chocolate. Gayle still had dim memories of white snows from her childhood, pre-Trinity fallout, but dark snows had been a companion for too much of her life to wish for anything else. Children ran slogging through the alleyways, hurling balls of frozen slush, building snow-people, and knocking them down with fists, claws, tails, and energy blasts.

Gayle walked outside in her puffy overcoat to find old widowed Mr. Elmore, pipe-cleaner arms scraping the ice off his jeep, tufts of wispy gray hair poking out from beneath a hole-ridden woolen cap. Mr. Elmore couldn't have been more than 60, but by anyone's measure the man looked ancient. He had been one of the first émigrés to Herotown, not a Super himself but married to one. Unlike so many spouses who fled from their now-pariahed partners, he had stayed, stayed through three children who grew up only to die (one in a street fight, one at the hands of Peace Officers, and one from the Orange Sickness), through his wife's death from the weight of old age and sadness. No law had ever kept him here. Even now, he could walk right up to the gates, submit to a genetic scan, and stroll back into the world of normal, free, sane people. But for fifteen years, he never had. Herotown was his home, he'd say simply, and return to the silent corner of his silent room and sit without speaking.

"Good morning, Mr. Elmore," Gayle called out cheerily.

Mr. Elmore waved with feeble joviality. His other hand continued to chip at the ice that imprisoned one of his tires.

"Here," Gayle sauntered over, "let me help you with that."

Gayle bent down, secured a grip on the chassis of the jeep, braced herself on a non-slippery patch of pavement, and heaved. The jeep lifted into the air, snapping its icy bonds into a million sparkling shivers. As she watched the Jeep flop around in her grip, felt nothing more than a small pull at her muscles, she realized she needn't even have exerted as much as she did. Then again, a week's absence was long enough to have to re-learn certain things.

She set the jeep gently down as Mr. Elmore watched, impassively, with the mute contemplation of one who had already seen too much. He inclined his head silently, which Gayle took for the gesture of thanks that it probably was. She didn't need words. She didn't need anything right now. Gayle literally skipped up down the street, waving to familiar faces whose names she still didn't know, and to utter strangers whose names she never would. Some waved back, some jeered, some walked on without noticing, but they were all her brothers and sisters. Today, at least, Gayle belonged.

As the morning passed she rushed several crowds of youngsters, crashing their snowball fights by gathering ridiculously immense snow-boulders and hurling them to rain clouds of wetness their way. They laughed, they cursed, they hurled their own projectiles back at her. When no one was looking, Gayle would randomly lift mailboxes, only to set them gently back down again. She didn't want to cause any real havoc. She just wanted a little fun. Wasn't even she entitled to that?

Could she, perhaps, even be entitled to a little something more? Visions of the end of last evening wafted up like the smell of warm cider, strangling her brain and her heart with feelings she was convinced she had forgotten. Beneath the now-soaking wet pads of her mittens, her right hand could still feel the lingering remnants of Detective Roland's firm, long handshake, not really a shake but a squeeze, as they left the hospital where they admitted Buzz. She could close her eyes, and see projected onto her lids, like little movie screens, the eagerness in Roland's expression when they made their "date" for tonight. Well, a joint investigation. That was as close as superheroes got to dating, wasn't it?

So many questions, so much ambiguity, such a small fire—Gayle had to savor the wisps of smoke from the sparks, breathe on the embers carefully—too much or too little and it would blow out entirely. Gayle surprised herself with the hunger she felt inside, to see him, speak to him, have any contact whatsoever, especially physical, even if it was just his hand in hers again, his shoulder brushing against her as they parted goodnight. Each momentary brush felt like a Friday morning all over again.

As Gayle found herself lifting her third senior citizen's trapped automobile this morning, she suddenly paused, sedan in hand, as a jab of self-consciousness knifed into her stomach. What would Roland think if he was seeing her right now, seeing this 140 pound woman lifting a 2,000 pound vehicle over her head, grinning goofily, while a crowd of onlookers murmured commentary?

Would he murmur too? Would he recoil? Would he turn away? Or worst of all, would he go on talking to her as if nothing had happened whatsoever, all the while some secret machinery shifted in his head to label her "freak," and she would never know? Her smile fled. She put the auto back down sullenly, deaf to the thank-you's from its owner. Suddenly Friday had fled, the snow melted, and Gayle again found herself being sucked into the pavement, some inner voice of hers screaming unheeded calls for aid. She walked through the crowds alone again, wondering what hope sustained them, sustained people like Cima in the Freakside market. They had the *Spandex Scene*, they had their black snowfalls,

111

they had their powerstunt games . . . and Gayle had her stupid schoolgirl fantasies about finding love.

Idiot. The walls around Herotown would fall first.

Now, past nightfall, the Stallion had left those walls nearly an hour. Gayle could almost pretend they didn't exist. But they did. They existed right here, right in the back seat of the van, right between where she and Roland sat conferring over the case.

He was saying something, but the words shattered beneath Noctyrne's shout of triumph.

"Got him!" she said. "The scent is strong, team, very strong—he's somewhere on this very block!"

GAP pulled the Stallion into a sudden swerve, running them up onto the sidewalk and scattering the small conglomerate of shoppers making their way past a fashionable Uptown boutique, holiday cheer on their faces suddenly transformed to indignation, and then, when they caught sight of the van's occupants, terror. Some ran, and some whipped out their pocket-phones, mostly likely calling the police or Peace Officers. The Friday Knights piled out, indifferent. They were fully authorized, and they had work to do.

"Scanning for heat signatures," GAP announced as he climbed into his battlesuit. Servos whirred, scanners hummed. "We've got about 1300 human beings on this block, Noctyrne. Can you narrow it down any further?"

"This way," she hissed, and leapt forth into the darkness, her body shimmering and fading into the cold night air.

"How does she . . . ?" Roland whispered. "I mean, is she . . . ?"

"A vampire?" Noctyrne suddenly appeared behind him.

Roland flinched, but, to his credit, did not cry out. Gayle tried to respect that.

"Just call me a creature of the night," she purred, running a long white finger along Roland's neck.

Gayle felt her own blood boil. Noctyrne had already taken one man she loved. Wasn't one enough?

Then she chided herself for her silliness. Noctyrne was playing, as she always did, even in the middle of a mission.

Combat Wombat begrudgingly put his computer under the seat and ambled out to face the task at hand.

"Where is this guy already?" He shifted in his Wombat Suit, patting at the dangling protrusion on the posterior end. "I'm freezing my tail off here."

"Close . . ." Noctyrne's voice issued from the darkness ahead. "Somewhere in this building."

GAP scanned the skyscraper before them. "Minstar Plaza. Home to three dozen small companies. Even as vacant as it is at this hour, it'll take hours to search manually."

Gayle held her arms tight to her chest, partially against the cold, and partially against the thought of hours passing. She only had three, maybe four of them left before midnight, and then her super-strength would flee for another seven unbearable days.

"Inside, somewhere towards the top," Noctyrne announced. She waited outside the glass doors expectantly.

"I'll try and tap into the security computers and unlock the doors," GAP began, when the sound of shattering glass interrupted him.

Inside the lobby, security alarms flaring, Combat Wombat picked himself up from where his flying leap had landed him and shook the glass shards off himself like a dog shedding water. He turned to his teammates and grinned. "You do that, boss man. The rest of us will go find the perp."

Somewhere inside his suit, GAP sighed.

Gayle led the way, followed by Roland. GAP followed once he had disarmed the clanging alarm, which by now had no doubt alerted not only their quarry, but everyone for blocks, to their presence.

"Um, anyone forgetting something?" Noctyrne tapped her foot impatiently outside.

GAP turned and bowed as much as his bulky suit would allow him. "We invite you in."

Noctyrne licked her fangs and smiled. "Thanks for the courtesy to the vampirically challenged. Now we're in business."

She led the team up flights of stairs, across corridors, through lobbies both empty and populated with extremely disconcerted looking night-shift janitors, down stairs, through other corridors, up more stairs. Noctyrne did not so much walk as glide ahead of them, with Combat Wombat, on all fours, nipping at her heels. Gayle and Roland jogged after them. She could hear the detective's lungs beginning to protest, but he never voiced a complaint. His hand continually hovered by his waist, near his holster. GAP brought up the rear, lumbering along, scanning as he went, and muttering synthesized "sorries" to any hapless building inhabitants whom they blew by. GAP was always the best at "apology duty."

Wall to wall carpeting covered every floor—drab sky blue on some levels, red or green or floral patterned on others. The halogens that lit the hallways actually looked to be in working order. The restroom doors bore elegant brass locks, for which you presumably required a key from some self-important receptionist. For fractions of a second, it all whirled past Gayle's eyes as she ran by, flickering images of the background scenery of a life that could have been hers, if not for Fridays.

"This room!" Noctyrne cast a dramatic finger at a set of expensive looking doors, bearing the unmistakable sheen of real oak, not pseudowood. Or at least, they were expensive-looking doors for a few moments until Combat Wombat slammed his way through them. Then they became expensive-looking splinters.

Beyond their wreckage, a conference room spread out in all its bureaucratic glory. Sweeping curves of white formica formed a semicircular table, peppered by extremely ergonomic-looking chairs, each bearing notepad holder built into the armrest. The chairs, all swiveled to attention facing a dropdown flatscreen monitor, looked ready to have an important meeting all by themselves, no humans required.

Except one human was indeed present. He was standing facing the wall-length windowglass at the far end of the room, apparently engaged in an act of staring out at the skyline when Combat Wombat oh-so-subtly announced the team's entrance. He swiveled quickly to face them, and Gayle had about four tenths of a second to ponder whether this might in fact be some sort of trap.

Then she saw his eyes. Or rather, what *should* have been his eyes. The sockets bore not eyeballs but patches of ebon void, dotted with miniature stars and galaxies that flowed and swirled at dizzyingly different rates. Gayle did not even face the question of whether or not to look away—the gaze was captivating, *hungry*, drawing her consciousness in like light to a black hole. *Need* filled her mind, every possible need she had ever felt in her life: lack of food, of sleep, of friendship, of respect. Lack of sexual satisfaction, of meaning and identity, of clean laundry. Lack of confidence. Lack of her parents. Lack of Waley. Lack of normalcy. Lack of being exceptional. Lack of peace. Lack of air.

Just as "lack of consciousness" loomed high on the list, she felt a cold metal arm brush against her face, so hard that she nearly fell over.

"Gal Friday!" George's synthesized voice bellowed.

"Who? Whuh?" Gayle felt the annoyance of a sleeper awakened from a particularly intense, though not necessarily pleasurable, dream.

"What happened to you?"

"I . . . who?" She scanned the room. GAP and Roland were still present. Combat Wombat, Noctyrne, and the mysterious stranger were gone. Gayle felt a chill, and traced it to a gaping whole in the picture window. More shattered glass. More of Craig's work?

"That man stared at you," Roland was saying, although his voice sounded miles away, "and then you went all . . . I don't know . . . spacey. We all turned our attention your way, and the perp used that time to smash his way out the window."

"To smash his . . . what?" Gayle blinked, finally shaking off her trance. "But we're at least ten stories up!"

"The man's either a Super or suicidal," said Roland. "Your two friends went after him while we stayed with you."

Something in Roland's voice, in the impatient twitch of his hands, seemed to want her to be fully aware of the sacrifice he had made in remaining.

"All right," said Gayle. "So what are we doing here waiting? GAP, do you have him on scanners?"

"Affirmative," he said, craning his metal head this way and that. "He's . . . . above us! He's climbing the building's outer wall!"

Gayle stepped tentatively to the window, grasped the conference table with one hand for an anchor, and forced herself to look down. Sure enough, the tiny forms Combat Wombat and Noctyrne were pacing the streets below, searching fruitlessly for their quarry.

"GAP, get them on the watch-com and tell them where to look," Gayle flung herself away, into a run, out into the hallway.

"Where are you going?" Roland called after her.

"To the next floor. I'll head him off at the pass."

"*We'll* head him off, you mean," said Roland. "I'm not letting you go off alone, not after what just hap—"

Gayle was already out of range of his voice. Muttering a mild curse or three, he took off after her.

*   *   *

Of course, Gayle had no idea what floor the perp was trying to reach. She just needed to get away, away from that stupid fear of heights, away from that man and what his eyes had done to her, away from Roland and his . . . his . . . . being Roland. Why had she been such an idiot, why had she jumped at the chance to have him along? He was a distraction, a terrible one. She couldn't explain it, but something inside her was convinced that the perp's mental mojo wouldn't have thrown her for such a loop had Roland not been present at the time.

Up the stairs, into the next corridor, down the next hall. Locked door. Well, Craig wasn't the only one with super-strength—not tonight. Gayle grabbed the handle, gave a twist, and tore it loose from its mooring, along with a good chuck of the doorframe itself. Just as effective, and far less messy. Cautiously this time, she opened the door, peered in, her eyes squinting in the dim light.

Nothing. Nothing she could *see*, anyway. Was he hiding here, under cover of darkness? The room didn't feel cold. The window wasn't broken. He couldn't have come in here. She would have to go up another floor, go around . . . and that would take too long. She knew what she had to do.

Steeling herself, she stepped up to the window, closed her eyes, took a deep breath, and threw a punch. This window joined its predecessors this night by shattering. Without giving herself time to think, Gayle reached into the folds of her trenchcoat, pulled out her grappling gun, craned out and fired. The cord flew up, up, up to the top of the building. A distant clank was soon followed by the whir of her gun's winch and tightening of the cord.

Here went Gayle's stupidest move of the day.

She should have waited for the others. But Noctyrne and Craig had ten or eleven flights to climb, and at the rate GAP moved, climbing a single flight might take him just as long. Who knew where Roland was. The perp would get away unless she took this into her own hands.

The movies make this look so damned easy . . .

Gayle did not so much step as leap out the window, and then screamed, yes, damn it, screamed, as she felt herself fall. She clung to the gun from which she hung suspended so tightly that her fingers began to make depressions in the steel grip. The backswing then brought her back to the side of the building, and she let loose a breath as she felt her feet collide with the concrete wall.

All right. Don't think. Don't look down. Just walk. It's just like walking. Just like walking. Except you're doing it up the side of a skyscraper.

One foot in front of the other. At first slow and methodical, then faster, then faster again. The faster she went, the sooner this would all end. Vertigo kept her from looking up. Very bad. How would she know if she encountered her quarry?

Wind whipped at her trenchcoat. Her Friday Knights signal cufflink started beeping. Well, tough. There was no way she was going to let go a hand to answer it.

Up, up. Gayle could *hear* the city screaming at her—the automobile horns, the plane and zeppelin motors, the monorail hum, the bird calls. She was a germ on its face, an unwanted bacterium that would at any second be expunged.

Up, up. Suddenly, her feet hit a gap where windowglass should have been. Again, against her will, she screamed. Then she felt the relief that came when a dentist finally removes his gloves and tosses his tools into the washbin. *It's finally ending.*

Forcing her recalcitrant knees to bend, Gayle pushed off, and let the backswing send her flying through the hole into this new room.

Unfortunately, Gayle's super-strength gave her a little more swing than she had bargained for. She went sailing through the room, through the wall at its end, and into some poor soul's office. File cabinets smashed, papers went flying, and the smell of ozone indicated she had probably shattered a computer monitor.

Shaking her head to bring the world back into focus, Gayle's vision shimmered in and out. Shapes were moving. What were they?

"Hold it right there!" she called out in her "confident" voice.

Footsteps. Receding. Dammit!

She took off at a charge, out of the office, into a hallway, just in time to see a human shape disappear around a corner.

Pumping her super-charged legs for all they were worth, Gayle sped after him, rounded the corner into a cul-de-sac, watched as elevator doors in began to close.

"Oh no, you don't," she said, rushing forward and thrusting her fingers into the narrowing gap. With a heave, she ripped them apart, the screech of protesting metal echoing throughout the entire corridor.

"You are under arrest," she called out, into an empty elevator car.

"What?" she blinked.

Then the blow came from behind.

Gayle fell to the floor, her world a mess of sparks. What had happened? Today was Friday. Her super-strength still held for at least another few hours. How strong was this perp, anyway?

Instinctively, she rolled aside, just in time to avoid another blow from a fast-moving red smear. Fire extinguisher. He had hit her with the fire extinguisher.

"Bad . . . . move . . ." she growled, flailing her arm out in a karate swipe. She felt the blow connect, slicing the weapon in two, releasing a devastating cloud of CO_2 into the air.

Fortunately, Gayle had prepared herself. With eyes closed and breath held, she barreled forward, seizing the man and hurling the two of them out of the cloud's reach. She wrestled him to the ground, feeling him squirm beneath her, coughing madly. He let loose a shout of frustration. Instinctively, Gayle opened her eyes.

Mistake.

The galaxies and stars stared back at her. For an instant, she got a closer look at the rest of him—dark features, unkempt black hair, angular face, taciturn remains of what might once have been a nice black leather jacket and suede pants. He looked of foreign origin, and when he spoke, his voice confirmed it. Of course, by then, it was too late for Gayle to do anything about it.

His face drew nearer, his lips hovering above hers. She could smell his breath, thick with mint, blasting at her with every cough.

"I sorry," he said in thick Bulravian-accented English, stopping inches from a kiss. "You are not who I need."

He tossed her aside and ran down the hall.

Gayle didn't know how much time passed until she regained control of her actions. The yearning pangs still beat inside her, yearning for every possible thing she didn't have, for everything she had but not in the way she wanted it. She shut out the noise, focused on the one thing she wanted immediately—that man's head on a platter.

As she ran down the hall, Gayle's watch beeped. She tapped it quickly with one arm. "Gal Friday," she panted.

"This is Noctyrne," came the voice. "Where have you been? The perp's still on your floor. We've got all the exits covered, and GAP has cut power to all the elevators."

"I'm on his tail," Gayle replied. "He must be in one of these offices," she scanned the rows of doors. "Just a matter of finding which one."

Time to put those detective eyes to work. The perp didn't have any keys that she knew about. That ruled out the doors with locks. What doors weren't locked? They all were, except the office she had come from through the window, which, if Noctyrne was right, someone on the team had covered . . . the elevator she had come from, which had no doors at all.

Doubling back, she rushed through the still lingering cloud of CO_2, stun gun raised. Having been under the man's spell twice now, she knew she had enough reflex time to fire off a shot even should he bamboozle her again.

"Freeze!" she said, only to find the muzzle of a gun staring right back at her.

With instincts honed from training, she dropped to the ground even as the gun shot, leg flailing to knock over her opponent. She felt the satisfaction of the blow connecting, heard the telltale cry of pain, in a voice she recognized all too well.

"Detective!"

"Arg!"

Detective Roland lay crumpled up in a heap in the elevator car. Above his head, two suede-covered legs were disappearing up through the maintenance access hatch.

"What happened?"

"I came down through the hatch and had him," Roland struggled to speak as he nursed his possibly shattered leg, "and then you came up out of nowhere . . . I almost . . . you almost . . ."

"I'm sorry," she breathed, and, before doing anything stupid like crying or taking him in her arms and cradling him, Gayle leapt up and grabbed the perp's shoe.

"You . . . get . . . back . . . here," she pulled, and his body came hurtling to the ground, a little more forcefully than she intended. The entire car shook with the impact.

Face to the floor, he began to rise, but Gayle's boot on the back of his neck arrested him.

"*Don't* move," she growled, "and whatever you do, do *not* look up at me. You are under arrest on the charges of assault and resisting duly authorized personnel of the law. You have the right of statement. You have the right to trial by a military tribunal."

"Shut up with your so-called rights," the man spoke into the car floor. "I am not citizen. I have, how you say, diplomatic immunity."

"I have, how you say, half a mind to smash you right through the floor of this car," Gayle pressed her foot harder against him. "Do you realize what you made me do?"

"Easy, Gal Friday," Roland braced himself against the hand rail and hauled himself to his feet. "I don't think anything's broken except my pride."

"Who said I was speaking about you?" she shot back, but the relief in her eyes almost brought tears.

A thunder of footsteps heralded Combat Wombat. "What? Where is he? Did I miss all the action?"

"Afraid so," said Gayle. "Here he is, wrapped and ready, if the Detective doesn't mind me doing the honors?"

Roland reached to his belt and tossed her a pair of handcuffs.

As she bent down, the Bulravian man twisted, craned his neck . . . and made eye contact with Combat Wombat.

"Urrgg," said the hero, and doubled over, papier maché mask pulling him to the ground.

Seizing advantage of the distraction, the man threw off Gayle's foot and scrambled on all fours over the hero he'd felled, out into the hallway—

—only to slam right into GAP. The *clang* echoed painfully throughout the hall. He staggered, swayed, and fell backwards to the ground, stunned.

"Thanks for saving the last blow for me," GAP chuckled. Noctyrne swooped in behind him. "Looks like another victory for the good guys?"

"About damned time," Gayle clamped Roland's cuffs on the man's wrists. "We need to go on cases more often. I'm getting way, way out of practice with this."

Adrenaline sang a song within her. She had done it. *They* had done it. The Friday Knights had captured their first honest-to-goodness super-criminal. Yes, a horde of questions still hung in the air, but for now, she wanted to start dancing. She had half a mind to take Detective Roland by the hand and start to swing. Where was he, anyway?

Roland was climbing out of the car, rubbing his injured leg and looking disapprovingly at the torn steel doors of the elevator. "So is this the normal amount of property damage you people cause during a given mission? I'm estimating somewhere up into five figures by now, not counting my own medical bills."

Gayle felt the little elevator inside her guts take a plunge.

Noctyrne arched, giving voice to what Gayle could not. "Well, that's gratitude for you."

"Snordwell industries will reimburse all the affected parties," said GAP, "including, if necessary, you, Detective."

"That's not my point," said Roland, patting down the unconscious man's form. "If this scumbag is telling the truth about diplomatic immunity, then all of this has been for a fat lot of nothing."

You say that as if that's my fault, Gayle thought to herself, suddenly sullen. Then again, she *had* injured Roland. He had a right to be annoyed. But then again, he *had* almost shot her, and she wasn't holding a grudge. Then again, could he be feeling out of his league here? Was the irritation in Roland's voice his pain speaking, his wounded ego, or . . . or . . . was it a slow recognition of just who and what Gayle really was?

Suddenly she wanted to cry.

Stop it! You're overthinking. That damned hypnotic gaze hadn't exactly helped her worries.

"Damn it all to hell," said Roland, adding a few stronger imprecations as he removed the passport from his captive's jacket pocket. "His name is Ehat, and he's a Bulravian dignitary. A diplomatic attaché to the Humanitarian League, the only world organization that still admits Bulravians since the embargos. We'll have to run the numbers, of course, but I've seen these kinds of passes before. It looks legit."

GAP took the pamphlet and ran it through his scanners.

"Bulravian dignitary?" Noctyrne cocked her head. "Why should that even matter? Aren't we, y'know, at war with them?"

"Not officially," Gayle frowned, forcing her mind back to practical matters.

"We have troops there. That's what matters."

Gayle didn't feel like an argument. "They're just advisors. The State and the other Allied forces have placed embargos on Bulravia, for refusing to honor the international superhuman segregation treaties and create Herotowns of their own. But until now, we've been content to let the Skovakians fight a proxy war for us. Why waste State resources when the Skovakians have been itching for a chance to invade their neighbor for decades?"

Gayle couldn't take her eyes off Roland's hands as they nursed his injury. How could he *not* be furious at her, scared of her? How could some part of him not agree with the nine tenths of the world that wanted to lock Supers into ghettos, that was ready and willing to support military action against countries that didn't?

"We got im?" a woozy Combat Wombat rose, slowly returning to consciousness after blurting out a few "whereisthebastardI'lltearhimapart's."

"Mm-hmm," said Gayle.

"So now we have all the pieces." He tugged at her arm. "Let's start putting the them together. I need to get back to the Stallion, to my computer—"

"The pass checks out," GAP announced. "And the law is very clear. We have to return this man to the Bulravian embassy."

"What?" Combat Wombat cried. "No freaking way!"

"For once, I agree with him," said Noctyrne.

"The law is the law," argued GAP. "We follow it. End of story."

"Well, this particular law's going to be tough to follow," said Gayle, "considering how the Bulravians closed their embassy in Mesopolopolis once the embargoes began. Are we supposed to ship him all the way back to Bulravia?"

"No," said a new voice, snapping all associated heads around. "You turn him over to me."

All turned, tensed for renewed battle, and didn't quite relax when they saw the source.

Nearly seven feet tall, clad in blue spandex lined with jagged yellow streaks, Thunderbolt didn't need to announce his identity. Everyone knew the members of the Superior Squad.

"I . . . I . . . ah," GAP stammered, as if he were somehow smaller than this non-armored man before him. "It's an honor to meet you, sir. I mean, a pleasure. I mean, an honor and a pleasure—"

"Nice mess you've made here," Thunderbolt's voice rumbled like a series of small explosions in a tin can. "But I'll take it from here. This man is wanted for crimes against the inhabitants of Superion City."

"Oh, stow it," said Gayle, unimpressed. "This case is under our jurisdiction, Thunderbolt. I didn't see you putting any of those mighty Class 6 powers all you Superior Squadders have to use in helping us during the fight. Or earlier, during any of his previous assaults. Why now?"

"Until now," Thunderbolt's eyes grew cold, and ozone crackled in the air around him, "this man had never assaulted a Super before. Until now, we did not care what he did to the Normals in this pustule of a city. But just three hours ago, he attacked our ambassador, Liana Golden. That makes this our business . . . and our duty."

He cracked his neck audibly. "Are you amateurs now . . . satisfied?"

Noctyrne arched. "Where do you get off calling us amateurs?"

"Oh really," said Thunderbolt. "According to city records, you've been tracking this man for days. It took the Superior Squad all of three hours to locate and apprehend him."

"Hey," Combat Wombat tensed, "last I recall, *we* apprehended him."

Small crackles of lightning danced across Thunderbolt's eyes. "Ah, the Great Traitor's nephew. I'm amazed that fake animal hide of yours isn't adorning someone's living room by now."

Combat Wombat surged, but GAP and Noctyrne held him back.

"You say that within clawing distance," Craig spat and hissed. "I dare you! I dare you!"

"Little man," said Thunderbolt coldly, "I would fry you where you stand, but I fear *papier maché* makes a poor conductor indeed."

Craig howled in rage.

Gayle tensed. This was quickly spiraling out of control.

Beside her, Detective Roland stepped forward. "Now hold on, Mister . . . Thunderbolt, is it? This is a joint investigation under the authority of the Mesopolopolis Police Department—"

Thunderbolt turned to Gayle and to her spoke right over the detective. "You work hand in hand with those who would imprison or destroy us, and then you wonder why I call you unworthy?"

"Some of us believe in upholding laws," Gayle countered, speaking right into his eyes. "Some of us learned in school that those who flout them tend to be called *villains*."

Thunderbolt's face contorted. His fists clenched. Aha. *That* got to him.

"Laws," he forced the words out of his mouth, "such as the Lee Act? Bah. Superion City wants nothing of those laws."

"Oh really?" said Gayle. "Would Captain Omega agree?"

Again, the fists clenching. But this time, Thunderbolt smiled. "Captain Omega believes in expediting matters," he said, producing a docket from a pouch and handing it to Gayle. "I believe you will find all our authorization in order."

"Seal of the President?" Roland blinked as he looked over her shoulder. "Just how important is this man we've caught?"

"If you don't know," Thunderbolt sneered, "then that's all the more reason to hand him to those who do."

"We *could* do that," said Noctyrne, flicking her hair playfully with one hand as she helped hold Combat Wombat with the other. "Of course, then, you'd probably want the information that one hero named Buzz got from Bulravia. It's kind of a necessary companion piece to the prisoner, don't you think?"

All eyes turned her way.

"What?" Thunderbolt's voice sank to a whisper.

"Y-yeah," Combat Wombat finally stopped struggling. "You'll probably want the information I filched from his data disk. Of course, you don't seem to have a warrant for *that*—"

The dark hallway suddenly flashed into a brilliant, blinding glare as Thunderbolt roared. Thunder shook the entire office building. "What do you know about this data?"

"Enough." Gayle quickly stepped in. "Enough to trade you custody of this man for it."

"Unacceptable. You are either bluffing or incredibly stupid."

"We could always share our information," offered GAP.

"Naw," Combat Wombat sneered. "We `amateurs' can't possibly have any answers he doesn't."

"Yeah," Noctyrne cooed. "I'm sure whatever we know, or think we know, is old news to the high and mighty Superior Squad."

"Might as well just give him the perp and call it a day," said Gayle, smiling at the twists of skin taking shape on Thunderbolt's face.

"Perhaps," the Superior Squad hero rumbled, as if every syllable were torture, "we can work out an . . . arrangement."

"Our precinct back in Downtown keeps a couple of safehouses handy," offered Roland, "for witnesses under protection. One of them's only a little way from here, across the river. It would make a much better site for negotiations than this hallway."

"We're fine with that," said Gayle. "Right, team?"

As one, they nodded. All eyes turned to Thunderbolt. The snort he gave would have to suffice for consent.

"See," Gayle whispered, elbowing Roland not-so-gently in the ribs, "we occasionally *do* resolve matters without violence."

The detective gave a snort of his own. It lacked the reverberating echo of Thunderbolt's, but Gayle found disturbing similarities . . . an observation that, she feared, neither man would appreciate hearing from her.

INTERLUDE

"Thomas has him."

"Thanks in no small part to those heroes you called `small-timers.'
They did what we couldn't. They captured Ehat."

Cerebellum stroked the protruding lobes of his skill gingerly, as
if to manually seal in the frustration. "By necessity, we have had to
keep to the shadows. We cannot risk compromising our standing just
yet. That is the only reason we failed to secure him."

"Of course."

"And you do realize that these Friday Knights now know too much.
This matter has to be handled very delicately. Thunderbolt should
have let me approach them."

"They know you. They know your powers. They'd be too suspicious
of you trying to pull some telepathic trick."

Sarah's great silver wings beat once, twice, carrying her from the
gangplank circling the top of Minstar Plaza building to roost on the
radio antennae above. The fragile filament looked like the weight of
even the thinnest human being would snap it, yet Sarah balanced
atop it effortlessly, dealing no damage.

"In another world," she called down to her teammate, "we would
be giving them a medal."

"As Thomas would be the first to tell you, this isn't the world we
want. But if we succeed, it soon will be."

Sarah, the Silver Peregrine, stared out at the steel forest of
skyscrapers, then gazed up, up, to the pale gray face of the moon,

marred with blue smears. One of them, the Sea of Tranquility, beckoned her home.

"It's not a *fait accompli* just yet. We still have to get Ehat to Superion City."

"You sound almost hopeful, Sarah. But which alternative are you hopeful for?"

Sarah did not reply.

Courts are the universally recognized place of law and order. For those arrogant enough to think their superhuman abilities permit them to somehow transcend the constraints of the system of law and order, the best thing we can do may be to grant their wish—deny them the court, let law and order fall away, leaving only justice.

—Senator Augustus Lee, campaign speech for the Presidency

MARLA

"I can't believe we're meeting like this."

"Why? Because you work for opposing counsel? Or because you dumped me two years ago, here, at the Shining Star Restaurant?"

Tenzin Myata looked out across the lights of Mesopolopolitan skyline, out to the Phoenix River which divided Uptown from Downtown, then to the mustachioed maître d' hovering expectantly at the elevator door . . . anywhere but at Marla Arliss. She wore a plain black dress, Tenzin a simple orange robe.

"It is of course agreeable to see you once again," said Tenzin.

"Even if Assistant Attorney General Holloway's office wasn't paying for the meal?"

"This money is my own."

"Oh." Marla quickly stared at her drink.

"You look very healthy."

"Thanks," Marla's hand moved to adjust the strap of her dress, then, thinking better, receded. "You look well yourself. I suspected Holloway would have worn you to the bone by now."

"He is indeed a strenuous taskmaster," said Tenzin, "but a handler soon learns the habit of any wild animal, and consequently, learns the

129

appropriate moments to duck, pull back, and, if necessary, appease, in order to engender compliance."

Marla allowed herself a wry smile. "I don't think Holloway would appreciate that analogy."

"No, I suspect he wouldn't."

Silence permeated in the air between them like humidity, even as, beyond the glass dome of the restaurant, winter winds howled and blasted the poor birds that dared to climb this high.

The waiter, in a token gesture, re-filled their practically untouched water glasses.

"So why did you ask me here, Marla? Here, to the Shining Star Restaurant, of all places? Something about the Shandon case, yes?"

"Yes. I think I've come close to figuring the whole case out. And that's what scares me."

"Oh?"

In the center of the dining area, a short, stocky pianist wearing a top hat began tapping out *The Night We Parted* in soft, almost subliminal tones. If Marla had owned a firearm, she would have shot him.

"I'm telling you this as a friend, and a friend only. Private communication, not for legal consumption."

"I can make no guarantees, Marla. You know how I feel about duty—"

"Yes, I damned well know how you feel about duty, Tenzin."

"That wasn't fair. My decision to take that job at the Attorney General's office—"

"Look, forget it. I'm sorry. This isn't about us. Or rather, it is, but in a totally different way."

Tenzin inclined his head slightly, a gesture for her to continue. Marla grit her mental teeth against the pianist's crescendo, forcing herself to focus on the matter at hand.

"I assume Holloway's office has run the data from the Michelis email by the appropriate chemists and biologists?"

"Yes. I brought said data to them myself."

Marla would've done that too, if public defenders had easy access to those kind of resources. But she knew a few things herself. "Remember my cousins? How they're both biotech engineers?"

Tenzin nodded.

"I know enough. I think I can predict what theories those scientists are going to come up with."

"You mean about the electrical anomalies in the water samples from Rhadamanthus Planum?"

"Yes. And you know what theories I'm talking about, too."

Expression vanished entirely from Tenzin's face. Marla recognized this as a sign he was contemplating.

"What you allude to," he finally spoke, "is merely only one theory of many."

"But the only one that exonerates Commander Shandon."

"That does not matter. Holloway has already assembled a team of scientists to refute it."

"And I could assemble a team to support it, just the same," she lied. "But I don't want to."

The music stopped. Tenzin's eyes widened. "I am not sure I follow you, Marla."

"Don't worry," she waved her hand dismissively. "Look, Tenzin. As you reminded me countless times when we dated, I don't know nearly as much as I should about karma. But I figure you have to owe me some sort of cosmic retribution for dumping me cold two years ago at this very spot."

"Actually, it was the next table over."

"Stop evading."

"This is not the courtroom. You are not cross-examining me."

"No, no I'm not," Marla said, and paused to take a small sip of water. "I'm asking you a favor, Tenzin."

She put down the glass and touched his hand as it rested upon the table. Tenzin fought the urge to flinch. Her skin, cold and moist from the water glass, enveloped his own like home. In that touch of skin to skin lay all the smells of Mesopolopolis Heights, the bright colors of the prayer flags fluttering from their apartment balcony downtown, the rush of the cold winds through his nostrils, so different from the humid clouds of his home. Ice stung his eyes, and only his years of discipline kept Tenzin from breaking down in tears right there.

The music started up again. Zolotusky's Third Symphony, Second Movement. Marla's hand withdrew.

"Tell Holloway we'll plea bargain," she said softly. "He can send his team of scientists home. Shandon will plead guilty to criminal negligence, on the condition he doesn't go public with the email."

Tenzin's face paled slightly. "I . . . admit that I am still confused, Marla. This email, and the theory you refer to, are your strongest arguing points for a complete exoneration. Doubtlessly, we would still manage to beat it, but without the email on the table you have no chance at all."

"You'll have to trust me on this," Marla spoke directly into his eyes. "I've thought long and hard, and finally figured out that there's something much larger at stake here. Larger than Shandon, larger than us, larger even than Holloway's ego."

"Holloway's ego is the issue. He will not want to accept criminal negligence. He would rather fight you, scientific witness to scientific witness, to obtain a murder conviction. He is willing to take the chance."

"Then here's where the favor comes in. Do whatever it takes to convince him that if he brings in the email, he'll provide a sure way for Shandon to go free."

"He may be willing to take that chance. He could consider such arguments a bluff, a risk."

"True. From me, he would. He'd be dead wrong, of course, but he'd still take it as a challenge. But you, Tenzin—he listens to you. You can change his mind."

Tenzin paused. "I . . . do not know if my animal handling skills are quite so accomplished."

Marla's voice took weight. "Then let me give you a motivation, Tenzin. Beyond just karma."

Despite himself, Tenzin blushed. "If . . . if you are suggesting . . ."

"Oh please, Tenzin. I'm over you. Your mind's not quite so pure as you'd like everyone to believe."

"Then, what—"

"Come with me, and I'll show you."

She offered her hand. He hesitated, fearing the sensation, then jabbed his arm out and clasped what she offered like a drowning man.

"Part of the uncertainty generated by the Second Heroic Age stemmed from sheer overpopulation. Until then, the average, informed State citizen could reasonably expect to memorize the ranks of the superhuman . . . The Amazing Elite, the Frontier Challengers, the Crimson Crusaders, and a handful of others. You could name the heroes, name the villains, and every culture recognizes how the ability to name grants power and, through that power, security. By the Second Heroic age, superhuman numbers swelled to the point where such knowledge, distinctions, and thus, security, became the purview of hobbyists only. After the mutations brought on by Trinity, the task became simply insurmountable for anyone without the resources of the Metahumanics Commission itself. Thus the uncertainty that plagues us in the present day . . ."

—President Augustus Lee, *Mending the Breach*

GAYLE

"No pressure, Craig . . . but you have ten minutes to crack the code on that data-disk."

Combat Wombat addressed himself in low whispers and peered intently into the screen of his laptop computer, small white pixels reflecting against his corneas, readily visible in the darkness of the Stallion's interior. His shoulders hunched inward as he curled over the machine. Riding shotgun gave him a little more stretch room, but not much. As the Stallion sat five tightly, six was out of the question, so George had stalwartly volunteered to sit in the storage compartment, where he normally stored his GAP suit, leaving Gayle to drive and Craig to ride shotgun. Noctyrne and Roland kept their prisoner under watch in the back, a blindfold tied securely around his dangerous eyes. Ehat slept silently, betraying no snores or grunts, not even shifting in his sleep. Once or twice Roland checked his pulse, just to confirm he was still living.

How hard had he hit George's suit, Gayle wondered? Did he require medical attention? To give him up to a hospital would unleash a torrent of red tape, and Thunderbolt's executive release order held the trump of all red tape measures. The Friday Knights had to keep this in their court if at all possible. Once the power-players stepped in, people would start to get squashed.

That was how the world supposedly worked. That was certainly the only real law of Herotown when Gayle and George were growing up, up until the day that Nik came back in town. Nik, another reason why Gayle hated her childhood. Back home in Mesopolopolis, bullies were flesh and blood. Along with his sociopathic tendencies Nik boasted M-6 ratings on strength and invulnerability, the highest you could go on the Scoper Scale. His superpower made him solid steel, as impervious and cold and merciless as the metal on his body. Rumor had it the Peace Officers had busted him once already for trying to cross the border, and he'd come back to tell the tale. Nik never bothered coming to school, but after classes were over, boredom would occasionally lead him to the yard to entertain and terrorize the masses. Today he was hurling rocks high in the air, super strength accelerating them to speeds that burned them to a crisp.

Nik stood at nearly two meters, and atop a hollowed-out wreck he was even taller. The wreck was probably a tank or APC or some other abandoned piece of Annihilus Bay hardware. At this point, who knew? The military had scuttled everything of value and burned anything that that remained when radiation floating over from Trinity Island forced them to abandon the Bay, the Flats, and most of what would soon become designated as Herotown. Supers had a higher radiation tolerance, the politicians assured the public, who, judging from how most of them voted, didn't seem to need much assurance.

"The people of the State aren't stupid," Gayle's father used to tell her, "and they aren't cruel. They're just scared, and scared people sometimes do awful things. But they'll come to their sense eventually." But they didn't, because fear was more powerful than sense . . . Gayle knew that for a fact, because she feared Nik more than anything.

The metal boy clutched an orange in his iron talons (squeals from the base of the wall suggested that the orange was not originally Nik's property), and the glowing embers that passed for his eyes scanned the streets before him as he packed snow around the edges of the fruit, took careful aim, and then hurled it at a passing dog. The sickening *thuk* that followed was unmistakable, and the poor creature hopped for several paces before realizing it now had a hole in its torso. Muttering a half-formed yelp, it spasmed and fell to the ground.

Nervous murmurs welled up in the crowd. A few kids laughed. Gayle felt like vomiting. Somehow she became aware of George at her side.

"Someone has to teach Nik a lesson," he said to no one in particular. Or was he speaking to her?

"Yeah, right," Gayle said. "Why don't you do that, right after you get rid of the Peace Officers?"

"First things first," said George, and returned to his sketchbooks.

Gayle was growing annoyed. Didn't George know his place? They weren't in civilization anymore. This was Desperation Flats, Herotown, the jungle. Everyone had to know the pecking order to survive, and you just had to accept that no matter how many rungs on the food chain you climbed, it didn't matter, because at the very top sat the Peace Officers, so what was the use?"

Gayle peered over his shoulder. George's drawing was nearly complete. What on Earth was it?

"You're not serious, are you?"

"You heard me," George said flatly

"You think you can take him?"

"If this invention works, yes."

"Invention? Invention?" Gayle laughed out loud. "This is Nik we're talking about. He's invincible!"

"He's only invincible," George said, "if no one stands up to him."

Gayle shook her head. This couldn't be happening. The grasshoppers didn't just decide that the bottom of the food pyramid was bad real estate and hop a plane to the level above the cougars and bears because the view was better there. This wasn't pretend. Things just didn't happen that way.

"It's Friday, Gayle. You could help me."

Gayle blinked. "What? How?"

"I saw your secret spot, Gayle, with my tele-glass invention. You think you're the only one who watches people? I see you lifting boulders and automobile parts every Friday, in your yard or in alleyways, when you think no one can see. You've got power, Gayle. You can help me fight him."

"No way," said Gayle, indignation giving way to incredulousness. "Even the kids with superstrength aren't a match for Nik. He's gonna be a supervillain someday. He tells that to everyone."

"We don't need superstrength," said George. "All a hero really needs is strength of heart."

"You'll need a coffin," said Gayle, "if Nik hears you."

"So let him hear. Are you on his side now?"

Gayle paused. She was on *reality's* side. Some things were just non-negotiable. Relocations. Bullies. This wasn't make believe. George fancied himself an inventor, but inventors couldn't rewrite the world. Could they?

Nik's gang was drawing near, and George receded into the shadows. Gayle had quite a walk ahead of her to get home before dinner, especially in the snow. As she turned to leave, she felt a sharp tap dig into her shoulder from behind.

"Did the sparklehead just say he could take on Nik?"

Oh, no, thought Gayle, it had begun already!

"Shhhh!" Gayle said, turning to the thin, wiry girl questioning her.

"George didn't know what he was talking about." It was a futile gesture, for Frezia immediately swiveled and passed on the information to the kids behind her, and those to the kids behind her, and then it happened.

"Hey, curly-locks. Look at me." Even if Gayle somehow had amnesia and didn't recognize the raspy voice, the smell of charcoal would have heralded Nik's arrival just as effectively. Nik's tinfoil-like bangs scraped small scratches across the dull, lustrous chrome that was his skin, and two irregular red spheres glowed brazenly from their sunken pits to call themselves his eyes. The piece of iron held fast between his ivory teeth looked like it could take off any minute, like a guided missile, and pierce the guts of anyone he chose. *This* was what George thought he could defeat? Nik wasn't human, and he wasn't even superhuman. He was something beyond anything they could reckon.

"I'm talking to you, girly," drew closer, omnipresent thugs flanking him on either side. Strength attracted strength. The faces and names changed, of course, because Nik's armies were infinite. That's what George didn't understand, what her father didn't understand . . . the bad guys always outnumbered you.

"What do you want?" Gayle tried unsuccessfully to keep the warble from her voice.

"I hear that you and the sparklehead were talking about me. That true?"

Gayle tried her hardest to remain silent. She really did.

"Hey, I asked what you little feebs were saying. Don't make me ask a third time."

There was no resisting. Gayle had no choice. She told him everything. They shuffled off, off to make an example of him. George would die. George would die, and his death would press upon on Gayle's conscience for the rest of her life. She could blame it on the world, of course, but she knew better. She waited until it was safe to move, and then she waited a bit longer, and then finally she scampered out of the tank alcove and watched Nik and his gang close the distance between them and George.

She had to bear witness. It was the least she could do. Gayle slipped and nearly fell on the icy ground, watching Nick's gang advancing, their larger and thicker legs making far better time than George's could. She wanted to scream, but the blood in her own head drowned her out.

Damn it for being Friday! That it was all happening today made it even more unfair. Today was the one blasted day she wasn't supposed to be afraid.

They caught up to him right by the old rifle range. At least four other kids fell into step behind Nik, but there might as well have been a thousand, or a million. If necessary, Nik could probably call up more from thin air. George turned at the sound of their footsteps, and, seeing recognition in the eyes of their prey, the pack broke into a run.

George, amazingly, held his ground. He made no motion to run or defend himself or anything. He just stood ramrod straight as Nik's gang enclosed him. No hint of fear showed in his eyes as the assault commenced, and Gayle found that the most horrifying part of the entire spectacle. It was one thing to see a tiger come flying at an antelope. That was scary. It was another to see the antelope suddenly grow five extra eyes. That just shouldn't have *been*.

George pulled up the thick folds of his coat, revealed belt buckle of ridiculous proportions, and depressed a button in its center. A flicker of golden energy mushroomed up around him, and for moment Gayle dared to hope that George somehow was capable of magic.

Then the flicker sputtered and died, and fear washed in torrents across George's face. Reality. As always. Gayle felt a tear come to her eye, and then it began.

One of Nik's goons grasped George's backpack with both hands and hoisted him in the air. Another delivered a gloved fist into the stomach of his target. George doubled over, grasping for breath, and they hurled him to the ground. It didn't matter that George wasn't fighting back . . . one thug grabbed each of George's arms as he lay tangled, leaving the torso and waist area wide open for Nik's approach. They held his arms because that was their nature, those were the rules. George was the one who was cheating, even as his coat was torn from him and flung into the street. He wasn't struggling, and he wasn't screaming or making any noise whatsoever—at least, none that Gayle could hear from her location.

Amused or irritated, Gayle couldn't tell which, Nik approached George, seized the belt, and made some disparaging remark that she couldn't hear. Curiosity overcoming fear, she crept closer. Nik ripped the belt buckle clean from its straps, buckling George's body in the process, and smacked it across the captive boy's face. George's skin reddened from the blow, blood started to well, blending with the silver of his stupid radiation suit and the black of the smeared snow.

Nik was going to kill him. For no other reason than that he was different, that he had tried, even in theory, to oppose him. Gayle's father had tried to fight the Lee Act. He had been stripped of his tenure, expelled from the University, eventually exiled to Herotown, and all because of two things—that he had tried to fight back, and because of Gayle. Now George was going to die for the exact same reasons.

Gayle couldn't let that happen. She didn't have "strength of heart," she knew that. But it was Friday. She had something.

With a swift motion, Gayle shucked off her backpack and charged the assemblage, roaring incoherently. Nik had just enough time to swivel his slow, ponderous form to face her before she slammed headlong into him. It felt like hitting an iron wall. With an audible clang that stayed in Gayle's ears long after impact, the two fell to the snow. Nik's goons, startled, let go of George's limbs and fell to the sidelines to observe.

Her head ringing, Gayle could barely register that she had the advantage, and by the time she did, she had lost it. Nik recovered and wrapped his arms around her in an iron bear hug. Gayle gasped as she felt the wind leave her lungs, and struggled uselessly to wriggle free from his grasp. It was no good. His arms shook and quivered slightly, but Gayle's super strength, especially without a good breath, wasn't enough.

She was dimly aware of him calling her a very, very vile name, and then he had lifted her up in the air, and by the time she adjusted to that, he had slammed her to the ground. Perception had fled, breath had fled. The whole world existed in the form of a spinning smear. Even Nik's voice seemed far away.

Self-preservation, fortunately, had ways of bypassing conscious thought. Gayle kicked out a leg in instinct, and felt a satisfying clank, followed by an even more satisfying shout of pain. So she could hurt him. It was possible. Nik could be hurt. Why had that thought never even occurred to her before?

Nik seemed just as surprised. His gravelly voice almost sounded as if it were pockmarked by tears. "You're gonna die for that, bitch!" he roared, and dove for her.

Gayle rolled out of the way, and the heap of metal landed with a shatter in the snowpile where she had been a second earlier. She scrambled uneasily to her feet, then kicked his fallen form again. Jabs of pain lanced through her foot, but Nik cried out as well.

She suddenly thought of Nik's gang, and turned to look to them, but they were staring, open mouthed, evidently as surprised as anyone else. Instinctively, she realized they weren't a threat. Without Nik, were they ever? What was it her father had said? "They're not cruel people. They're just scared, and scared people sometimes do awful things."

The reverie proved her undoing. Nik was up again, and Gayle barely had time to react as he hurled a blow. It glanced her on the side and sent her spinning to the ground. Redness blanked out her gaze. Had the punch connected, she surely wouldn't have survived.

Long before she could refocus her senses, he was on her, his weight crushing the life from her bones, his arms pushing in on her shoulders and starting to snap them. Gayle surged and kicked with all she had, but she was still flesh, and he was still steel, and all her bravery was going to just get her killed, just like she always knew it would, how could she have been so unbearably stupid . . .

How was she still thinking thoughts? Shouldn't the life have left her by now? Or was this one long, extended moment of death? That would explain the golden glow . . . she was finally being carted off to heaven, which, of course, would be *anyplace* other than Desperation Flats . . . .

She felt Nik's weight lift off her as he floated away, and she dimly wondered at how that was backwards, and how she was supposed to be doing the floating. But she was still on the ground, and Nik was up in the air, far up in the air, in a cloud of sparkling gold bubbles, flailing and yelling and, yes, crying, crying out for help, for answers, for . . . his mother. His mother.

Once more, her father's words echoed. "Scared people do awful things."

If Gayle's arrival and challenge to Nik had jostled the bully's gang, this new vision sent them positively into panic. They fled the scene, leaving Gayle alone . . . with George.

"It worked!" he was grinning stupidly through a haze of blood, his fingers manipulating the severed belt buckle's controls. "It worked! Portable antigravity! I knew it! My dad'll be so proud!"

Gayle struggled to her feet, wishing the world would cease wobbling from this angle to that.

"Why . . . didn't you do that earlier, you jerk?

"I'm sorry," George said. "I tried. If you hadn't stepped in, I wouldn't have had the chance. I'm afraid the design still needs some revisions and fine tuning . . ."

On cue, the bubbles flickered and burst, and Nik fell from the sky, screaming, into the waters of Annihilus Bay.

"Oh no," George frowned with real trepidation. "Can he breathe underwater?"

"What the hell do you care?" Gayle's eyes widened. "He tried to kill us."

"Heroes don't kill," George scolded her, as if she were an incontinent puppy, and he ran to the edge of the firing range to peer into the waves beyond. Nik was splashing, his iron form dragging him down. George fumbled with his belt, and the antigravity field sparked to life again. Deaf to Gayle's protests, George remotely lifted Nik out of the bay and onto one of the many floating pieces of debris that littered the waters.

"You're insane," Gayle shook her head.

"And you were amazing," George coughed, as if suddenly remembering his injuries. "I knew you were a hero inside. I knew you would come help if I needed you."

Gayle didn't want to answer that. She helped wipe the blood from George's face, and he took her back to his father's laboratory to get them both cleaned up. William Snordwell II was even thinner and more anemic looking than his son, and even less connected to reality. With the injured children taken care of, he returned almost immediately to his latest project.

"He's even more obsessed than you," Gayle muttered as her eyes took in the bunsen burners, laser torches, and general clutter of the workshop.

"This is nothing," said George. "You should have seen our lab back in the city."

"You were relocated too?"

"No, we came here by choice," George said, not without some pride.

"Whaaat?" Gayle fought the temptation to smack the boy whose life she had just saved. "Why? How?"

And then George explained, explained how the world's most brilliant and wealthy inventor and industrialist had risen to the top of the world, only to watch the military employ his designs at Annihilus Bay, and again to create and equip the Peace Officers, and to enforce the Relocations, and to keep the Herotowns in check. He railed, he protested, he refused to design another weapon for his contractors, and when they threatened to sue and jail him, he jailed himself first by moving here. He divested from all the public portions of his company, sold his stocks and properties, and took all the liquid assets he could glean to Herotown . . . here to rebuild, here to do penance for his wrongs.

Jail, you see (George explained), was supposed to be about rebuilding and doing penance, about making rights out of your wrongs, just like heroes were supposed to be about standing up and winning against impossible odds, and somewhere among all those supposed-to-be's, Gayle fell in love with him. Not a loud, demonstrative love, and not even the torrid, tempestuous love she would come to know when she met Waley not long after.

Gayle's love for George could never be acted upon, any more than love for a teacher or a poet. Gayle loved George for what he showed her, what he reminded her of, how, at the small cost of some bruises and broken bones, that the world could be different. She never did find out what happened to Nik . . . some say he left town, became a Supervillain, and was killed by a Bloodhound Gang. Others claimed the Peace Officers actually recruited him to join a Gang. But Nik was gone, he didn't matter. He had served his purpose. He had been the vehicle by which George had taught her hope.

Somehow that hope guided her, sustained her, through school and through Waley and through all the hopeless weekdays and surreal Friday nights, through the black snowfalls and irradiated foods, through all the realities of life as a super. These days, as an adult, George's money sustained her body, but her soul would have died long ago without the sustenance he had inspired in her. If he were to abandon his GAP suit and other gadgetry that earned him a Class C rating for cybernetic enhancements, he was only Class M-1 in superintelligence, and those were the borderline cases where you might even be able to live on the other side of the Wall, but he willingly chose the Herotown life, as his father did—to save the world from here.

Gayle knew that, without even really realizing it, George had accomplished an even greater feat than world-saving. He had taught a sad, cynical, lonely girl to brave the darkness and cradle the fragile light within.

Something about the way the Stallion's headlights feebly stabbed into the dark of the night streets reminded her of that as the Friday Knights, the team she and George would form over a decade after that fight in the snow, went about trying to preserve that fragile light, through all the unforeseen complications of that task.

2

"Come on, come on . . . it's got to be *one* of these ciphers . . ." Craig scrunched his face as he hunched over his laptop.

Gayle searched the skies listlessly through the windshield. Somewhere up ahead, Thunderbolt was flying, indifferent to the laws of gravity as well as the laws of Mesopolopolis. She almost yearned to see the looks on the faces of police-chopper pilots, or wealthy socialites living in their skyscraper apartments, as a Super soared brazenly past them. To think that in Superion City, such sights were the rule and not the exception . . .

Craig cursed, kicking the floorboards with such force that the metal dented.

"It's hopeless," he said. "I'm never going to be able to unlock this all before we reach the safehouse."

"Stay with it, Combat Wombat," Gayle tried to sound soothing. Ever since Thunderbolt had mentioned Craig's relation to Twister, she'd seen the changes in her friend's bearing . . . the increased listlessness (even for Craig), the furrowed brow. He was trying to prove himself.

"Ever since Thunderbolt showed up with that executive release order, I've been trying all sorts of state department schemes. I don't know all their encryption patterns, but I'm making some headway. The data headers look like a GlobalCom call, but none of the usual telecom protocols are present . . . this is a proprietary data structure."

"Um, ok," said Noctyrne. "Sure. Whatever you just said. Can't you, like, crack part of it?"

"It doesn't *work* that way, Noctyrne," said Craig. "Data is either encrypted or it's not. The best I can do so far is get the headers. Descriptors of what the data fields are. Unfortunately, those don't make a lot of sense. The destination of the call seems to be somewhere in Bulravia, but the source . . . splen, it just doesn't make sense."

"Maybe our starry-eyed friend here can help us out," Noctyrne elbowed their captive in the stomach. "Hey, you! Wake up time!"

"Careful," Roland surged forward, one hand already reaching towards his holster. "We don't know what other powers he may have."

A wordless groan issued from Ehat's mouth, and then a string of what sounded like nonsense syllables.

"Is that Bulravian?" asked Roland.

"I don't think so," said Gayle. "I'm hardly fluent, but the language doesn't have those hissing noises and glottal stops.

"Hello," said Noctyrne. "English, please. English."

His head perked at the sound of her voice. "Are you who I seek?" He flexed his arms, presumably to try pull his blindfold off, only to find his hands bound behind him.

"Easy there, buddy," said Roland. "Georgie Porgie time is over."

"You cannot threaten me," the man said softly. "I have diplomatic—"

"Yeah, yeah, so we've heard," Roland grasped him roughly by the shoulder, jerking him back so the detective could talk directly into his ear. "But unless you want us to ship you out to sea, toss you overboard, and let you swim back across the ocean to Bulravia, you'll be a good little boy and help us with a problem."

"I cannot help you with anything," said Ehat.

"Hey," Noctyrne said, "we have a hard time believing you came all the way here just to hit on random Mesopolopolitan women. You've got to know something that makes you important enough to be connected to a top secret data transmission from Bulravia."

At the sound of that, Ehat cocked his head. He quickly tried to suppress the motion, but Roland caught it. This man was no accomplished spy, that was for certain. But who was he?

"Combat Wombat says that file's something like a telephone call," said the detective. "You wouldn't happen to have made any calls in between trying to kiss the girls, now, would you?"

Ehat man shivered. He opened his mouth, lips trembling. "Please," he said, "I need . . . I need . . ."

"A cold shower, evidently," said Noctyrne, but she evidently didn't hear the subtle high-pitched tingle, as if a computer monitor had suddenly been turned on in the room. Combat Wombat, with his animal senses, might have, if he wasn't so focused on his work.

But Gayle sensed it immediately. She felt it in her lungs, her liver, whatever organ it was that secreted heartbreak. Her breath grew short, the road ahead swam, and her arms had to overcome a sudden weight to turn the wheel.

"Hey, watch it!" Craig shouted as the Stallion swerved barely in time to avoid running into incoming traffic off the Platinum Bridge that led into Downtown.

"Trouble, Gal Friday?" GAP's voice crackled in on the intercom.

"Nuh, no," Gayle shook her head, blinking her eyes. What was happening?

Ehat's mouth remained open, his skin quivering, his whole body stiff as if someone were running a small electric charge through it.

"Hello . . . Georgie Porgie . . . back to Earth . . ." Roland shook him, but he remained transfixed.

Gayle felt as if oxygen itself had somehow grown heavier. Breathing became a labor, an irritating task that she just wished would be over with. All she wanted was release, one final release that would . . .

"NO!" Ehat suddenly screamed, throwing himself forward into the seats ahead, knocking into Gayle's driving posture and causing the Stallion to swerve once more.

"Dammit, Gayle," Combat Wombat shouted as the laptop fell over and out of his hands. "What's gotten into you?"

Ehat shouted again, in Bulravian, and began flailing his head back into the seat, again and again, as if in seizure.

"Stop it," Noctyrne and Roland held him fast. "You're not getting out of here . . ."

"I don't want . . . me out," he snarled. "I want . . . *it* out . . . but it doesn't want her . . ."

"It?" said Roland. "It doesn't want who?"

Gayle suddenly felt the pressure release, and she gasped, breathing greedily. Then she pulled the Stallion violently to the side of the curb, threw it into park, unbuckled her seatbelt, and spun around to face the back seat, all with such swiftness as to appear as one solid, fluid motion.

"Whatever the hell you're doing," she lunged forward into the back seat and seized Ehat by the shirt, pulling him forward, "*stop it!*"

Again, she saw Roland recoil slightly at her ferocity. This time, she was too angry to care.

Ehat grimaced, in far more pain than he should have been. "Not . . . me . . . it . . . ever since . . . call from . . . Europa . . ."

"Europa?" said Noctyrne. "Is she another one of your little sweeties?"

"The Europa mission." Gayle could have slapped her. "Shandon's command. Remember?"

"Europa . . . mission," Ehat spit out the words as if trying to upchuck them. "Call . . . to . . . Doctor Michelis . . . from the *Santa Maria* . . ."

"Neville Shandon?" Roland raised his eyebrows incredulously. "The Space Murderer? Give me a break. You ask me, Commander Shandon's guilty as sin of murdering his fellow astronauts, but even I have a hard time believing he made you assault those women."

"*Need*," Ehat cried, stretching out the vowel sound like a tantruming four year old.

Despite herself, Gayle flinched.

Seeing her reaction, Roland stepped in, pulled Ehat from her lagging grip back to the seat again.

"I've seen some sickos in my time," the detective jostled Ehat, "but you're a whole new breed."

"Yeah," said Noctyrne, fangs suddenly bared. "Even your blood's probably slimy. But don't think that'll stop me if you try anything again . . ."

"Hold on," Gayle whispered, hoarse. "Hold on. Let him talk."

But all Ehat seemed capable of saying was the word "need," again and again, to the point where sobs began to wrack his body.

"Guys," GAP's voice broke in on the intercom again. "Thunderbolt's circling for a landing. I think he thinks we're trying to pull something on him."

"No!" said Craig. "He can't burst in yet. I've suddenly got an idea!" He rushed back to his laptop, fingers a blur, keys cracking under the rapid fire impacts. "Drive, Gayle. Just drive!"

Slowly, still shivering a bit (from what?), Gayle returned to face the wheel and put the Stallion back in drive.

"It worked," GAP said. "He's returned to his old position and heading."

"Whatever you're trying, Wombat," said Roland, "you'd better make it quick. The safehouse is just around the next corner."

"I'm trying the United Space Exploration data formats," he said. "USE employs a few standard encryption schemes. If Georgie Porgie's not just some whacko, then—"

He paused. "Wow." Data suddenly streamed across the screen. "Wow."

"What?" Gayle pressed. "What is it?"

"I'm not sure," Combat Wombat whispered, "but I think our friend here . . . or part of him, anyway . . . may come from a lot farther away than Bulravia. About 400 million miles farther, to be precise."

3

Thunderbolt stood with arms crossed, dominating the safehouse living room like some giant wooden Indian. The dim light gave everything else in the room a muted feel, from the tattered green couches to the flaking psuedowood grandfather clock, even down to the smudged shininess of coffee table books (a haphazard pile that included a home gardening guide, *Cats Throughout the Ages*, and President Lee's best-selling autobiography *Mending the Breach*), but the cobalt blue of Thunderbolt's costume managed to catch the stray light cast off by the lights of GAP's battlesuit. Roland refused to turn on any of the battered bronze lamps—safehouses weren't safe, he reminded them, if people knew they were occupied.

The only other light in the room issued from Combat Wombat's laptop, where his decryption program was finally achieving some success. The Friday Knights' primary mission, he had told them as the Stallion pulled to a halt, was to keep Thunderbolt occupied for the several minutes it would take to complete that operation, so he actually had something to tell the Superior Squadder.

That wouldn't be difficult, considering how GAP kept yammering words of admiration. "This must remind you of the search for Doctor Nefarious' hidden fortress . . . Please give our regards to Captain Omega . . . Was the Swamp Creature from Sudanam really a thousand feet tall?"

Gayle wasn't sure how much of it was an act. George had *posters* of the Superior Squad hanging in his bedroom, for pity's sake, or at least had them until Noctyrne complained that she was jealous of the Silver

Peregrine's picture. Gayle had always thought that silly, but just the same, shuddered to think of what would happen if Thunderbolt called in his female colleague to this little conspiratorial meeting. One flash of the Silver Peregrine's platinum eyebrows and George might hand over Ehat, the datadisk, and half the team's finances without a second thought.

Thunderbolt, for his part, answered questions in gruff monosyllables. Like Captain Omega, he clearly saw his role as a duty, a burden, a calling, and not something to boast of any more than a beaver boasted of a dam, or a bee of a honeycomb. Others admired a hero's work . . . a hero did it because he was born to. That was the Superion City way. Sometimes it scared Gayle a little.

She resisted the urge to cast glances at Combat Wombat, so she let her eyes rest uneasily on Ehat, tied up in the corner under the continued watchful glares of Detective Roland and Noctyrne.

Ehat seemed indifferent to his surroundings. The fevered state he had experienced earlier in the Stallion had quickly subsided, and now he sat impassively, occasionally cocking his head as if listening to unheard words.

"Enough," Thunderbolt finally pushed GAP aside—there were not many beings that could do that easily—and strode up to where Ehat sat tied.

"On your feet, scum," he bellowed. "Face me with some passing remains of dignity."

Ehat rose languidly.

"Do you have any final words before I execute punishment for your inexcusable assault on Ambassador Golden?"

"Whoa," Gayle rushed in, "what about a trial, what about—"

"Superion City has all the evidence it needs," said Thunderbolt. "Video records have proved him guilty."

"You folks really don't do much to help the cause of Supers down on Earth," said Detective Roland. Gayle snapped around in surprise.

Thunderbolt looked as if he was going to explode in response, and Gayle rapidly interposed herself. Fifteen years ago she had risked her life to save George, and nowadays she had learned to show none of her former hesitation.

Of course, she also knew Thunderbolt's type. Whatever else he was, he was a hero. He wasn't about to seriously harm an innocent, even one who challenged him, but Gayle's presence made sure he wouldn't even try roughing Roland up. Thunderbolt would never lay a hand on a fellow hero. At least, Gayle hoped not.

"I will not even dignify that with a response." Thunderbolt seemed satisfied with that, and returned his attentions to Ehat. "Well? What have you to say for yourself?"

"She was not who I sought," he said simply. "But I am getting closer."

Thunderbolt surged forward and, with the speed the matched his namesake, slapped Ehat across the face. The Bulravian man's head lolled, and Gayle rushed in to grab the taller hero's arm.

"Stop it!" she said. "This wasn't the deal!"

"I want to hear why," Thunderbolt surged. "I want to hear why he turned against his own kind."

If Roland was thinking *oh, so assaulting Normals isn't crime enough*, he was smart enough not to say it. Gayle thanked the Spirit Above for that. She could only prevent Thunderbolt from mauling one person at a time. Heck, if it kept him distracted, she could keep up this dance all night.

"I need," Ehat said hoarsely. "I need."

"What does that mean?"

Ehat remained passive.

Thunderbolt reared his arm back again. "Tell me, or I swear by the Cape and Mask themselves, I will burn you to cinders!"

The crackle around his eyes spoke that this was no idle threat.

"Wait!" said Gayle. "Wait!"

"Stay my hand, woman, and you risk suffering the same fate. Those who defend villains must be counted among them."

"This man isn't a villain," Gayle arched defiantly. "I'm one of his victims myself, dammit, and I'm telling you that!"

This drew stares from everyone in the room. Even, damn it, Craig.

"I . . . felt his yearning," said Gayle, "more than once. He's right. He . . . needs. I can't explain it."

"Gal Friday," GAP drew near, "are you sure you're all right? You were under the influence of his power, after all . . . perhaps he planted some sort of subliminal suggestion—"

"I don't need a subliminal suggestion to know what loneliness is!" the words tore themselves from Gayle's heart without her even commanding it. What the hell did George know, with his fiancée and his fantasy world?

"I understand need," she cried out. "A need for someone, anyone, who understands, who can fill that terrible gnawing *void* . . . and I understand how painful, how frustrating it is, when you think you've found a match and . . . and . . ."

Don't look at Roland. Don't look at George. For pity's sake, don't look at Thunderbolt, you're starting cry . . . look at . . . . look at . . .

Ehat. Thunderbolt's blow had knocked loose his blindfold. The stars and galaxies swirled unbidden.

Contact.

Gayle felt the yearning once more, with every cell of her being. Only this time, she understood it.

4

"Gayle! Gayle! Wake up."

The smell of ozone pooled in Gayle's nostrils. She coughed, and her breath tasted like the aftermath of a blown-out birthday cake.

"What happened?"

"Thunderbolt," said the voice over her shoulder, Roland's. He was cradling her. The room all around them was a solid black scorch. GAP's armor sizzled with stray sparks, and Naomi's hair was standing on end as she helped George exit it.

"Thunderbolt's gone," said Roland, his voice dripping with defeat. "His tantrum fried Combat Wombat's laptop, all except the data disk itself, which was protected. We had no other choice but to give him that only copy, like we'd promised. He took Ehat with him."

"What?" Gayle exclaimed, trying to rise to her feet. "How could you let him—"

"Let?" Roland helped her up. "Let? It was all we could do to keep him from incinerating Ehat right then and there," said Roland. When Thunderbolt saw Ehat use his mind-mojo on you, he let loose and started blowing up the furniture. He tossed GAP and Combat Wombat aside like feathers, and only Noctyrne draping herself across Ehat's body kept him at bay. We gave him the disk, the prisoner, everything if he only agreed not to kill him."

"Oh splen," Gayle grumbled. "Freaking splen. Idiots!"

"Don't worry," George, now out of his suit and being soothed by Noctyrne's ministrations, weakly raised a reassuring hand. "We made

153

him swear the Superion Oath. Thunderbolt would never break that, not even in a rage."

"No, no, no," said Gayle, shrugging off Roland, "can't you see that was all an act?"

"A what?" said Roland.

"An act," said Gayle. "Thunderbolt played you all . . . played us all . . . for fools. We walked right into his hands. Who's to say he didn't plan that all along? He got everything, and we're left empty handed."

Gayle kicked over the charred remains of Ehat's chair. It fell into splinters with a less-than-satisfying clatter.

Combat Wombat growled, shaking the useless hunk of his laptop. "I had it all decrypted, all of it, and now my own copy's wiped from the hard drive." He hurled the wreck to the ground, stamped on it, kicked it.

"I can't believe it," he howled. "We finally, finally get a case . . . something big, something titanically *huge* . . . and we screw it up. Like we always do."

He turned to his leader. "Why the hell are we kidding ourselves, George? We aren't heroes. We're just Supers. There's a difference."

Craig reached up, seized his *papier maché* headdress, and with a sickening rip, tore it from its moorings. He hurled it to the ground with a soft clumber that almost brought a tear to Gayle's eye.

"You're just overreacting," said George. "I'm sure that, once Thunderbolt calms down, he'll be willing to share some information with us—"

"What?" Noctyrne, cradling him in her arms, suddenly let him drop. "George, are you out of your mind? We were played, George. Gayle's right. Buzz was right. We're just a bunch of idealistic screwups."

"This isn't happening," Gayle raised her hands to her head. They felt strangely cold against her temples. She turned hopefully, helplessly, to Roland. "And you? Have you given up, too, Detective? Which do you want to do now, fear us or ridicule us?"

Anger bubbled up inside Roland, making small, brief protrusions in the skin of his neck and cheeks. His brown eyes blazed.

"What I want," he finally forced out, "is to solve this case. It's still open. Even if it isn't still ours. Something stinks about this Thunderbolt fellow, and I don't trust him with this investigation."

"Well, neither do we, Detective," said Gayle, unimpressed, "but in case you haven't noticed, we have nothing now. No perp, no disk, nothing to show four our efforts but lumps, bruises, and in my case, a headache that runs through my whole body . . . ."

Her voice trailed off.

"Gayle?" asked George. "Are you all right?"

"Maybe," Roland muttered, "she's just working up the strength to insult me again."

"No!"

"Hey, I was just joking—"

"No, no, no, wait . . ." She raised a finger to silence the world. "Wait . . . my whole body . . . head . . . my heart . . . what Ehat did to me. Every time he did it, I understood a little more, and that final time . . . that final time it clicked."

"So what," Noctyrne whined. "With the case now in Thunderbolt's hands, our jurisdiction's ended. Our city permits have now revoked. We have to return to Herotown."

"Only if we're caught," Gayle smiled wickedly. Then, remembering who was in the room, she turned to Roland. This was the test. This was the big test.

He stared at her, those deep brown eyes that enthralled and infuriated her. *Don't fail me, please don't fail me, please, just this once, be who I think you are, who I want to believe you are . . .*

Roland stared down at his scorched brown suit, at the smoking remnants of his shoes, at the badge in his pocket, still crackling with charge. He was taking an inventory, she could tell, an inventory not just of his physical person but of his values, of his identity. She didn't envy him. But she wanted him to finish, quickly.

Finally, Roland's eyes rose to meet Gayle's. His jaw was set. She feared that posture as much as she treasured it. Then he said three words.

"I'm with you."

Something inside Gayle sang. She spun on her heel, cast her newfound radiance to her beleaguered teammates. "Well? What are we waiting for?"

"I don't know," Combat Wombat grumbled, still unconvinced. "How about a course of action? How about a plan?"

Gayle was not daunted. "I've got one." She turned to George.

"Saddle up the Stallion, GAP. We're headed to the Mesopolopolis Penal Dome."

"What?" Noctyrne gasped. "Has that guy's stare-vision made cheesecloth of your mind, Gayle? It's crawling with law enforcement! No offense to present company," she cocked her head at Roland, "but isn't that the absolute *last* place we want to be?"

"Not if we want to meet the man we have to meet." Gayle was already bounding for the door.

"Gal Friday, you're not making sense," said George. "We're with you. Believe that. But we need to know—"

"You'll know when I tell you on the way. There's no time to lose." Triumph blazed behind her eyes. "We're still in this game, team. The good guys can still win the day."

I do not regret attempting to appeal to our universal humanity. Some would have you think "universal humanity" is only "universal" for those untouched by horror. I disagree. I say that a time of horror is the most crucial time of all to remember the ties we share with other human beings.

—President Arthur Stevenson, resignation speech

MARLA

"So you think you've figured it out."

"Yes, Commander," Marla Arlis sat on end of Shandon's cot in the Penal Dome, while its traditional occupant sat on the other. "Yes, I think we have."

Tenzin Myata stood perfectly still at the far end of the cell, but his eyes kept wandering—the equivalent for him, Marla knew, of madly pacing back and forth.

"We've figured out what we found while drilling on Rhadamanthus Planum, on Europa. Those anomalous electrical signals. They weren't just random, Commander, were they?"

"Yes," said Shandon. "Yes, they were."

"No," said Marla, "you're lying. The patterns in sample Lieutenant Michelis analyzed. The sample that never made it back home. The indications he found."

"Look, I'm a murderer, all right?" Shandon muttered. "It's all my fault. I won't be needing your services any longer, Miss Arliss. You're fired. Good day."

"I don't believe that, Commander. Especially not now. And I don't think opposing counsel does either."

"Do not presume to speak for me," said Tenzin. "Stop stretching it out, Miss Arliss."

He turned to Shandon. "I beg your forgiveness, Captain. You don't have to say a word to me, and your counselor should have already advised you of that, were she not so caught up in this fantastic theory—"

"Not a theory," said Marla, "but the only rational explanation, based on the data."

"Which is—"

"Which is that those electrical patterns you noticed in the water," she said with the eagerness of a child displaying a treasured Christmas present, "they were some sort of life form, weren't they? An alien life form. The first proof that we're not alone in the universe."

Tenzin closed his eyes and exhaled, his gesture of frustration. "Ridiculous, I know. She's trying to build a defense that these creatures were either sentient, or if not, at least somewhat aware of their surroundings, and somehow acted in self-defense, killing your shipmates. She seems to feel there is data enough in Lt. Michelis' transmission to indicate this. Sadly enough, that theory just might persuade a jury. Count yourself lucky."

"Well, I don't," Shandon blurted. "To hell with her theories, I was there. There was nothing alive on Europa except me and Michelis and Al-Awadi. And then just me, after I . . . I killed them."

"No!" said Marla, stepping up to him. "No, Commander, I don't believe that."

"I don't care what you believe," his voice rose to childlike pitches. "You're supposed to be on my side here."

"I am, and that's why—"

"Just go away! Go away, Counselor, or I'll call for the guard—"

"You didn't kill anyone, Commander," she pushed herself far inside his bounds of personal space. "Those life forms did."

"This is preposterous," Tenzin scoffed.

"These life forms acted, in some sort of self defense," Marla talked right over him. "They responded to Michelis' and Al-Awadi's drilling. There was no malfunction in the equipment. What killed Michelis and Al Awadi wasn't you, and wasn't even negligence. What killed them was living in that water sample."

Marla didn't think a human being's skin could grow quite so white as Shandon's did.

"No!" Shandon cried, pushing back from her, leaping to his feet, however unsteadily. "No, you can't say that. You can't go into a courtroom and say that, I won't allow it! I dismissed you, damn it, you have to go now, you have to—"

His legs began to shake, forcing him to sit back on the cot.

Marla didn't know who looked paler, Shandon or Tenzin.

"I . . . I . . . do not understand," Tenzin blinked, looking from Shandon to Marla and back. "Commander, why abandon this defense, however flimsy it might be? As I said, it might be enough to instill reasonable doubt in the minds of a jury . . ."

"I think," Marla spoke softly, "it's because the Commander doesn't want to have any more deaths on his conscience." She reached out, took Shandon's hand, felt the sweat pooled there. "Isn't that right, Neville?"

Shandon let loose a breath he must have been holding for three months. "They're intelligent, you know," he said, stumbling, finding the bed with the back of his knees and settling down. "I . . . felt them. Felt them in my mind, or somewhere, as they killed Michelis and Al Awadi. They were curious, they were scared, they were angry . . . they were lonely . . . and afterwards, they were regretful. They gave me emotions, impressions . . . I don't know how else to explain it."

"Rubbish," Tenzin whispered. "Absolutely unprovable."

"It doesn't *have* to be provable," Shandon wheezed, his voice a creak of grating gears. "Don't you see? It just has to fire up the public. Once the news hits that aliens may have been responsible for the first deaths of human beings to reach the outer solar system, do you know what will happen? Can you even conceive?"

Tenzin opened his mouth, then paused. Realization crept along his face, through the veins and blood vessels on his bald head. He muttered a small prayer in Tibetan.

"I can see now why you didn't trust me," Marla said. "I was so focused on how your conviction would hurt the space program, so insistent on playing that angle to get you to talk . . . but that could only have produced the opposite effect. I didn't realize just what it was you were scared of."

Marla, of course, knew, with equal mixtures of guilt and indignation, what she was scared of. She was scared of how humans would lose yet another yard of ground next to Supers. It was so unfair! Now they would have to, because the other alternative was so much more frightening . . . .

"I still do not understand," Tenzin said, trying to regain his footing. "You do not know . . . you cannot know . . . what our reaction would be. You have no right to keep such a discovery hidden from the people of Earth."

"No right to keep it hidden?" Shandon arched. "Counselor, I have no right to *reveal* it. Look at history. Look at what we do to our fellow human beings. Look at what we did to the Inuit, to the Islanders. Look at the Herotowns. Whenever we encounter something new, different, and potentially dangerous, we lash out. We destroy. We look for any possible excuse . . . . and my trial will give the best excuse of all. Retribution. Revenge. Holy War."

Marla grit her teeth when Shandon mentioned the Herotowns. Surely, surely that wasn't the same thing as what happened to the Inuit! Her ancestors, the colonists, invaded, and everyone knew that was wrong. But the Supers . . . *they* were the invaders here. No one invited them into the human gene pool half a century ago, no one asked for their assistance in managing crime and poverty, and certainly no one asked for Trinity. Who could argue with Trinity?

Tenzin still seemed stuck on the particulars. "But the space program is so underfunded," he was saying. "How realistic is the fear that—"

"We'd find the money," said Shandon. "When it comes to war, we always find the money. We'd toss enough nukes at Europa to split the moon wide open, kill every living thing there. Can we even afford to take that chance?"

"That's why you wiped the sensor logs," said Marla. "That's why you jettisoned the sample. And that's why you're willing to sacrifice yourself, even deal a blow to the space program," her voice wobbled slightly, "to plead guilty, rather than let this all come to the public light."

"Believe me," Shandon pulled himself up to his full height, "I'm not anxious to be a martyr, Miss Arliss. That's not why I joined the Space Exploration Corps."

"But you don't have to be," she pleaded. "People could still listen to you, if you explained the whole story. You were the first human to walk on Ganymede!"

"A routine mission," said Shandon. "The computers did all the work."

"You were decorated at Annihilus Bay!"

"I was a terrified eighteen year old who knew how to fly a plane, and pressed a button that dropped bombs because I was too scared to stop pressing it. I have no right to ask history to remember me for anything like that, and I refuse to have it remember me as the man responsible for turning humanity towards genocide."

He sighed. "Assuming, of course, whatever lives in those light patterns on Europa isn't strong enough to fight back. I don't know which scenario scares me more. But yes, I'd rather be a small martyr than let Michelis and Al Awadi become big ones. That's the last thing they would have wanted. I know. They were my friends."

For a moment, in that posture Shandon held, Marla could indeed see the bearing of an astronaut, the pride and horzionlessness of that long-lost generation that lived and died before Trinity, in the first Heroic Age or even earlier, before the coming of the Supers. Then it faded, collapsed along with Shandon's body, back to the cot.

Marla wondered how the space program would suffer from Shandon's conviction. It would recover, no doubt . . . but now she was beginning to wonder if that was a good thing. Well, she and Shandon only had power over this piece. She, Shandon, and Tenzin.

Marla found Tenzin's gaze. "He's sacrificing his freedom, I'm sacrificing my case . . ."

She paused. What more was she sacrificing?

"Now it's your turn, Tenzin," she finally concluded. "Do whatever you have to. Make sure Holloway keeps that email off the table. So far, only a few eyes have seen it. Let's keep it that way, all right?"

Tenzin stared vacantly at the cell floor like a man lost. What did the teachings say, the teachings? His ears had grown deaf to the centering voice of wisdom inside. He needed to meditate. Never mind that, he needed to hop a plane to the Kingdom of Tibet, to confer with the Lamas and honored elders, even though he had never, ever done so in his life.

Finally, he raised his head. "I do not know. I do not know what right I have to withhold information that is not mine to own. The knowledge that we are not alone in this universe . . . its effects, positive or negative, are too staggering for one mind to comprehend. But so too are the effects of human violence."

"I . . . I am afraid," said Tenzin. "I am afraid of any alternative. At minimum, even if I convince Holloway to take criminal negligence, he will grow enraged, Holloway always makes sure someone pays for his ill moods. My career . . . my career will be over."

"Some things are more important than career," said Marla. "I tried to tell you that two years ago, at the Shining Star Restaurant. You didn't listen then. Maybe you will now?"

She held his gaze, searched for some sign of the man who had held her hand as they walked across the Mesopolopolis River, who sang to her as the sun rose across the harbor, kept her warm on those frozen January nights. She found something, some uncategorizable pattern of light, and took that as a start.

Wordlessly, she took his hand.

At that moment, the door to the cell door opened, and the worst possible voice, the voice that still haunted Marla Arliss' nightmares.

"Commander Shandon," said Thunderbolt, "prepare to be judged. You, and any who would defend you."

INTERLUDE

The Silver Peregrine's eyes blazed with white-cold fire. "What in the name of the Spirit itself is Thomas doing?"

"You saw, Sarah," Cerebellum said calmly (but his eyes were closed, and Sarah *knew* that was a sign he was upset), "Ehat wouldn't cooperate. Not even with my mind scans."

Sarah paced the top of the skyscraper. She didn't even know which one they were standing on this time . . . they all started to blur after awhile.

"So he's kidnapping *Neville Shandon?*"

"I read Ehat's mind, or what passes for it now. Beneath all the static of the two entities, I pulled out the image of the person he was seeking. Neville Shandon. He's the only one who might get Ehat to cooperate."

"And if Shandon can't? If Ehat doesn't?"

"You know what comes next."

"Dammit, this has gone too far! We're crossing the line here with a jailbreak."

"We had to cross it sometime."

"This is going to get the Normals involved. Their military, and all the other resources they command. They'll be prepared for our next phase. It'll turn the whole plan upside down . . . turn it into a bloodbath!"

"Perhaps," said Cerebellum, eyelids squeezed tightly shut. "But it's not like anyone can stop it now."

Sarah beat her wings, launching off the roof of the skyscraper and into the night sky. "We'll just see about that."

I see no hypocrisy in the formation of Superhuman Resource Units. So-called "Bloodhound Gangs" are far from instances of sending foxes to guard the henhouse. Rather, they are cases of sending foxes to kill each other, so then hens don't have to waste their ammunition.

—Ryan Spudnick, Associate Director of the
Metahumanics Commission

GAYLE

"Ok, we're on the Mesopolopolis Expressway," said Noctyrne at the wheel of the Stallion, "and no Bloodhound Gangs yet."

Just the fact that Noctyrne had to *say* that didn't make Gayle feel very reassured. But then, she could occupy herself with other things during the minutes it would take to reach the Penal Dome.

The city's largest construction project before Herotown was the Mesopolopolis Expressway. It snaked around Uptown and the adjoining Federal District, standing at 1,000 feet above ground level on hollow, rigid pillars with steel columns and beams reinforcing the perimeter to resist the toll of wind and weight. Funding had run out a decade ago before it could be extended to reach Downtown, although some construction had taken place in the intervening years: ever since Trinity, the city had constructed various guard boxes and crows' nests midway up several pillars to dissuade attacks by superhuman terrorists.

The Expressway could lead them through Uptown to the Federal District right up to the Penal Dome in less than half an hour. That left thirty minutes for any number of possible bad things to happen, before some definite bad things did.

If Roland felt any such tension, he wasn't showing it. He seemed too occupied with Gayle's own distraction.

"Amazing! So these are normal skin cells?"

"The kind that fall off us all the time," said Gayle, holding up a tire iron to use as a pointing stick. The roof of the Stallion's interior made a poor movie screen, but GAP's suit projectors put on a decent enough show. With Noctyrne driving now, the rest of the team was free to take in the science lesson.

"In this case," Gayle pointed, "these are skin cells from our favorite Bulravian national, Ehat, that fell onto our clothing when he grappled with us. However, if GAP would be so kind as to zoom in with his Suit's microscope lenses . . . ."

The image complied, and a crackle of dull amber energy pulsed around the organelles of the cell.

"Is that image out of focus or something?" Combat Wombat squinted.

"No," said Gayle. "The cell looks blurry because of a foreign energy field. Separated from its source, the field is already starting to fade, but you still can't miss it."

Roland nodded, staring with the kind of hunger with which he stared at everything. "So what is it?"

"That, Detective," said Gayle, "is what reached out to my mind three times, to see if I could help ease its loneliness."

"What?" Roland gaped, as if someone had just told him Reindeer could fly.

"Waitaminute," Combat Wombat began to fidgeting with his hands, as if putting the pieces of his thoughts together manually, "could that field have come from Europa?"

"Yes," said Gayle, "I'm almost positive. I think it came via the transmission you were trying to decode from that disk. Somehow someone aboard the *Santa Maria* sent it to Bulravia for some reason, and this man Ehat got . . . for lack of a better word . . . infected."

"Infected? By an, ah, energy field?" Roland looked like he wanted to take notes.

"By a lifeform," said Gayle. "I think this energy field is alive, and inhabiting Ehat's cells."

"Eeew!" said Noctyrne, shaking so that her silk costume shivered. "That's revolting!"

"Fascinating is more like it," said GAP, and with a resistance borne of long practice Gayle denied her impulse to take his hand and pull him in for a closer look.

"An energy based lifeform with the potential for cohabitation with a human biosystem," he said with the glee of a six-year-old opening a Festival present. "In spite of what are no doubt completely separate and divergent evolutionary paradigms . . ."

"Not to mention completely different physiologies," Gayle added.

"Physiology?" George chuckled. "Physiology isn't even the issue. Physiology assumes we're dealing with matter to begin with."

"Which might suggest that, in terms of consciousness, energy is the only real currency."

"Yes!" George's eyes lit up, and Noctyrne shifted in that "ants are crawling up my costume way" she had, brown eyes focusing far harder on the road then they had to. Gayle felt those small maggots of guilt seep into her heart, and she yearned to dash them to mulch. Wasn't Gayle allowed to enjoy the little moments with George, didn't she have a right to *that much*?

"Two consciousnesses sharing one form," said George. "The discovery of a lifetime! The potential applications are staggering—"

"Whoa," said Roland, "slow down. Before we start making plans to market the thing, let's remember, Ehat didn't look terribly happy to have it inside him."

"Nor," said Gayle, coming back down to Earth, "did the alien appear to enjoy its environs either. I can vouch for that—again, don't ask me how—but I *felt* its loneliness, an empty, hollow, *searching* feeling that almost shook me apart. This lifeform isn't villainous, isn't hostile. I'm not sure it knows where it is or how it came here, and it seems desperate to connect with another of its kind."

"And it tries to connect with cute girls?" asked Combat Wombat. "Is this, like, a cute chick on its own world, or something?"

"I don't know," said Gayle. "I'm dealing with impressions here . . . I don't think the alien really has thoughts in the same manner we do. But one thing it has in common with humans is emotions. Ehat's a human being, and maybe . . . I don't know . . . it's confusing his desires with its own. Maybe Ehat's brain is getting the yearning signals for the alien, and translating it as a desire for human companionship."

"Wow," Roland ran a hand through his hair, "that's certainly the strangest motive for a perp I've ever heard, Gal Friday. But I have to admit, it fits the facts. But what did he mean when he said the ambassador wasn't who he was seeking, but that he was getting closer?"

"I only have vague impressions," said Gayle. "But I think he was trying to make his way to the Penal Dome. I think he's seeking out Neville Shandon."

"Kissing every girl on the way to him?"

"I don't think these creatures understand the slightest thing about corporeal gender, Detective. All they understand is desire."

"Ok, ok," said GAP, "so Ehat, or whatever is controlling him, is seeking out the an accused space murderer for some reason. Well, I doubt Thunderbolt's going to listen to that reason, or any `little lost alien' plea. He looked ready to execute him right there."

"Do they . . ." Roland checked his speech. "I mean, does he . . . will he . . . do that?"

"I don't know," Gayle pursed her lips nervously. "Captain Omega would never stand for summary execution, but then, I don't know if Thunderbolt's acting with his blessing or not. He's always been the wildcard of the team."

"Silver Peregrine's the voice of compassion," GAP said, a little too wistfully for either Noctyrne or Gayle's liking. "The others just kind of look to one of those three for direction. They're a very efficient team, you know. Just the proper balance of attitudes and attributes."

"Yeah, Thunderbolt's *reaaal* balanced," Combat Wombat grumbled.

"Focus, guys," said Gayle. "Look, as of now, Thunderbolt has us at a disadvantage."

"No, really?"

"Yes, Combat Wombat, and in more ways than the obvious. He has *information*. Whether he knew the whole story to begin with or was just bluffing us, he now has the disk, and the info on it will probably tell him exactly what's living inside Ehat. Until we know that information as well, we won't know what Thunderbolt plans to do, and whether or not we need to intervene. The only other place to get that information, the only other person who would have it, is Commander Neville Shandon, and fortunately, we know exactly where he is."

"The Penal Dome," Noctyrne shivered. "Ick. Why are we even bothering? I mean, our pass has expired, our case has been transferred to Thunderbolt's jurisdiction . . . what more can we even do?"

Gayle stammered. If she had to *explain* it, what was the point—

"An innocent man's life may be at stake," GAP said slowly, and Gayle could have kissed him. "We can't take the risk that Thunderbolt won't mete out punishment on the alien, whether it's actually guilty of some crime or not . . . not to mention Ehat himself. We can't allow innocents to suffer, be they human, Super, or some other life form entirely. The whole point of heroes is to prevent that."

Gayle scanned the van's interior with a smug exhaustion.

"Someone," said Roland, "had better tell that to Thunderbolt."

The Stallion continued in silence for several minutes.

*   *   *

Silence most assuredly did not reign at the Mesopolopolis Penal Dome. By the time the Expressway brought them close enough to look out and see the steel and concrete hemisphere rising up from like a blister on the fingernail peninsula of South Shore, the Friday Knights could spot the angry lights of helicopters swarming above the perimeter while red lights stabbed up to meet them in the night air. The "thuppa thuppa" of their rotors provided bass for the pounding "awooga-s" of the prison siren, audible even a half mile away through the Stallion's closed windows.

"Splen," hissed Combat Wombat. "Something's up at the prison. So much for sneaking in unnoticed."

"Oh, like you're Mister Subtlety, anyway," said Noctyrne. A bitterness had recently seeped into her voice. "Look, this is stupid. We're already in the city illegally, and now that there's some police action going on down there—"

"More than police action," said GAP. "I'm tuning into the police scanners now. They've called in the military. And the Peace Officers."

"Oh, that settles it," said Noctyrne. "The next exit, we're getting off and speeding back home."

"No!" said Gayle, wishing her voice hadn't just risen to that whining pitch. "We can't, Noctyrne, not when we're so close—"

"Are you deaf, Gal Friday?" said Combat Wombat. "Peace Officers. As in, the folks who shoot us. For all we know, they're alerted to our arrival—"

"That's impossible," said Gayle. "No one knows we're even coming." She turned to GAP. The team leader. Her George.

"GAP, you can't expect us to turn away from the case at this stage. There are too many loose ends, too much unaccounted for. Innocent lives are in danger!"

George opened his mouth, and Gayle's soul soared with the expectations of whatever words would have come next. But the roar of a jet engine drowned them out.

All eyes inside the Stallion turned to watch two fighterjets swoop down the edges of the City skyline, swoop gracefully down between the monorail tracks, banking before they would scrape the Expressway ramps. The blue flare from their retro-jets lit up the streets below as they maneuvered for a landing on the prison grounds. As if arrested in their flight by an invisible hand, the jets shook and hovered, white clouds of detritus billowing up from the ground below as their VTOL engines brought them to an even parallel with the landing pad.

The jets' aerobatics, however were not what commanded the Friday Knights' attention, were not even what caused George to swallow whatever words of reassurance or inspiration he was about to issue. For another aircraft was approaching, and it became clear now that the pair of fighterjets merely served as its escort, its honor guard, its harbingers. The new craft seemed as ungainly as its predecessors were graceful, a dull gunmetal gray to the fighterjets' shining white fuselages—gray save for some very distinctive red markings. Bricklike with bulbous protrusions, the craft did not so much land as sink, stumbling between the Expressway ramps and actually shearing off an exit sign in the process. Metal screeched in pain as the sign crumpled beneath the aircraft's hull, snapped loose from its moorings, and protested with a million sparks as it plunged dozens of meters to smash against the streets below.

Indifferently, the transport aircraft dropped through the air to the prison grounds, passing beneath the dome's apogee and falling out of sight. The red markings on the hull, however, combined with the brazenness of its approach, told the Friday Knights all they needed to know.

Noctyrne pulled the Stallion to the side of the expressway, letting the other automobiles roar past it. Inside, no one dared speak. Finally, Combat Wombat was brave enough to whisper the thought dominating all the Supers' minds.

"A Bloodhound Gang," he breathed.

2

"They can't be after us," Gayle was trying to say, but the voices of her teammates drowned her out. Combat Wombat was yelling various obscene imprecations against the government, Noctyrne was practically apoplectic with hysterical cries, and GAP kept attempting the impossible task of calming both of them down simultaneously.

"Look, we need to settle down, regroup—"

"*You* regroup," Noctyrne took a swipe at him. "We have a wedding in six months! We have a life we're trying to build here. How can you ask us to risk all that on a stupid pointless—"

"Risk is part of the equation—"

"Screw your equations! Maybe if you looked up from them once and awhile you'd—"

"Hey, there's no need for—"

"We're all gonna die!"

The din swallowed Gayle's words, Gayle's very existence. She felt as if she were sinking into a sea of concrete, just like in her dream, just like when she reached her hand out to Waley and he ignored her, leaving her to sink, sink, with hand outstretched . . .

. . . . and then suddenly, a hand clasped hers.

Detective Roland.

"—hear me?"

"Er?" she turned around, searching for his voice in the tumult.

"I said, can you hear me?"

"Yes," she cupped a hand around her ears, "yes, you're right beside me. What?"

"I was saying," he cupped a hand around his mouth, wincing at the Wombat War Cries bellowing from Craig's voicebox, "we need to find out what's going on. Someone needs to do some reconnaissance here. As the only person who those Peace Officers won't shoot on sight, I volunteer. I know a few guards at the Dome. Maybe I can get some information."

"Good idea," Gayle had to shout—Noctyrne's words had dissolved into incoherent bat shrieks—"but I'm coming with you. At least as far as the prison grounds."

"What?" asked Roland.

Gayle didn't know whether he asked out of disbelief, or whether he just couldn't hear.

Gayle motioned for him to exit the vehicle. He crawled out, with Gayle at his heels, even as chaos continued to roar within. Their departure went completely unnoticed.

"You can't go alone," she said as she felt the night air whip her face, her hair, her trenchcoat. "If there's a crisis down there, you'll need someone to protect you."

"Protect me?" Roland arched. "There's an entire contingent of Peace Officers down there, not to mention police, military—"

"Exactly," said Gayle. "Who'll protect you from them?"

Roland opened his mouth in indignation, then paused. He searched her face, and she smiled.

"You've got to stay here," he repeated. "You know that."

Gayle opened her mouth, but he quickly talked over her, "I mean, someone has to calm down the Knights, ready them for whenever I . . . we . . . . I . . ."

He paused, eyes searching the air between them for the right words. Gayle followed his gaze, nervously, expectantly.

"I . . . I wish I could take you with me," he said. "You're . . . you're a good partner, Gal Friday. What I mean is, we work well together. I mean, what I mean is—"

Gayle put a finger to her lips, pulled up close to him, and, with the roar of automobiles around them commingling with the shouts of her teammates from inside the Stallion as musical accompaniment, she leaned over and kissed him on the cheek.

He flinched slightly as she approached, not quite realizing what was happening until after the moment had already passed. Then he looked up at her, her sparkling blue eyes, the nervous smile on her features.

"This is insane," Roland finally breathed. "I mean, this situation, this entire case, the past three nights, you, me—"

Gayle put a finger to his lips now.

"Ssh," she said. "Insanity's our stock in trade. Welcome to the life of a Super."

Then, so as not to pull him close, she shoved him away. Not quite aware of her superstrength, she accidentally pushed him a good two meters back. He dove out of the way of an angrily oncoming bus.

"Spirit Above, no!" Gayle rushed towards him, feeling her heart crack, but he put up a reassuring (or warding) hand.

"It's . . . all right," he coughed. "I'm getting used to this."

Something knotted in Gayle's gut, finally erupting in a laugh. The scene seemed a little ridiculous.

"Good," Roland smiled. "That's the attitude. You stay here, keep them from killing each other. I'll report back as soon as I'm able."

With that, the detective took off down the Expressway, ran up to an auto that was slowing to take the off-ramp and flashed his badge. After a brief exchange with the driver, he got in and took the wheel. Gayle looked on, meters away, with a mixture of admiration and jealousy. Roland had been so, so wrong two days ago (two days? It seemed like two years!) back in the restaurant in Herotown, when he said Supers had the real power. Far from it. One day a week, Gayle could lift autos, Combat Wombat could tear them apart, GAP could invent a better one and Noctyrne could stop them with nothing more than her looks . . . but only Roland could just hold up a badge, summon a commanding voice, and demand that the System obey him. No super-powers, no gadgets, just the coat of authority and the strength to use it.

That was what made Normals so dangerous, according to some of the more strident editorials in the *Spandex Scene.* Seeing Roland in action, Gayle begrudgingly began to see that point of view. Normals, some of them anyway, possessed *authority,* the invisible power to command multitudes. Multitudes in the billions, the *Spandex Scene* was quick to remind, compared to the mere thousands of supers, most of whom lay locked away in Herotowns, or huddled in their own affairs on the Moon. Gayle had studied law. Gayle knew all the ins and outs of authority, yet couldn't wield even a smidgeon of it. For all her intellect (or what everyone kept telling her was such an intellect), the only way she could wield authority was the cheap way, the way that got you locked up or hunted by Bloodhound gangs—authority via brute strength.

With an angry heave, she lifted the Stallion up by its bumper and shook. One by one, like stubborn nuts stuck to the bottom of a can, her teammates fell out, dazed and cursing.

"*Stop it!*" she shouted, and, to her surprise, they listened.

"We're heroes, for pity's sake," she said as they sat bewildered on the cold pavement of the expressway breakdown lane. "We don't turn tail and run at the first sign of trouble! Detective Roland's just gone down to get us some more information, and when he returns we'll have a better idea of what we can do. For now, we have to wait."

"Spirit *Above*, Gayle," Noctyrne was frantically brushing the street grime off her costume as if it were acid, "we know you're keen on the Detective, but don't drag us into your little love games if they're going to get us killed—"

"*Love games?*" Gayle roared, swinging the Stallion high overhead like a club. "Do you have any *idea* the kind of love games I've had to put up with since you and George . . ."

Noctyrne produced a small squeal, and flung her hands to her mouth. Combat Wombat grabbed her shoulder savagely.

"Hey Naomi," he hissed, "do not . . . argue . . . with a woman . . . swinging . . . a truck."

"Gal Friday," George rose, looking so naked and vulnerable without his armor. "Gayle. Please. Put the Stallion down. It's been a rough night, and we need to calm down."

"Calm down?" Gayle cried, still swinging away. "Since this case began I've been kidnapped, attacked by hired killers, hypnotized three times, smashed in the head with a fire extinguisher, and oh yes, scaled the side of building, which was the worst part of all, believe me—except maybe for the fact that, ever since I met Roland, I've been forced to think about all the things I usually try and keep buried, and every time I think about them, I find reason to doubt my sanity, my place on this team, and in some moments, whether I even should be alive right now. Do you understand? *Can* you understand?"

"We'd understand you a lot better," said Combat Wombat, "if you'd put the truck down."

"Please," added George, searching into her eyes.

And that did it. Even the brute authority fled, and Gayle felt her muscles grow lax. She eased the Stallion to the ground, then savagely shut her eyes to keep back tears.

George, her George, most assuredly not her George, walked forward and reached out his meat-slab arms with an almost robotic awkwardness, as if he were still wearing his two ton metal GAP suit. Then he embraced her, and the warmth of human flesh was unmistakable.

"I'm sorry," she snuffled into his shoulder. "That was probably very unprofessional. All of it."

"You're allowed," George whispered hot breath into her ear. After a pause, he added, The fact that any of us have the sanity we do right now is pretty damned remarkable. What little we have, we usually owe to you."

Gayle pulled away and allowed herself a chuckle. "Now, despite everything, *that* is the strangest thing I've heard all week."

They embraced again, and if Noctyrne had reservations she kept them to herself. She drew nearer, put an arm around Gayle from behind, and held her teammate close.

Combat Wombat drove his hands into his pockets. "Hey, I am not joining your crunchy little group hug, ok?" An uneasy smile spread across his face as Gayle's eyes found his. "I like ya. I'm sorry. Let's stay with this. There, are you happy?"

"With you all?" Gayle felt tears burn hot tracks across the freezing skin of her cheeks. "Yes. Yes, I am. Even when aliens and Bloodhound Gangs threaten."

"Good," said George. "Now you three get back in the Stallion where it's warm, and I'll put on the GAP suit and use its telescopic vision to see if I can gather some information of my own."

Nods all around, a few handshakes, and then, with the immediacy of actors once the houselights rose, the Friday Knights went back to the work of being heroes.

4

"Good news," Roland's voice said over a secure comm-link with GAP's suit. "The Bloodhound Gang's not after you guys. The bad news is that they're after Ehat."

Roland's voice sounded patchy, barely audible over the roar of the helicopter blades, the hum of tank motors, and the cacophony of voices in the background. GAP did his best to filter the transmission on both ends, but both parties still had to ask the other to repeat themselves at several junctures.

"That makes sense," GAP replied. "Considering the presence of all those Air Force types, it looked like something related to our extraterrestrial-influenced friend."

"Well, our friend's been busy," said Roland. "According to officials on the scene, Ehat broke into the Penal Dome and kidnapped Shandon, along with two lawyers who were visiting him."

"What?" Gayle piped in. "How could Ehat break in? When last we saw him, he was Thunderbolt's captive."

"According to the Warden's statement," said Roland, "Thunderbolt tried to stop Ehat but failed. He took off in pursuit."

"*What?*" Combat Wombat cried. "That little scrawny Bulravian guy, beat up Thunderbolt?"

"Depends if he used that hypno-vision," said Noctyrne.

"I don't know," Gayle bit her lip.

"You've got good instincts, Gal Friday," Roland replied. "Some of the guards here are telling a different story. They say *Thunderbolt* broke in and did all the kidnapping. But no one's listening to them."

"Makes sense," said GAP. "Who'd suspect a member of the Superior Squad? They're the only super team the City respects."

"Well, they're not giving Ambassador Golden much respect," said Roland. "She's here, right now, and demanding this case be turned over to the authority of the Superior Squad. She and the military commander are having quite the argument, but he's standing pretty firm."

"If Captain Omega wants to send in the Superior Squad," said Gayle, "no one's going to be able to stop him. Not even Bloodhounds."

Roland's voice warbled . . . or maybe it was the phone connection. "I can't say I want to be nearby if it comes to a fight between heavy hitters like that."

A fight. Between the Superior Squad and the government's thugs? All the Friday Knights shivered at the thought. In the fifteen years since Trinity, through the Lee Act and the relocations and all the laws and policies regarding Supers, the Superior Squad had never come to blows with the authorities. Even during the Freehold Massacre eight years ago, when Peace Officers opened fire on unarmed protestors who were illegally operating a commune in the suburbs that housed Normals and Supers together, the Superior Squad stood down, remained neutral.

It was that incident, of course, that prompted Captain Omega to break the Squad's contract with the city government, and relocate, along with some select Supers, to the moon, where they built Superion City. But never did Omega or any of his teammates raise a hand against the law.

Captain Omega and Mayor Ironheart, now in his third consecutive term in office, maintained an understanding. The two had literally fought side-by-side, as Ironheart had commanded one of the battalions at Annihilus Bay, and, or so the papers said, the two shared the mutual respect of old comrades-in-arms. If Mesopolopolis ever needed heroes (and it did, almost weekly), Ironheart could place a call to the moon and they would arrive. Presumably, if the Superior Squad needed some leeway, Ironheart could make the law look the other way, much to the chagrin of some critics in the *Times*, not to mention Cardinal Maxtor of the Church of Humanity.

But this case went beyond Ironheart, beyond Mesopolopolis, up to the highest echelons of the State itself, if Thunderbolt's note was to be believed. Would the mayor be able to protect his city's heroes? Would he even try?

"The Bloodhound Gang's just sitting around," Roland was saying. "One of them's got a portable satellite dish. I think they're waiting for some sort of transmission."

A few moments pause. Then Roland returned.

"Jurisdiction, that's it," he said. "They need the files with Ehat's energy signatures so they can track him, like we've been doing."

"But that authority got signed over to the Superior Squad," said GAP.

"As Thunderbolt was oh-so-proud of showing us," Combat Wombat added.

"That's right," said Roland. "Part of the argument with Ambassador Golden seems to be revolving around her refusal to sign it back over and give the tracking signatures to the Squad."

GAP zoomed in on the conversation, projecting the image holographically so his teammates could share in the view. Gayle saw the pride in Liana Golden's bearing. Could a six foot tall woman with shining gold skin carry herself in any other fashion? Yet there she was, surrounded by Peace Officers in armor as tall as GAP's suit, brandishing plasma rifles the size of treetrunks, and she neither cowered nor capitulated. Gayle wasn't a good lip reader, but the Ambassador's eyes and posture said it all—that power didn't lie in guns or in superstrength, but in will and determination. *That* was the way a Super should carry herself. Hell, that was the way any human being ought to carry herself. Gayle became suddenly conscious of her own slouch, and fixed it.

"They're going to be at this for awhile," said Roland. "Welcome to the less-than-glamorous side of policework—the red tape."

"Red tape or not," said Gayle, "she can't hold them off forever. If they can't get the tracking signatures without a mess of hassle, they'll just take new scans. Either way, since we already *have* the signatures, we can get a head start."

GAP nodded his metallic head. "That's right. Combat Wombat, Noctyrne, and I will start the search."

"Hold on," said Gayle. "What about me?"

"You wait here," said GAP. "Join up with Roland when he gets back, and see if you can manage to catch Ambassador Golden alone. She might be willing to talk to a fellow Super."

"Excuse me?" asked Gayle. "You're assigning me diplomatic work all of a sudden?"

"It's needed work," said GAP. "Don't forget that we're not the only ones with those tracking signatures."

Gayle paused, stomach suddenly knotting. "That's right. Thunderbolt and the Superior Squad have them as well."

"And authorization or not," said GAP, "they'll be on this case. What's more, they probably know more of what's actually going on than we do. Which is why, as you told us earlier, we have to even that score. We need someone to talk to Ambassador Golden."

"You're our best diplomat," Noctyrne smiled, and everything in her posture spoke an attack. Here? Now? Of all places? Couldn't she put this aside? Then again, Noctyrne might have just been telling the truth. Combat Wombat was right now hard at work stalking a small cluster of rats on the roadside, licking his lips in anticipation. George blubbered whenever he spoke to any attractive woman, even Noctyrne—Liana Golden would have his tongue in knots. And Noctyrne never left George's side, which meant . . .

"Ok. Ok. I'll do it."

"Good," said George. "Besides, you know, in about an hour . . ."

Gayle's eyes narrowed as the words punctured her heart. Could he be *that* dim?

"I know very well the limitations of my powers, GAP," she spat back, and could he really have been as shocked as he looked?

Gayle smiled weakly, and George, wanting to believe the expression, took her up on it. Noctyrne didn't notice the whole exchange; she was busy grabbing Combat Wombat by the shirt collar. Well, at least Gayle could enjoy the small victory of Noctyrne not being around to see her so crestfallen.

But she couldn't leave Noctyrne on these terms, not when the other woman was rushing off into danger. Heroes didn't do that. *Friends* didn't do that.

Gayle forced herself to take one step, then another, until she had covered the ground in-between her and the young vampire. The young, gorgeous vampire, with the flowing black hair that would never loose its sheen, would never tangle like Gayle's, would never need three rinses and two conditioners to prepare it for a half hour of frustrated combing. Noctyrne, with model-perfect posture and blemishless skin and the love of one of the greatest superheroes on Earth . . .

"H-hey," Gayle forced the sound through reluctant vocal chords. Combat Wombat had just scampered off behind a guard rail, leaving the two alone. Alone with the roar of autos and the wind that buffeted Gayle left and right, but passed through Noctyrne as if she were made of mist.

Noctyrne didn't so much turn as slide to face Gayle, always cutting a perfect profile against the night sky.

"What?" she hissed.

Despite herself, Gayle flinched. Something in Noctyrne's hiss must have acted on a biological level. Something in those red eyes, with their streaks of . . . pink?

"Look, Noctyrne . . . . Naomi." Gayle fidgeted. "I'm . . . I'm sorry for what I said earlier. While swinging the truck."

"Oh?" Noctyrne shrugged with practiced indifference. "I haven't a clue what you're talking about."

"Come on," Gayle stamped, "don't make this any harder for me than it is. I blew it. I'm sorry. I shouldn't have said—"

"It's so unfair," Noctyrne hissed again, and Gayle zoomed in on those beads of liquid near her eyes. They didn't look as much like tears as they did cranberry juice, and the extremely watered-down variety at that. Noctyrne's chest didn't shudder. Her eyes didn't narrow. She didn't hunch or show any of the other symptoms of crying. Yet what else could it be?

"What's unfair?"

"George," said Noctyrne. "He's so brilliant. I mean, every few hours he invents something else, Gayle. Every few *hours.*"

"I know," Gayle smiled hopefully. "Can't figure out how to tie a trash bag, but can invent a nuclear-powered trash compressor over dinner."

Noctyrne didn't smile. Instead, more pink streaks came falling. "I hate it. And I hate that I hate it, too."

"Hate it? What do you—"

"Do you have any idea how *intimidating* this all is for me, Gayle? I mean, I went to school before I got bitten. High school, some junior college. I'm not a total idiot. But around him, I feel like one."

"But—"

"No, Gayle, let me finish! It's not just the brains. It's that . . . that thing inside him," Noctyrne pounded her own chest with such force that Gayle couldn't believe she didn't double over or cough. "I mean, with masks off, we all have our own separate lives and skills, right?"

Do the masks ever come off? Gayle wondered silently.

"But here, in costume, on the job . . . we're supposed to all be heroes, right? It's not the powers that makes the Super but the Super that makes the powers, and all that Captain Omega nonsense?"

Given our recent run-ins with Thunderbolt, thought Gayle, *I'm not sure members of the Superior Squad are best people to cite . . .*

"It's like no matter how hard I try, I'll never be the hero he can be just by breathing!" Noctyrne began to wail. "It's like every second I'm with him, I'm living on borrowed time. Like any day now, he's going to wake up and realize how . . . how . . . how positively *inferior* I am. I hate feeling inferior. To him. To you."

"But Noctyrne, how can you say that when—" Gayle blinked, paused. "Wait, to me?"

"Yes, to you, Gayle." Noctyrne bared her fangs, but the cranberry tears were flowing unabated. "George deserves better than me. He deserves someone like you. Suma Cum Laude and all that from Mesopolopolis University. Spouting the same kind of `all for one' and `save the world' hero stuff that he does, on demand. He needs someone like you, not some stupid little waif like me . . ."

The rest of her words were lost as she collapsed into Gayle's arms. Gayle took her awkwardly in a hug, as if holding a glass porcupine, unsure of how much damage a tight embrace would do to either of them. Noctyrne felt like she weighed less than a beachball . . . but then, with Gayle's strength still Super, how could she really tell?

Gayle found herself stroking Noctyrne's hair and whispering

soothing words, an infuriating reflex when all she wanted to do was slap her.

You really are *an idiot!* Gayle somehow couldn't find the voice to tell the other woman. *Here you've got the unconditional love and generosity of the wonderful man on Earth, and all you can do is whine about it?*

It was like someone who lived on a beach complaining about the sound of the water every night, or the owner of a skyscraping penthouse apartment grumbling about fear of heights. No, it was even worse than that. *She's too terrified of losing what she's got to even enjoy it.*

"Gal Friday? Noctyrne?" George's voice called obliviously over to them.

Noctyrne snapped out of Gayle's arms, and her tears had vanished. No mascara runs, no lines in the face, no bags around the eyes. Just gone. Gayle wanted to envy that, but suddenly she couldn't.

"We're ready," said George. Noctyrne and Combat Wombat drew up on either side of them. Just like that, they were a team—ready to take on evildoers, to save the innocent . . . all without Gayle's help.

What had Noctyrne been complaining about again? Gayle had suddenly lost the urge for all apologies.

"We'll keep in constant communication," George was saying to her, almost apologetically.

"Yeah, yeah," said Gayle, weakly waving them on as they peeled out and tore off down the Expressway.

Noctyrne had been jealous? Of *Gayle?* George's fiancée was not only an idiot, she was insane.

There she stood, Gayle Fellman, Gal Friday, 5'6 and 140 pounds, 26 years old and dressed in a trench coat freshly stained after only having been dry-cleaned a night earlier, holding a crumpled fedora to her chest as the winter wind whipped the folds of her clothing into tiny billows. Automobile exhaust threatened to strangle her lungs as, feet planted on painted pavement, she craned her neck to the darkness above Mesopolopolis. Clouds had rolled in, hiding the lights of the giant towers, the folds and crisscross of their latticework obscured by the shadows of even taller buildings. Gothic gargoyles loomed, laughing at the icons atop all the different Churches—the Orb of the Keeper church, the Ankh of the Osirians, the Eye of the Kabbalists, the Pentagram of the NeoPagans, even the DNA Helix of the Church of Humanity, and more, tiny sculptures of human belief mocked by powers older and darker. Ebon monoliths above, endless void below, deafening wind punctuated by the engine noises all around her.

Far out, at the edge of her vision, lay the only light source that really punched through the haze, and it came from that terrible boil on the face of the city that was the Penal Dome. Tiny helicopters still circled, searchlights still probed the night, klaxons barely audible at this distance whined away. The stink of machinery and human waste and polluted air cocooned her, threatened to lift her up off the ramp and hurl her into the abyss below, or, worse, catapult her into the colder, blacker void of space above.

This is the world I keep pledging to save?

The tall monoliths of the city didn't care. The city's true guardians, inside their battlesuits and helicopters, didn't care. The people scurrying above and below, to and from loved ones, in search of loved ones, in search of pain and pleasure to give and receive—none of them cared. None of them even knew this one, tiny slip of a woman in a dirty trenchcoat generations out of fashion was even standing there, a speck hidden amongst infinity, waiting quietly until the tiny spark that made her special fled for another week.

She wished George would come back. She wished she could erase Naomi's voice from her head. She wished Roland would get here soon. But part of her wished, even began to *believe,* that they had all forgotten about her. How could they not, when the city was so vast and she was so small?

Roland wouldn't forget about her, would he? She wanted so desperately for him to be an anchor. Being around him, catching even the hints of his respect and desire for her, made her feel *human* for the first time since she'd been with Waley. Human, and not a costume, not a set of university degrees, not a genetic scan pattern, not just one other small outcropping jutting out meekly amidst a sea of steal and concrete . . .

An automobile engine drew perilously close, and Gayle, shocked out of reverie, threw herself aside, shielding her eyes from the glare of its headlights.

"Detective?" she called out.

Something was wrong with the automobile. It was larger, more expensive, than the one Roland had driven, jet black and devoid of any stylized contours or markings save a silver triangle on the hood. The rear passenger's side window lowered, but in the darkness Gayle could see nothing of the interior.

"Get in the back," a male voice from inside. Not Roland's. Not George's. Not anyone's that she recognized. A slight warble shook the tones, as if they were coming across a radio transmission.

"Excuse me?" she said, muscles tensing. She still had an hour of superstrength left, damn it all. If some joyriding punk wanted to try something, she would take unfathomable pleasure in wrapping the metal of that auto around his—

"Now, Gal Friday," he repeated, his voice unmistakably altered through some sort of synthesizer. "You've wasted too much time already. I only have a few moments to tell you the only information that will keep you, your friends, and possibly the entire city alive."

5

Gayle sat down in the passenger seat, feeling the material bend and mould around the contours of her back and buttocks. After all the abuse she had taken today, her body was sorely tempted to just lay in this mysterious plushness and fall right asleep—that is, if her adrenaline hadn't been pulsing strong enough to shatter her aching bones and muscles.

She scanned the back seat—plush and empty. An opaque glass divider separated her from the front of the automobile. This did not look good.

"Okay, she said, keeping one foot securely out the door and on the pavement, "what do you want?"

"Close the door," said the voice.

"I'd prefer to keep it open—"

"Close it!" the voice hissed, accompanied by what sounded like microphone small feedback.

Oh well. In for a cubit, in for the wad . . .

Gayle closed the door gingerly, hoping to somehow prop it so it wouldn't lock. A soft "clatch" sound from the mechanism told her this plan hadn't worked.

"Right," Gayle said softly. "This is where I get gassed, right? Or electroshocked? Or, dare I imagine it, told I've just won the lottery?"

"None of the above, I'm afraid," said the voice, and for just a moment, Gayle thought something in the cadence sounded slightly familiar. But when next he spoke, her mysterious host's voice remained alien.

"You're in way over your head, Gal Friday. All of you."

"Gee," Gayle shifted uneasily, "I really needed a mysterious informant to tell me *that*."

"I think you do. I think you lack any true conception of how far this case reaches."

"The President. Superion City. Europa." Gayle shrugged. She fought the urge to chuckle—it was like talking about how one would spend a fortune should one ever inherit it.

"There's a war brewing out there."

"Excuse me?" asked Gayle. "You mean, the manhunt? The Bloodhound Squad?"

"Barely a battle. A spark, if you will. Of course, all a raging inferno needs is a single spark, properly positioned, to begin the ignition. And then, war."

Gayle eyed the divider between them. One good punch, with her super strength behind it, would shatter even bulletproof glass to shards. But she didn't know where her informant's head lay . . . if she punched in the wrong spot, she might accidentally injure or kill him.

"Are you saying we're somehow going to get involved directly in the war against Bulravia?" Gayle asked. "That we'll stop using Skovakians as proxies?"

Silence.

"Look, you yourself told me time was limited. Why the game of twenty questions? If you've got something to tell me, just say it—"

"A war is brewing between Supers and Normals," the voice said hurriedly, as if the words were foul-tasting pills to be swallowed. "In Bulravia, in Mesopolopolis, on Superion City . . . everywhere where there are human beings. Not just tensions, not just conflicts in foreign lands over Supers' rights . . . but all out, full scale war."

Nausea crept into Gayle's innards like honey from an old jar. "What? Why? What evidence do you have that—"

"Captain Omega is losing control over his people," the voice interrupted. "They've been developing a secret weapon for years now, and recent events are almost certainly going to propel them to use it ahead of schedule. The effects may not be nearly as devastating as they plan, which will only mean the Normals will have time to respond adequately . . . and Annihilus Bay will look a children's street game of Heroes and Villains compared to what will come next."

Even over the sound of her thundering heartbeat, Gayle took note of his reference to the street game. Whoever this man was, he knew about life in Herotown.

"Who . . . who are you?" she demanded, wondering why her voice sounded so much weaker than she intended. "How do you know all this? How can I trust you? And why are you sharing this with me?"

"Too many questions," said the voice. "The only question I'll answer is the one whose answer you already know. Why am I sharing this with you? The same reason anyone parts with a valuable . . . because he wants something in return."

"And that would be?" Gayle asked uneasily.

"I need you to save the man named Ehat, and the entity to whom he plays host."

"Saving them was our plan all along," said Gayle.

"I know. That's part of why I chose you. I need you to save them and bring them to me."

"What?" asked Gayle. "Mister, assuming we can even find him, pry him loose from Thunderbolt, and spirit him away before the Superior Squad, the Bloodhound Gang, the military, or anyone else gets him first, why on Earth should we give him to you?"

"Because you want him to be safe. I can provide him with safe haven. In fact, I am the only man on Earth who can."

"And I'm just supposed to take your word on that?"

"You have no alternative. As you so eloquently put it, he will not be safe with the authorities, Normal or Super."

"That's not good enough," said Gayle, leaning forward, pressing her face to the barrier, trying and failing to see anything through the smoked glass. "I need something more."

A pause.

"Be careful when you ask for information, Gal Friday. You may regret it."

"Yeah, yeah," Gayle still couldn't shake the tremors in her muscles. Was it just the sensation of her super-strength beginning to wear off?

Was some device in this mysterious automobile exerting some sort of effect on her? Or was it just plain, simple, undistilled fear?

"Very well. I will tell you the true nature of Superion City's plans, the full extent of their capabilities. I will also tell you one more piece of information, because it directly impacts your safety, and your safety, for now, is necessary for my plans."

"I'm touched," Gayle muttered.

When the voice spoke again, Gayle listened intently. When she heard the first piece of information, her heart wavered, to the point where it pushed at her stomach, made her feel like vomiting. But it was the second piece of information, seemingly far, less significant, that sent her, despite her resolve, despite her wariness and determination to project a strong front, into uncontrollable sobs of grief.

"A hero acts in the service of humanity."

—Captain Omega, *Justice for All*

"'The service of humanity,' he says. We're not arguing that. But which individuals among humanity, and what said service entails, and who decides all of this . . . those are the questions he doesn't answer, and that's what makes me uncomfortable."

—Ella Ducharme, former State Poet Laueate

MARLA

1

Marla Arliss had done everything right. Crossed every T, dotted every I, studied every night when her classmates went partying—not that she would have even known what to do had she ever joined them, of course. But what good did partying do? Resisting peer pressure, alcohol, drugs, pushy boys, none of it had ever proven difficult, largely because the temptations had never really presented themselves. How was poisoning yourself with liquor until you vomit supposed to be tempting, anyway? How was running off with some sweaty, overzealous, barely shaven boy in a fraternity blazer supposed to be romantic? Others surely looked to Marla as a model of temperance and resistance, but in truth, Marla had never even felt much that needed resistance. She was a good girl. She followed the path, got good grades, went to law school, and that was that. That was life, wasn't it?

So how, how and why had she ended up here? Thirty years old, single, employed in a thankless job, cowering in the gum and beer stained bleachers of Mesopolopolis Stadium in the Federal District, alongside the one man for whom she had ever felt temptation, and paid the worst of prices for it? How did she end up clinging to him in fear as a spandex-clad nightmare tore the night air around her asunder with electricity, each arc jolting closer and closer to her frail, unprotected form?

"Remain calm," Tenzin was telling her, even as sweat coated his own brow—sweat, even though the night air had to have dropped well into the negative temperatures.

Marla wanted to answer, wanted to spit some caustic comeback, but her lips gibbered, her eyes watered, her nose ran. This was what her life had come to? This was how it was most likely going to end? Why? It wasn't fair!

"What do you want from us?" Neville Shandon demanded. Even gaunt and wan from weeks in prison, crouching against the winds in his billowy orange prison jumpsuit, he managed to look confident, imposing. Marla wanted to look like that. Why was she here blubbering while he stood up to that . . . that thing . . . that had captured them?

It spoke.

"You?" Thunderbolt rumbled, each echo cascading across the empty bleachers of the stadium.

The hero's unearthly height made him stand out even more as he stood on the empty playing field, closed for the season. Security guards, whom Marla's continually increased tax dollars were supposedly paying to protect City structures and facilities against Superhuman terrorists, were nowhere to be found. Uncut grass and disused sporting equipment stood mute audience to Thunderbolt's every word.

"You have nothing to offer, human. Your only value exists for persuasion."

"Persuasion?" said Shandon. "I don't understand."

"Of course you don't."

Thunderbolt turned his back on the astronaut and the two lawyers, and concentrated on his fourth and final prisoner, the man who sat, unshivering, motionless, staring into thin air as if hoping to rend it wide open with his gaze. Marla had made the mistake of looking into those bizarre eyes of his earlier, during the flurry of her abduction, and had paid for it with unconsciousness and a terrible headache that, even now, threatened to erode the lining of her skull.

He didn't seem so threatening now, but Thunderbolt still skillfully avoided eye contact as he approached him. "Well? This is the human you loved so much, the one you wanted so much to reach. You will do as we asked you, now, or he will die."

The star-eyed man sat in silence, unmoved even by the power of Thunderbolt's voice. The lightning storm around him might as well have been the distant pop of children's' sparklers.

Thunderbolt shook him by the shoulders. "Well, Ehat? Have you been listening to me?"

"Stop it," Shandon staggered up to them. Marla, even through her fear and discomfort, was impressed with the astronaut's courage. When Thunderbolt had broken them all out of the Penal Dome and carried them away on a plume of electric energy, the speed and vertigo of the ride had shaken them all past the point of standing comfortably.

"Are you really worth this trouble?" Thunderbolt shook the silent man. "Are you really worth all of this damned sacrifice? What more do you want from us before you'll do ask we ask?"

"Stop harassing him," Shandon pressed. "What do you want from that poor man? What did you ask him?"

Thunderbolt continued to ignore him. Shandon drew close, bent forward as if to make some sort of physical grapple—but even as he began the motion, a spark of lightning, traveling so fast that Marla only saw the aftereffect as a streak on her retinas, arced into the astronaut's body. He cried out as every limb shook, every hair stood on end.

"Stop it!" Marla found her voice suddenly, even as Tenzin pulled at her sleeve desperately.

"Marla," he said, "you are both being foolish. The only thing we can do right now is wait and—"

She shrugged him off violently. Holding fast to the aisle rails for balance, she approached Shandon just in time to catch him as he fell back into her arms. His eyes lolled backwards as a moan issued from his chest.

Tears continued to stream. Marla didn't care. Something hot and lightning-like had suddenly fired up in her as well.

"You," she growled to Thunderbolt's turned back. "You really are as bad as they say. Rumor has it that Mayor Ironheart's only your puppet, that he calls the Superior Squad in every time there's a disaster, so you all keep on making sure there are disasters so you're `needed.' Here, here's the real you! The Church of Humanity was right! You're nothing but monsters, monsters pretending to be heroes!"

Thunderbolt turned. Marla suddenly found herself very unprepared for that, especially when she was the lightning glowing white hot in his eyes. He let loose a cry with the full thunder of his voice, a wave of sound that battered her, Shandon in her arms, like a tsunami.

"How *dare* you?" the Hero roared. "How dare you judge me, judge any of us! You are at fault. You have twisted what it means to be a hero! You, with your Herotowns and your Lee Act, your Freetown Massacre, your wars . . . you have destroyed the very fabric of heroism!"

Small, soft crackles issued in rapid sequence from the vicinity of Thunderbolt's head, and Marla tensed, expecting another attack . . . but when she saw his visage twist, his eyes narrow, his cheeks scrunch . . . could he have been . . . crying? No. Impossible. It must just have been a side-effect of his powers.

"We used to act to protect all of humanity," Thunderbolt bellowed. "Now we have to act to protect ourselves. Do you think we want this? Do you think we *enjoy* this?

"You certainly seem to be enjoying it," Marla spat back, unsure of where this sudden boldness had sprung from. Tenzin was gazing open mouthed, as if she somehow presented a more horrifying image than Thunderbolt. Fine. Let him. Arrogant self-righteous bastard.

"This will all be over soon," said Thunderbolt, and Marla felt as his words weren't really directed at her. "Sooner than we had planned. I had hoped to live to see it, but now . . . now perhaps I'm glad I won't."

"What?" asked Marla. "What are you talking about?"

"Any moment now," said Thunderbolt, "one of two parties will arrive. If it turns out to be your military and their precious Bloodhound Gang, then there will be blood indeed, and carnage, and we all will die . . . but not before I ensure that dozens die alongside me. If, on the other hand, the Superior Squad gets here . . ."

He paused, and again the crackling, popping sound issued forth from his face. "Then the only death will be mine. Someone will have to take the fall for this. I cannot let their name be besmirched, not at this crucial stage."

Thunderbolt swiveled in place, stared daggers at the silent, sitting man. "Well? Are you satisfied with that?"

The man with stars for eyes gave no answer.

Thunderbolt seized Neville Shandon, shoved him roughly into Ehat's frame. The astronaut bucked, straightened himself out, reached forward to keep the Bulravian man from falling over.

"You," Ehat turned to him. "You are the one I seek."

"I . . . I am?" said Shandon. "I don't understand. I don't know who you are, or why I've been taken here—"

"Understand," said Ehat, and his eyes opened wide. The galaxies exploded into miniature big bangs, billions of particles shooting outward, making contact with each and every rod and cone in Neville Shandon's eyes. Somewhere, in a place that was not a place, in a time that was no time at all, Shandon stood before a great sea of light, coalescing into columns and pillars that twisted like taffy . . . aligning briefly into the most intricate of skeletal shapes, then shattering into clouds of glitter . . . swirling into seas at his feet, pseudopods of light that tickled his arms and hair.

Then, as if the chemicals on photographic paper were finally settling into a developed picture, the landscape bled in around him. Gone was the stadium and the spires of Mesopolopolis, replaced with icy plains that stretched into craggy white mountains against an infinite black horizon, dotted with the light of a billion faint stars. He should have been gasping for breath, should have felt the cold of space steal his life away instant by instant, but standing on the surface of Europa again seemed as natural as walking in the fields of his family's farm.

Looming in the sky where clouds should have been hung a ball of brown and green and yellow, bigger than the sun, bigger than anything any human was ever meant to see. Jupiter. King of the Gods, almighty judge, with his massive red eye, large enough to swallow the entire Earth several times, bearing down on Shandon's infinitesimally small figure.

"A courtroom," he said slowly, understanding intuitively. He had escaped one trial, the lesser trial, only to face his true one.

What could he hide from this judge, this jury? How could he justify his terrible mistake? He was a murderer, just not in the way his own people believed. He had killed members of another species, a crime which humanity had yet to recognize as a crime at all, save in the courts of individual conscience. Was that where he stood now? Was this all some fevered hallucination, brought on by the unreality of his real life?

Commander Neville Shandon, United Space Force, first human to walk on Ganymede, Gold Phoenix medal recipient for bravery in the Battle of Annihilus Bay, stood naked and helpless before the eye of a god, and laid himself prostrate before it.

"I'm sorry," he said. "I take responsibility. I should have been more careful, should have been open to the possibilities of life on Europa, life unlike our understanding. I should have made some manner of reparation. I tried, with my silence here on Earth. But it wasn't enough. Please, take whatever retribution out on me you will. Just spare my people, and forgive them. They do not understand, and may never."

Shandon knelt down, bowed his head, tensed for whatever executioner's axe might fall. He felt something tickle the hairs at the base of his neck.

"Arise, Neville Shandon. You are forgiven. That is why I came to seek you. To forgive you, and to apologize for the lives we unwittingly took."

"You . . . you weren't seeking retribution?"

Shandon heard no answer, and when he dared to rise to look up at Jupiter once more, he was staring at the bleachers of Mesopolopolis stadium, and the giant blue-clad form standing between him and the stands.

"Yes, human," Thunderbolt was sneering, "you've figured it out. I wasn't seeking retribution for Ehat attacking our ambassador. In fact, he never even committed such an act. I needed an excuse to find him, and once I did, I learned he wanted to find you. So he's found you. Well?"

Shandon looked around, blinking. Had any time passed, by the others' reckoning? Ehat had closed his eyes, had settled back with a contended expression. Shandon was afraid to acknowledge him.

Thunderbolt tapped his foot expectantly. Marla and Tenzin held themselves against the winter gusts. A terrible silence followed. Terrible silence, interrupted by the howl of winds and the distant rumbling of engines. Someone was coming.

Thunderbolt tensed, opened his mouth to speak, when a high pitched whine rose up in the air, accompanied by a flash of silver that Marla's brain barely had time to register before it hit the ground. A plume of smoke rose up, plunging the stadium into inky clouds.

Marla coughed preemptively, shutting her eyes against the burn she knew would come a second later . . . yet somehow didn't. She heard growling noises, an impact of bone against bone, an animal cry—and then the unmistakable cry of Thunderbolt's voice, calling out in pain.

Marla tensed. She should take advantage of this. She should run. She was a lawyer, not a policewoman, and certainly not a Super. Shandon was still within arms reach . . . she should grab her client, help lead his semiconscious form out . . . but where was out? And what about Tenzin? Could she trust him to take care of himself?

She had heard stories of Bloodhound Gangs, read the testimony of those who had seen them. They were the meanest and nastiest of all Supers, those with the deadliest of powers, recruited and trained and brainwashed to kill, kill, kill, not only their quarry but anyone who got in the way. If they had arrived, Marla didn't want to be anywhere near.

Something grasped her left wrist, something cold and bony, and she shrieked. With a strength and savagery she didn't know she possessed, Marla lashed out with her right fish, connecting in a knuckle-shattering blow that made her cry out as much as her opponent. The shriek that came back at her was female.

"Run!" Marla shouted to Shandon, and the astronaut, barely in command of his faculties, wavered a bit before launching himself forward, into the smoke, in the direction of the shriek. Spirit above, how could he be so brave? Barely conscious, yet fighting to save her? How could this have been the same weathered, defeated man who she had counseled so many times in that prison cell?

Sounds of struggle. This was Marla's best chance to run, now, with no distractions and no encumbrances. She turned, swiveled on her bare heel (her shoes had fallen off long ago, on the flight over), felt the cold grass of the stadium sting and prickle her skin, then give way to cement. The aisle. Exits couldn't be far in this direction.

She trotted off a few steps. Then she stopped.

No.

Marla Arliss had based her whole life on doing the right thing, her whole career on defending the downtrodden, hadn't she? She couldn't abandon Neville or Tenzin, couldn't walk into that Church of Humanity the next morning and proudly join the declaration of her superiority to Supers, if she acted as inhumanly as they did.

Lightning arced up out of the smoke cloud, and the rational part of her mind reminded suddenly remembered how suicidal going back would be.

She took a step, hesitated, took another step backward, hesitated . . .

Then Neville Shandon fell backwards out of the smoke, a thin black shape atop him, snarling and hissing. Instinct made Marla's skin crawl, and instinct (she supposed later, looking back on it) made her lash out with a savage kick. She felt the blow connect, felt shivers of revulsion wrack her body (she had seen someone kick a dog once and felt nauseous for hours). When satisfaction suddenly swept in to wipe out the nausea, she kicked again.

The black shape shrieked, and Shandon, seizing the advantage, rolled over and reversed the position of the struggle. Either the smoke was starting to disperse, or Marla's eyes were starting to adjust, because she could now dimly make out the contours of a female form in Shandon's opponent.

"Get . . . off!" the form growled, and with a kick hurled Shandon three feet in the air. Fortunately, the angle sent him back to the grass, and not to the cement bleachers where he could have been killed.

Marla charged forward, eager to press the advantage, not having the slightest idea of quite how.

"You *idiots!*" the female form rose, and Marla saw black robes and hair billowing around white skin. "We're here to *save* you! Stop attacking us."

"Oh, right," Marla cackled, dimly aware she had passed beyond all reason. Wasn't that what Tenzin used to accuse her of, way back in the worst of their fights? Well, ha ha, Tenzin, you were right.

"Thunderbolt said he's really a hero," Marla shouted, "and now you say you're here to save us. Lady, if I can even call you a lady, I don't trust any of you."

"Fine," the woman turned away, "see if I care. Save yourselves. I'm going to go help Combat Wombat before he—"

A flying brown blur shot past the two women and into the bleachers, shattering the wood and showering them with splinters. Marla yelped as she felt her skin and clothing shred.

A low rumble began to rapidly approach, and Marla ducked out of the way just as a cocoon of lightning barreled out of the smokescreen, sheltering a barely perceptible human form within. Thunderbolt, murder in his eyes, was drawing nearer to inspect his handiwork.

"Craig!" the pale woman cried, looking from the shattered bleachers to Thunderbolt and back.

"I warned you not to interfere," said Thunderbolt. "I didn't want to kill you."

"Well, that makes one of us," the woman cried out, and hurled herself, arms outstretched, at the other Super. Marla could have sworn she saw membrane stretch out from the woman's arms, like bat wings, but just as her brain registered the thought, energy snapped from Thunderbolt's hands and blasted the pale form from the air. Fluttering like a discarded newspaper, she fell sprawled to the ground.

Marla stared in disbelief. She was the only other person standing now, the only one for Thunderbolt to turn his attentions towards, and indeed his face was turning this way. She should have run, damn it, she should have run! She could have lived, why was she so stupid and—

Thunderbolt suddenly crumpled forward, hit by some invisible blow from behind. Marla strained through the thinning smoke to see several small projectiles come hurtling his way, each one finding it's mark with a sickening thud. Caught off balance, Thunderbolt's cocoon of lightning flickered, faded . . . just in time to admit a giant metal man-form into his personal space.

"Hope those impact missiles tasted good," the robot, or whatever it was, threw a lumbering punch that sent the hero sprawling, "because here's dessert."

Marla felt her breath leave her. Someone, something, had downed Thunderbolt. How was that possible?

"Noctyrne!" the robot called out in modulated tones. "Naomi!" It lumbered forward, crouched as best it could by the fallen bat-woman's form. She gave a low moan.

Behind him, Thunderbolt had risen, was posturing for an attack.

Without even knowing why, Marla yelled, "Look out!"

The robot turned just in time to see Thunderbolt's charge, and maneuvered in what could only have been some bizarre judo move, taking the momentum from the hero's charge and hurling him across the playing field.

"Thanks," said the robot. "Now get out! I've already led the Tibetan man and Ehat to safety."

Ehat? That must have been the star-eyed man. Marla hadn't exactly had time to stop and get names.

"Who are you people?" she demanded, still, unbelievably, not running. She was beginning to wonder if she even could. "Are you a . . . a Bloodhound Gang?"

"Us? A Bloodhound Gang? No freaking way."

The new voice rose up from the bleachers. Caked in dust, face smeared with blood, a short, stocky man held his hands high, hands that tapered off into sharp claws.

"We're the Friday Knights. Don't any of you posers forget it."

"Combat Wombat," the woman ("Noctyrne," the robot had called her?) said groggily. "Either we're both dead, or we're both alive. You tell me which, ok?"

"You can't be dead, Sweetie," the robot rumbled affectionately. "Affectionately? "You're sort of undead to begin with. You know, the whole vampire thing?"

"Oh," she said. "Yeah. Right." She winced. "Well, I sure hurt enough to wish I could be."

The robot swiveled its head, light rays from its eyes sweeping the playing field. "Heads up," it said. "Thunderbolt's recovered and he's heading back this way."

"Go!" said a voice from behind Marla. It was Neville Shandon. His hands pushed rudely at her shoulders, and she bucked the pressure.

"Listen to the man!" said Combat Wombat. "This is no place for civilians. Go to find someplace safe and stay there. We'll find you after we finish off with blue-boy here, and ask you a couple of questions."

Marla didn't like the sound of that, and a look into Shandon's eyes confirmed he felt the same. Finally, with him tugging at her arms, she let herself trot, then jog, then run, up the aisle, across the walkway, out the north exit door and through the turnstiles into the street.

Behind her, the Friday Knights drew in close, readied themselves for battle. Thunderbolt charged forward, rapidly closing the gap between them . . .

. . . . and then, a hundred yards away, the entire south wall of the stadium exploded.

"No one expects you to save the world. But neither can you ignore the duty to try."

—Silver Peregrine, address to the graduating class of Mesopolopolis University

GEORGE

Few things can get the attention of four Supers about to fight, but a sudden, unexplained massive explosion usually does the trick.

As one, GAP, Combat Wombat, Noctyrne, and Thunderbolt turned to face the devastation. Six forms ran, scampered, and flew forward, like a twisted nightmare version of a sports team taking the field after halftime. No one recognized these new Supers, but then, no one had to. The red bandanas each wore told it all. A Bloodhound Gang.

"Hard as you may find it to believe," said GAP quickly, "we really didn't want to fight you, Thunderbolt. We've always looked up to you guys in the Superior Squad. I mean, really, we've wanted to *be* you. This has all been a terrible misunderstanding . . . how about, ah, a strategic truce, and then straighten things out with these Bloodhound Folk?"

"You cannot `straighten things out' with a Bloodhound Gang, you imbecile! Once the termination mandate has been activated, they will stop at nothing to destroy us. Their commission rises with each kill they score."

"Oh," said GAP. "I was afraid of that."

Thunderbolt looked rapidly left and right, searching the bleachers. "Where is he? Where is Ehat? He's gone! Now we're just going to die in vain!"

"A little fatalistic, dontcha think?" said Combat Wombat. "I mean, sure, it's six to four odds, but ten of us is probably worth one of them . . . wait, dammit, I meant one of us is worth . . . oh, hell . . ."

Noctyrne bit her lip. "I'm scared," she said, pulling closer to GAP. "I don't want to die here. Not for nothing."

"We saved Ehat," said GAP. "That's got to count for something."

"You have no idea who or what he is," said Thunderbolt. "In Superion City's hands, he was going to be our salvation. Now? We're going to die by the very system you've just helped ensure will live on. At least show enough dignity to take a few of them with you."

With that, he soared forward, lighting crackling all around him, yelling the famous Superion City battle cry, "For Justice!"

"Dammit," said GAP. "We needed him here, to formulate some kind of plan."

"Here's the plan," said Craig. "We fight, and don't stop till they're all out cold." With that, he raced ahead.

The Bloodhound Gang seemed content to hang back, to wait for challenges, and were not disappointed by the approach of the two heroes. The two of their members who flew, a male with bright green skin and a jet pack and a female with buzzard wings and skin to match, held back and waited for him to sail between them. Thunderbolt stuck an arm out in each direction, firing lightning blasts at each of his airborne opponents, both of whom dodged with ease.

Too late, he realized they had been a distraction. One of the Bloodhounds on the ground, who looked to all appearances like humanoid frog covered in spines, had positioned himself directly underneath Thunderbolt's flight path. With the hero's attention on the sky, the frogman shot forth a volley of foot-long spines from his skin. They jabbed up through Thunderbolt's skin and bones with a sickening "thuck" sound, and the hero let loose such a bellow that automobile windows shattered for an entire block around.

Combat Wombat's sensitive animal hearing proved his undoing as the scream washed over him in a wave of pain, sending him sprawling to fall head over heels in mid-charge. Most of the Bloodhounds held hands to their ears as well, but one, a woman seemingly composed entirely of animated liquid, sloshed forward and enveloped Combat Wombat in her aqueous form. His face pressed against her waves in a mask of horror, mouth open as she poured herself mercilessly into his lungs.

Thunderbolt fell to the ground like a brick, and the other Bloodhounds, still disoriented from his scream, nevertheless staggered forward, moving in for the kill.

GAP plodded forward on his ungainly legs, cursing the slow speed of his suit. Zeroing his targeting scanners on Combat Wombat's beleaguered form, he hesitated only a moment before activating the blowtorches beneath the suit's right arm. The flames spread over the watery-prison that was Combat Wombat's opponent, boiling her very form to steam. She cried bloodcurdling screams nearly as loud as Thunderbolt's had been, and GAP immediately cut power to the torches.

This was wrong. This wasn't a superhero battle. There was no banter, no clichéd repartee, no lame jokes. There was only pain and screams and soon, maybe death. This wasn't why George had built the GAP suit, wasn't why he and Gayle had formed the Friday Knights . . .

A moment's hesitation was all the Bloodhounds needed. The frogman fired off two particularly sharp and nasty spines GAP's way. Unable to pierce his armor, their impact nevertheless pushed him off balance, and the two airborne Bloodhounds seized the opportunity to swoop down and push him back the rest of the way. GAP fell down with a clatter, limbs flailing, unable to right himself.

The fifth bloodhound, a man whose facial features seemed practically undetectable beneath a bevy of scars, threw his arms forward to reveal "hands" that were little more than sharp blades. GAP didn't even have the luxury of wondering if those blades were responsible for the man's scarred condition before he felt the living knives scraping into his suit, searching for flaws and cracks.

Fear rose as the bladed man found the joints, the armpits, the neck. With every slash, sparks flew, and warning lights on George's internal display flashed alerts about breaches in the suit's integrity.

Another blow landed, severing an oxygen hose. George felt his breath grow short. In a few seconds, he'd have to take off his helmet to breathe, and then—

Noctyrne swooped down from nowhere, landing on the bladed man, clawing at him with her own talons. Raven hair tossed back and forth as her neck swiveled every which way, trying to find a spot to bite. In seconds, the flying Bloodhounds were on her, hauling Noctyrne off their teammate and tossing her into the sky. She twisted, shifted, started to glide, but they buzzed past her again, delivering blows to her lithe form.

They're working as a team, GAP thought with a sinking feeling. *We're not only outnumbered, we're out-coordinated.* Then his oxygen cut out completely, and the only thoughts he could form revolved around removing his helmet . . . damn it all . . .

The second he lifted it off, felt the cold air sting his lungs, the knife man hauled back and swiped his arm in an executioner's blow that would sure claim George's head.

Combat Wombat leapt into the way, taking the blow across his arm. He howled wildly as his impact brought the knife man down, and George suddenly felt the urge to vomit as he saw a small object spin away from them. The object was Craig's right hand, all the way up to the elbow.

The hand left a bloody trail across the grass, one which George barely had time to register before the frogman hurled another spine at him. George pulled up his armored arm just in time to deflect it. High above, the two fliers continued playing ping-pong with Noctyrne. Across from him, Combat Wombat was running on pure animal mode, snarling and biting and tearing at the knife wielder. Behind him, the water woman was beginning to collect herself again, pulling the billows of steam back together into a humanoid form.

Who to help first? Naomi? Craig? Himself?

"You will not win this day unscathed!" came a bellowing cry from behind him, and a bolt of lightning flashed forth to connect with the frog man. The Bloodhound squealed as his skin began to char, then fell shivering to the ground, fading in and out of consciousness.

Thunderbolt, bleeding profusely, raised a shaking hand and pointed it at the reforming water woman. Another blast, and water proved once again what an excellent conductor it was. She screamed as she burst into droplets.

"Behind you!" said GAP, and, raising his armored fist, fired an impact missile from the silo beneath it. The missile streaked towards its target, the Sixth Bloodhound, a thin but solid man dressed in military fatigues . . . who took it head on. The missile hit him in the chest and shattered like ice.

No, George thought sinkingly. *He's invulnerable.*

Thunderbolt turned around and fired a lightning blast. The awesome energy arced out, lanced against the Bloodhound's body. His military fatigues charred and crackled, burning away to reveal his bare skin . . . bare skin that betrayed not the slightest burn or wound. Slowly, silently, wearing a thin smile, the man advanced on Thunderbolt.

Enraged, the hero fired another lightning blast, accompanied by a sonic boom that shook the entire stadium. The energy hit the Bloodhound square in the face. His hair stood up briefly, his eyes closed against the glare . . . but he kept coming, unaffected.

Cursing, Thunderbolt fired yet again, and once again, the man stood firm, and by now he had covered the distance between them. The Bloodhound seized Thunderbolt's sternum with one arm, his head with the other, and, with a satisfied grin, began to twist. Thunderbolt's face contorted, straining against the other man's strength.

GAP, on the ground, wallowed and spun like an upturned turtle. It was useless. He wasn't going to be able to right himself without aid. To his left, the knifeman had gained the advantage on Combat Wombat, and Craig was desperately struggling with his one remaining hand to keep the blades away from his throat. Up in the air, the two flyers had each grabbed hold of Noctyrne's limbs—one the arms, one the legs, and were pulling in opposite directions with all their strength. GAP knew how far Noctyrne's regenerative abilities could be taxed, and they were reaching their limit.

GAP cursed himself for wishing his helmet were still on, so he couldn't hear Naomi's screams. He waved his arms uselessly in the air, trying to aim, but without the targeting scanners in his helmet he was as like to hit his fiancée as her assailants . . . or more likely, hit nothing at all.

Apparently impatient with his standoff, the invulnerable Bloodhound wrestling Thunderbolt dropped his right hand to one of the bloody spikes sticking into the hero's chest. Thunderbolt's face drew grim and tight, knowing full well what was about to happen. The bloodhound seized hold and twisted the spike, jiggled it back and forth, gnawed and tore at Thunderbolt's internal organs. The hero grit his teeth, closed his eyes, exerting every possible effort not to give his opponent the satisfaction of a scream. In the end, he failed.

As Thunderbolt screamed, his muscles went limp, and the Bloodhound seized the moment to return to his neck twisting grip.

"No!"

A new voice. GAP struggled to sense its source, only to find Commander Neville Shandon approaching at a full run. He flung himself at the invulnerable Bloodhound, raining useless blows upon his back. The Bloodhound reached out casually with one arm, as if swatting a tick, and cracked a fist across Shandon's face. GAP hear a sickening "pop" sound, and Shandon's body fell lifelessly to the grass.

Thunderbolt stared at the fallen astronaut, then back up at his opponent. His eyes flared white hot.

"You," he hissed, his mighty voice now barely more than a scraping whisper. "You disgrace us all."

With a savage motion Thunderbolt drove his fingers inside the smiling Bloodhound's mouth. Cocky, sure of victory, the invulnerable man hadn't expected such a move.

He wouldn't be expecting anything else again, ever. Thunderbolt let loose a lightning bolt *inside* the man's body. GAP watched in horror as the Bloodhound's form lit up from within, like a paper lantern, and smelled the sickening odor of cooked meat. Thunderbolt heaved a shrug, and the Bloodhound fell to the ground, dead, his insides burned within the invulnerable shell of his skin.

Thunderbolt collapsed to his knees, bleeding, a satisfied smile on his face. "I . . . told them . . . they would not leave this battle unscathed . . ." His eyes began to glaze in that euphoria before death.

"No!" GAP shouted. "Thunderbolt, stay with us! Help Noctyrne, help Combat Wombat . . . help someone . . ."

The hero swayed like a willow tree, rolling onto his side and breathing ragged, heavy breaths into the grass.

Okay, think, GAP pondered frantically. *You can't get up. You can't use your helmet's systems. What* can *you do?*

GAP reached out, feeling for anything he could use for a weapon . . . and seized upon Craig's severed arm.

This was no time for sentiment, no time for revulsion. George called upon every scientific detachment he could muster, raised the hand, and hurled the projectile, claws first, at Combat Wombat's opponent. The knife man, blades centimeters from Craig's jugular, suddenly gasped as he felt a pain come from behind.

The Bloodhound reached around uselessly to feel at the claws wedged in his back. Had he possessed actual hands, he could have removed it easily, but the knives, without the proper angle, proved useless. He cried out in pain and frustration.

Combat Wombat, seizing the advantage, surged forward with a head butt and knocked his opponent into swift and immediate unconsciousness. He growled, grinned at his handiwork, then looked with vague curiosity at his bleeding right stump. Smiling insanely, he turned to GAP.

"Hey, George . . . thanks for giving me a hand. Ha! Haha! Hahahaha!" His eyes rolled back, and he collapsed back to the ground, where he lay unmoving.

Noctyrne . . . Noctyrne was till in trouble. But GAP was out of tricks. How could he possibly save—

A silver streak dove out of the sky, screeching like a flock of a thousand angry birds. Faster than George's eye could follow, it impacted one of the flying Bloodhounds torturing Noctyrne. The vulture woman was down, and as the jet-pack man struggled to figure out what had just transpired, the silver form rushed him as well, knocking him to a painful landing below.

Noctyrne, sagged weakly into the arms of the newcomer, a platinum-haired woman clad in shining silver armor that included a hawkshead mantle. Two enormous wings billowed out from her back, proud and downy, not worn and mottled like those on her opponent. Two piercing silver eyes shone from her face, betraying an anger that overshadowed her unearthly beauty.

"Bloodhound Gang! You will stand down, in the name of Superion City!"

The Silver Peregrine had arrived. Could the rest of the Superior Squad be far behind? On any other day, GAP would have cried with relief. His favorite member of his favorite team! But here, now, with the dead and dying all around him, all George wanted was to hold Naomi close, to close his eyes and feel her and smell her and pretend the whole rest of the world didn't exist. Maybe, just maybe, if he did that, it would all be better in the morning. What had they accomplished? Where was the dream in all this blood?

"You don't have authorization!" shouted the jetpack man, still woozy from his fall. "We have jurisdiction here!"

"Ask me if I care," Silver Peregrine shouted as she swooped to the ground. The two surviving Bloodhounds eyed her warily but kept their distance. She let Noctyrne off on shaky feet, then strode towards Thunderbolt's fallen form, never quite taking her eyes off anyone else.

"Thomas," she whispered, although not too softly for GAP to hear. "Thomas!" She cradled his form, felt for a pulse, found a weak one. Her eyes began to tear.

"Don't waste your time with me, Sarah," his cough, rattled his whole massive frame. "You've got to find Ehat."

"I . . . I can't. A contingent of Peace Officers is approaching. They'll surely follow me, find him—"

"You must take that risk!"

"No," a deathly frown marred her face's soft features. "I can't let you die for nothing . . ."

"Then call in Cerebellum, and the others," he gurgled. "We'll make our stand here . . ."

Silver Peregrine stared up and around at the field of bodies. "Hasn't there been enough death in this place today?"

With supreme effort, as if he were lifting a forty ton tractor trailer, Thunderbolt raised his shaking hands towards her face. Unable to cover the short distance, they hovered in the air, and Silver Peregrine took them in her own, helped them complete the journey.

"I . . . I think I understand, now, Thomas," she whispered. "Seeing what they've done today, I think I understand what drives you, what drove us all to this insane course of action.

He gave a blood-addled chuckle. "I thought I understood it too, until that . . . human . . . Shandon . . . gave his life for mine. For me! When I would have seen him dead, had he not been of use to us. I do not understand. Help me, Sarah . . . help me to . . . to . . ."

Thunderclaps rose up again, and for a moment GAP thought Thunderbolt was exercising some last vestiges of his power. But then shapes eased into view, mirror images of himself begin to fill the field—Peace Officers, by the dozens, flanked by soldiers and police. A hundred rifles cocked at once, a hundred laser sights crisscrossed over their targets.

"Go, Sarah!" said Thunderbolt. "Quickly, before it's too late . . . warn the others."

His eyes lolled, and Silver Peregrine held him close, tears flowing freely, begging him to wait, not to go. Then the Peace Officers approached, seized her roughly by the arms, hauled her off his dying form.

"No!" she cried. "Give us another minute—"

"This is now a quarantined zone, Ma'am," one of the officers said tonelessly. "Hazmat teams need to assess the danger to the populace. Please step this way."

"No!" she cried again, struggling in the grips of the armored giants. She pulled and strained, tried to get some lift with her wings, but the two-ton battlesuits were beyond her power to drag. She sobbed helplessly as another Officer dragged Thunderbolt's form in the opposite direction. He mumbled curses but was too weak to offer a fight.

Officers lifted GAP up, brought him to his feet, commanded him to exit his suit. George was only too happy to comply. One of them began serving him a warrant for his arrest, citing all the expected charges about operating without authorization. George didn't care. He kept looking to Craig being dragged away in this direction, Naomi in that direction. Her eyes caught his, and he tried to look strong. He hoped she took confidence that his money, his connections, his intellect, would get them out of this. It was a confidence he lacked.

Why? What had this all been for? They never even found out about Ehat, but George suddenly found himself unable to care. The dream had died tonight, died amidst the splatter of blood and the severing of limbs. What had happened to Heroism? Where had it gone?

Then his eyes fell on the fallen form of Neville Shandon. Last of the great astronauts, accused "space murderer." He would never go to trial now. George suddenly felt thankful. Guilty or not, it didn't matter. Neville Shandon, that's where the dream rested.

George began laughing, first small chuckles, then outright hysteria.

"What the hell is so funny, freak?" a Peace Officer postured.

George surprised himself when he didn't feel threatened by the Officer's looming armored form. For one, his father had designed that very armor. For another, he was beyond caring.

"That man," George pointed to Shandon's corpse, even now being loaded into a body bag, "that man, was a hero. A true, bona fide hero. More than me, certainly more than you. He could have gotten away. From the battle, from his jail sentence. But he stayed. He stayed and died . . . for us. That's what heroes do, you know."

The Peace Officer slapped George with the broad side of his armored hand. George's teeth rattled, his glasses shattered. But even on the ground, tasting blood, his laughter persisted.

"To Neville Shandon!" he cried out. "The greatest superhero of them all!"

Someone zipped the body bag shut over Shandon's form, and the living were hauled away.

Certainly, the incident at Freehold was a terrible tragedy. But we must remember that we are at war, and in war, there are casualties among the innocent as well as the guilty. The State will of course launch a full investigation, questioning the commanders of all police and military units involved, but how can we not conclude that the blame for the deaths of the non-violent protestors lies squarely on the shoulders of those among them who used violence to further their aims? They are our common enemy in this continuing war for our security.

—Attorney General Halbert, following the Freehold Massacre

GAYLE

Gayle and Roland rode to the stadium in silence. Roland had given up asking why she wouldn't speak to him, why her skin was pale, why her eyes were watered. When he arrived to pick her up, an energy crackled in his eyes to match Thunderbolt's aura. He moved with fluid, bouncing motions, as if purpose had suddenly reawakened within him. Gayle supposed he was finally experiencing the chance to be a hero, to take part in something larger than himself.

Gayle couldn't bear to look, much less speak. Roland spent the whole drive to Mesopolopolis Stadium, the site of George's last transmission, peering over at her every few moments. Her face was stone.

A Peace Officer roadblock loomed up ahead, and, fearful of them discovering Gayle, Roland pulled over and parked on the side of the street. They exited the car and crept through back alleys, arriving at the Stadium just in time to watch the ambulances, prison trucks, and hearses begin to pull away. Whatever happened, it was over. From the way George's comm-watch wasn't responding, the ending didn't look good.

"Dammit," Gayle whispered from their hiding spot on a loading platform across the street. "What the hell went on? I should have been there."

"That's crazy," said Roland. "You would have been either killed or captured. Most likely the first, since you told me your strength would fade away at midnight, and it's 12:30 right now."

Gayle remained silent.

He put his hand on her shoulder. She shrugged it off violently.

"Gal Friday." He paused. "Gayle. Please, listen to me. I know this looks terrible, but there's hope. I have some contacts, some influence. We can find a way to free your friends, to get them out of this mess."

Still she remained silent.

"This isn't like you," he said. "This isn't like you at all. You don't give up."

"I guess you just don't know me," Gayle said softly. "Just like I don't know you."

"What?" asked Roland. "What's that supposed to mean?"

"I think you know," said Gayle, turning to him with tears in her eyes as the last of the Peace Officer armored personnel carriers rumbled past. "Ask yourself what you were doing eight years ago around this time. The scene must have looked very similar, didn't it?"

"Eight years ago?" asked Roland. "What on Earth do you . . ."

Suddenly, his face froze. His jaw dropped slowly. The energy of newfound heroism fled. He said, simply, "Oh."

Roland stared at the ground, then looked back up at her. "Gayle . . ." his lips trembled.

"Don't call me that," she said, pulling away.

"Gayle, listen to me!" he finally blurted out. "I was a fresh recruit then, barely eighteen. I was young and scared, and following orders—"

"That's the refrain of your type, isn't it!" she cried out to the sky, not caring who heard. "Following orders! I was only scared! Everyone's scared, that's it, right? Everyone's a poor scared kitten only hissing in self defense. Well, I'm sick of it! Sick to death! I'm sick of living this life, sick of this world, sick of what it's become and what it's going to become still!"

"People change," Roland insisted. "You're not being fair to me! Yes, fine, I was a cop at Freehold, during the riots, during . . . what followed. I don't know how you even found out—"

You're not the only one with detective skills, she wanted to sneer, but all she had the strength left for now was honesty. "I just found out barely an hour ago. Right before you picked me up. When were you planning to tell me?"

"You found out an hour ago? Who told you, how did you—"

"That's not important! I didn't want to believe my source, Roland, not even when he showed me documentation. I was hoping you'd deny it, hoping there was some mistake, but now . . . now that you've admitted it . . ."

She choked back tears, tried to keep transmuting them to rage.

"Listen to me," said Roland. "I was just a beat cop, called in for riot duty when the commune population began to turn violent. I didn't shoot anyone, didn't hit anyone . . . I just tried to get people to safety . . . tried, and didn't succeed very well at all."

"But you stood there!" she said. "You stood there as they killed us, just like they killed us today! A whole commune of unarmed people, Super and Normal alike, and the Peace Officers opened fire—"

Roland threw up his fists in fury. "Dammit, woman, will you look at the present for a moment? I'm trying to help you here, now—"

"Why?" she asked. "Why, to atone for your crime? Was that why you were being so kind to me, why you let me think you had feelings for me?"

"I let you think I had feelings for you because I did, and I do!" Roland shouted out.

"I don't even know what to believe anymore," said Gayle, turning her back on him. "Your case is over, Detective. Go on home."

"Like hell. The case may be over, but my responsibility isn't."

"What," she craned her neck back, "suddenly you discover responsibility? Are you telling me you want to be a hero now, too? It's a damned thankless job, Detective. Go find something more rewarding."

Roland seethed, wearing a look of desperate desire to somehow punch or shoot his way out of this. "I've said all I can," he breathed. "I'm not going to apologize for who and what I am. I never asked *you* to do that."

"How kind."

"You're being completely unfair. Were you waiting all along for some excuse to kick me aside? Was that it?"

"I have to go," said Gayle, her eyes welling with tears she thought she had cried herself dry of. She began walking away.

"Wait. Wait, Gayle, where are you going?"

"To do what I can to prevent Armageddon," she said simply. "Please don't follow me. I don't want to have to hurt you."

She heard him sigh softly behind her, and turned.

Though he said nothing, the shake of his chiseled features, the shudder in those damnable deep brown eyes, spoke, "you already did."

Breaking eye contact one final time, Gayle turned and forced her legs to walk, her arms to pump, even as a terrible gnawing part of her pulled with Ehat-like strength to turn back around, to go back to him, to beg his forgiveness. But she kept on forcing one foot in front of the other, walking down the alleyway, trying not to think about Roland and George and Naomi and Craig and all that she now knew. Her super strength was gone, her friends were gone, and she supposed now that she never really had Roland to begin with. All that remained was her case, her mission. Damn it all, she was going to see that through.

Roland might have said something more, but as Gayle walked he receded into the night, like the remnants of any finished dream, no matter how intense.

Creeping amidst the sidestreets, clinging to the shadows in the way that only urchins and former urchins of Herotown knew how, Gayle drew closer to the caravan of police and military vehicles, only as fast as the slowest of the troop transports. At every intersection, police and soldiers stood diverting late-night traffic (Gayle looked at the uniforms and forced herself *not* to think of Roland). Warning cones cordoned off the cycle lanes. Those few pedestrians walking the streets at this hour either huddled in small groups to rubberneck, or, more commonly, kept their eyes firmly on the ground and hurried to their destinations that much more quickly.

My fault, my fault . . .

Gayle had convinced the team to go save Ehat. They had all wanted to go home, to return to the half-lives they all led, even George . . . that should have served as a sign. After all these years, she still didn't "get it," and thanks to her ignorance, her friends were doomed. Roland should thank the Spirit Above that she drove him away. He should have trusted his fears. Gayle was dangerous. Sooner or later, people who spent time around her suffered and died.

The convoy rolled along like the spread of night, boasting enough firepower to make any rescue attempt an exercise in suicide, even with the super-strength that Gayle now lacked until a whole new week passed. She tried the Friday Knights' signal yet again, with no success. Fearing she might give away her position if anyone inside one of those vehicles detected the transmission and decided to trace it, Gayle gave up trying.

What to do?

Only one thing remained that she *could* do. Find Ehat and deliver him to her mysterious source, in exchange for that information he gave her. Spirit Above, that information! That information that robbed her of her last chance for happiness. Was that yet another risk of being a superhero detective—finding out information you never wanted to know?

She shouldn't owe that damnable faceless man in the black car anything. But he and Ehat were her only links to this case, to her friends, and to have them all in one place might at least give her an idea of what to do next. But how to find Ehat, if even the Peace Officers hadn't yet? And they hadn't, too . . . Gayle had doubled back to the Stallion earlier, hoping at least some of her teammates had made it back. She didn't find them, but did check the police scanner and heard the active APBs on Ehat. Had he somehow found a way to mask his energy signature?

Gayle would recognize him anywhere, even if he had. Parts of her head *still* ached from where he had tried to connect with her, on top of the fifty other headaches vying for dominance in her skull right now. If she concentrated, she could even shove the other hurts to the side and focus on just the ones Ehat had caused . . . .

Contact.

215

She felt him. There was no other way to explain it. She felt him as if he were a sixth finger of hers, a third leg. Wordlessly, she walked across the streets of the Federal District, around corners, boldly defying the denizens of the night as she approached the side of some sort of storefront. Flags sporting a crimson phoenix, symbol of the State, papered the bricks in a wild fashion, some adorned with graffiti bespeaking imprecations against Osiric. Years ago, the papers had referred to the Bulravian leader as Prime Minister Osiric, but now of course, he was merely Osiric, or perhaps "Damned Osiric," or worse. Ehat had picked here, of all places, to hide?

A maintenance door, locked, provided the only apparent entry, unless she felt like battling the iron mesh gate over the shop window. Two minutes with a lockpick from her utility belt and the maintenance door swung wide.

State flags hung everywhere, all shapes and sizes. Phoenixes on tee shirts, on caps, in cartoon posters for young children. Gayle dimly remembered her father telling her on his knee about the pride, strength, and passion of that bird, how even in the throes of agonized defeat, it would rise resurrected from its ashes, stronger and prouder than ever.

Cowering in a dark corner beneath majestic phoenix images sat Ehat, crumpled, crooked, staring out through the window mesh into the featureless night of the street. Bulravian, alien, in all possible ways, shaking beneath the symbols of the land that opposed his own. Were the tides of that force which men called nationalism tangible enough to be felt even when the specifics were incomprehensible? As if woken from a particularly captivating dream, he slowly, groggily turned to register Gayle's entrance.

"Ehat," she began. "Or whatever's inside you. I know what happened to you. At least, I know what someone *told* me happened to you. I hope you can confirm or deny it for me."

Careful to avoid eye contact, Gayle saw Ehat stared at her with something approaching recognition.

"Someone, a stranger, took me into his automobile. He told me that Superion City made contact with your race on Europa years ago, and told no one. I was told the Supers there, some of them, had been trying to convince your race to help them wage war against the Normals on Earth ever since."

"You are very alien to it . . . us . . . me," Ehat struggled to find the words. "Even now, as it . . . I . . . we . . . achieve closer connection, it . . . does not understand your ways. It . . . we . . . do not understand how you can so freely sever the connections between your parts."

Gayle forced the tears back with whatever shadows of superstrength remained. "Those connections aren't as strong as you think."

Ehat didn't seem to notice. "My . . . its . . . race only to maintain its own interconnection. The part of you that is Superion City asked us to destroy the part of you that is Earth."

"You refused."

"Yes."

"My source says the Supers on the moon wouldn't take no for an answer. When their telepaths failed to influence your alien minds, they instead influenced the United Space Agency to arrange the *Santa Maria*'s landing site to be right on top of your colony on Europa. They scheduled the drill, *engineered* an incident, in the *hopes* you'd wage war on Earth in retaliation. But you didn't."

"We made a mistake," said Ehat, making a half-sniff, half-humming sound that she soon theorized to be his best attempt at crying. "It . . . we . . . accidentally . . . severed . . . the connection to two parts of you."

"Two parts . . . you mean Michelis and Al-Awadi?"

"Sorrow consumed us. We sent part of ourselves, me, to travel back to your planet, to connect with you there and render our apologies, to tender our forgiveness . . . but this one, the one I connected with . . . the connection . . . took so long to make . . ."

"Some connections aren't meant to be," Gayle said heavily. "Sometimes two people, two life forms, are just too different. They carry two different sets of experiences."

"Not . . . too different," said Ehat. "One day . . . our two races . . . will realize our connection in harmony . . . we two, your race and ours, are all connected parts of a still greater whole."

Shouts from beyond. Sounds of engines suddenly rose. Were the Peace Officers looking for them? Gayle tensed.

"Nice idea," said Gayle, "but I think it depends on whether Supers and Normals from my race kill each other first. Do you know about Superion City's backup plan? Their failsafe?"

Ehat nodded, with the tentativeness of an infant trying out an experimental new movement. He spoke no words.

"I was told they're going to send a ship to Europa," Gayle prodded, "under the guise of investigating the Shandon case. They may have already sent it, for all I know. The ship carries an immense transmission antenna, the big brother of the kind that Lieutenant Michelis used, in which your alien part piggybacked a ride to Bulravia. Did Thunderbolt tell you any of that?"

"It was present in him . . . in his unspoken part . . . his thoughts." If Ehat, or whatever was inside him, was surprised or upset by those thoughts he had detected, he didn't show it.

"They're going to use it to make that happen again. To take creatures like your alien half, and forcibly transmit them into the minds of millions, maybe even billions of humans here on Earth. Imagine the chaos and death that would occur if every man, woman, and child on Earth suddenly became a host to one of your race! Civilization would fall apart within days. And I imagine whatever passes for civilization on your world would be in shambles too."

"Forced bad connections on all . . . could end us all," said Ehat. "But we cannot prevent it."

"Our people could," said Gayle. "I mean, people on Earth. If they wanted to. Thunderbolt must have been racing against the clock. If you recovered enough of your memory to tell someone of his plan, you could tip off the authorities here, thwart it—"

"No," said Ehat. "The part of you that is . . . Thunderbolt, Silver Peregrine, Cerebellum . . . didn't want to . . . force bad connections on all. They told me that. They wanted to use me as their . . . connection . . . to my people."

"You mean, like an ambassador?"

"Yes."

"If they could use me to convince my race to attack . . . to attack only certain places, certain times . . . they wouldn't have to resort to force bad connections all."

218

"Oh, wonderful," said Gayle. "So they just wanted a war instead of a double genocide, and that makes them heroes?"

Ehat didn't answer.

Gayle shook her head. "Something must have pushed them over the edge. They moved to the moon eight years ago in protest of events here on Earth. Their policy was to secede rather than make war. Why the change? And I can't believe Captain Omega would be in favor of this sort of thing. This has to be a rogue faction. If he found out, he would try and stop it. Right?"

Why would he, though? The simple answer, of course, was that he was Captain Omega. He would use any means he could to defend the weak, the downtrodden, those in need of protection. But who now fit the bill of those in need of defending? What if he had decided the real victims were the Supers of Superion City, and the real villains were the people of Earth, each and every last one of them?

Sirens wailed in the distance. Dammit! They had to move. But the ache screamed in Gayle's bones. But . . . but . . .

"But I'm tired!" she cried out. "I'm tired and hurt! Leave me alone! I don't want to go save the world now! Spirit Above, can you hear me? You've taken everything from me . . . my parents, my friends, Roland . . . enough! I give up!"

Gayle ran to one of the beams that held up the ceiling, pulled and tugged till her muscles screamed. It was no good. She had no more strength, she couldn't bring the store crashing down like she wanted to, to end it all. With a scream of rage, she punched the metal beam, then kicked it. Whimpering in pain, she collapsed to the ground.

Somewhere through the haze of hurt, she felt warm skin press against her forehead.

"I became a part of you," said Ehat. "I connected with you. With Neville Shandon. With Craig, with Marla, with others. You know about connection, moreso than many other parts."

"What on Earth are you babbling about?" Gayle spat back, feeling mucous run across her mouth.

"What you call heroism. What you call self-sacrifice . . . willingly exchanging some parts to preserve the endangered connections of others. We had no concept of this until we encountered you."

"I'm sorry," Gayle growled. "You're probably better off without that."
"You do not believe that," said Ehat.

Gayle tried to think of the big picture, the heroic picture. She struggled to put faces on those billions now in danger. George, Naomi, Craig—captured, perhaps even dead. Detective Roland—who she deluded herself into thinking she knew, when stars above, she didn't even know his first name. Her friends from the University—scattered to the corners of the State, never having visited her in Herotown. Mr. Elmore back in Herotown, and Cima, faces she saw and voices she heard. Waley, an echo in her heart, somewhere in the world where she'd never again see him.

"I want to believe it," Gayle cried tearlessly. "But I'm only one woman. I'm only half a Super. I . . . I've reached my limit. I've reached the end."

"No," said Ehat. "You have only begun."

The galaxies swam in his eyes as he drew closer. Gayle reluctantly but willingly met his gaze head on. His face drew close, the maw in his eyes sucking her very soul out, and she felt herself move into his arms, felt their lips touch . . .

"You are not alone," said a voice, either Gayle's or Ehat's or someone else's entirely.

For a moment, either a millisecond or a millennia, Gayle couldn't tell which, she felt *connected*. She could not tell where her flesh and mind began and ended, and where six billion other souls, maybe six times six billion, began. Years ago, joining in love with Waley had perhaps, perhaps, approximated this sensation, but the womb was probably far closer. Even to call it a "sensation" . . . that was the kind of injustice of calling the simultaneous explosion of every single capillary in her body a "sensation."

In the minutes afterwards, after the coughing and gasping, the vomiting and cold sweats of withdrawal, Gayle would try and recall specific thoughts, images, emotions, that clearly belonged to other people, other creatures, other senses for which she had no name. Like a memories from infancy, though, it had all fled, fled behind the worst kind of barriers—those that indicated that the memories had never been transcribed at all. All she remembered, all that she would remember for the rest of her days, was that, for the duration of that experience, she knew, *knew* with the certainty she had always envied in the religious and the artists and the couples in the throes of love like George and Naomi, that she was not alone. That she was a part of something greater.

And all of it, all of it would vanish, vanish amidst screams and chaos, if the rogue Supers from Superion City succeeded in their plan.

"You need to come with me," Gayle finally managed to say, after several failed attempts to restart her suddenly raspy vocal chords.

Ehat said nothing. Well, that wasn't a protest.

She took his hand gingerly, half afraid, half desperately wishing, that the connection would re-establish itself. It didn't. Flesh merely touched flesh, and all kept behind its respective barriers, as she led him out the door.

Keeping him silent was not the difficult part. Difficult was weaving in and out of alleys, staying in the shadow of skyscrapers, eschewing the pedestrian lanes and ducking behind mailboxes or potted trees whenever they heard sirens. Ehat asked no questions. He followed her every move with perfect obedience, never saying a word. The few people who passed paid them no heed, but the late hour meant hiding in crowds would be impossible, and once they were almost discovered when a patrol car passed perilously close and slowed down to match their gait. Gayle began to panic, wondering if they should break into a run, terrified of the sure pursuit that would follow if they did. But the car sped up again and vanished behind a corner.

Still, Gayle didn't allow herself the luxury of releasing her breath until she arrived at the rendezvous point, saw the fancy black car bearing the silver triangle emblem parked expectantly at the corner of the next street.

Gayle stopped, turned to Ehat.

"Listen. I made a promise to the man who gave me this information. In exchange, I would deliver him to you, so he could keep you safe."

Ehat stared impassively. Gayle didn't dare make eye contact again, but through the periphery of her vision she could swear she saw something in his gaze . . . something like . . . trust.

He trusted her. And why not? He needed to be protected. A Bulravian, a Super, an alien, in every way out of his element, lonelier and more vulnerable than even Gayle had ever been. He had been hunted by police, by Superheroes from the Friday Knights all the way up through the Superior Squad. Gayle suddenly realized that, in a sea of enemies, she was his only protection. She was his Hero.

She could not, would not abuse that responsibility. She had no idea who was in that car, what his motivations were, whether he was even a "he" to begin with. Taking chances hadn't paid off very well for her in the last two days.

"Come on," she turned to Ehat. "There's been a change in plans." She tugged at his arm. "Quickly."

Again without question, he came along, matching her speedier gait with his own. Behind her, Gayle heard an auto engine roar to life.

"Keep running," she said. "Even if I fall behind."

Gayle could *feel* the car approaching, gaining on their heels . . . a rough *thuk* sound demanded her attention, and she turned back to look as she ran. The car had jumped the curb, was running along the pedestrian walk. Its lights flashed to life, bathing the two fugitives in an incriminating haze.

He's not going to run us over, Gayle hurriedly reminded herself as she ran. *He can't. He needs Ehat. Unless, of course, he only wanted Ehat so he could kill him. But I doubt that.*

Then Gayle's heart skipped a notch. *Of course, I have no reason whatsoever to think, now that he's found Ehat, that he needs me alive anymore.*

Gayle found the strength to run faster.

The curves of the pedestrian walk, thankfully, limited the car's speed, but in seconds it would be on them.

Fine.

Gayle jumped, spun in the air, and landed in crouching tiger position on the hood of the auto as it sailed up to meet her. Her feet bounced and lost purchase on the smooth hood as it warbled beneath her, and she floundered for a moment, fighting to direct her fall forward so she could splay herself against the windshield. It worked. She both felt the car slow and break suddenly, unsure of just when that next curve in the walkway was coming.

If only I still had my super strength, I could just punch through the windshield . . . hell, I could just pick up and toss the car . . .

No. Gayle had learned long ago not to lament if-onlies where her powers were concerned. She didn't spend all those years training her mind and body just to dwell on sour grapes.

For the moment, she had the advantage. The driver was confused, paralyzed. Now was the time to act. Reaching into her utility belt, Gayle pulled out a small, screwdriver shaped device and, depressing a lever on the base, drove it like a stake into the windshield glass with all her strength. A satisfying *crack* told her the miniature sonic vibration generators in the device were working just fine. She hauled back and struck the windshield again. A spiderweb of cracks blossomed out from the point of impact. Another one or two blows, and she'd break right through.

That was when every goosepimple on her body suddenly exploded. Or at least, Gayle felt that way. Sight and hearing and thought blurred out in a cotton haze of pain, followed by intense vertigo and the distant notion that she was falling, although which way and onto what didn't seem to matter. A dull pain cracked across her shoulders, and if she hadn't vomited a half hour ago in the storefront with Ehat, she would have now.

By the time breath returned to her lungs, Gayle saw the auto's taillights receding around the next corner. She didn't have time to try and ponder what had happened, and only as she picked herself up into a shaky, halting run in pursuit did her mind coalesce enough to form theories.

Electrified hood. Cute. My mysterious source seems prepared for everything.

Except no one could be prepared for everything. It was time for another surprise. Gayle reached to her belt, pulled out a boomerang, and tapped a button on the bottom. Razor sharp blades flung outward from every surface but the one she held on to.

A sure bet I'm not going to catch this one on the return trip, Gayle thought as, rounding the corner, she saw the black auto driving Ehat up against the road divider like some cattle rustler.

Good. That forced the car to slow down. Gayle drew close, then hurled the boomerang with all her might. The blades greedily sunk into the left rear tire, and Gayle was rewarded with a satisfying hiss of air. Gayle pulled a second boomerang from her belt and scored a similar hint on the tire's twin.

If only I had more boomerangs . . .

The driver didn't seem to take notice, too focused on his (or her?) successful pinning of Ehat to the cement barrier. Gayle glanced around, tried to find onlookers, but the earlier departure of the convoy had cleared the streets. For all she knew, a curfew was now in effect. But just because she didn't *see* any eyes didn't mean eyes weren't watching this scene right now. Someone might be notifying the police, or the Peace Officers, or worse.

"Ehat!" she cried out. Jump on the hood, climb over the car! I've slashed the rear tires, so it can't follow you!"

Judging from his mute expression, Ehat either didn't hear or simply didn't want to comply. The car's rear doors opened as one.

As curious as Gayle was as to who or what might emerge, she had already prepared a preemptive strike. By the time the first leg stuck out, before the first foot even touched pavement, a gas canister from Gayle's belt was already sailing through the air, much like the one George had launched hours earlier to create cover at the Stadium. Inky clouds mushroomed from below, swallowing the car in their intangible maw.

Okay, Gayle, she thought as she rushed the curtain of artificial night, *remember the dimensions of the car . . . three, two, one,* jump!

Gayle lifted off the ground, reached out her hands, pulled back her knees, only to feel metal slam into her shins the second before she belly-flopped painfully against the rear windshield.

Dammit! Misjudged! Pain cried banshee wails from her lower legs. She dug her fingers into her palms, bit her knuckle until she drew blood, but it was no good. She had simply pushed her endurance too hard tonight, demanded too much of her body, to be able to shrug this off.

Whimpering, she felt herself slide off, body smearing against the metal in a desperate attempt to cling before landing rudely, ass first, onto the concrete below.

Where was that figure who was exiting the car? Am I on the same side as it was? Did it ever fully emerge, did it pull back in?

Gayle tried to back herself up, feeling for the divider, but every thrust of her legs turned into a spasmic flail. She let loose a low moan as her head began to swim.

No. I can't black out. I can't!

With whatever sense humans possessed that transcended sight and sound, Gayle became aware of a tall, lanky figure standing above her. If she couldn't see it, could it see her? Was it the ink cloud still hanging in the air at all, or had pain just blurred Gayle's vision away?

She felt helpless, exposed, vulnerable . . . she tried to raise herself on her arms, reach down to her utility belt, but her brain wasn't making the connections. She couldn't think of what to do next.

The figure loomed closer. Gayle's second to last thought was guilt for sending Roland away. Who would protect him when she was gone?

It made no sense. If she had wanted a rescue, she would have wished for George or Craig or Naomi. If she was feeling guilty about leaving someone defenseless, it should have been Ehat. But for no readily explicable reason, she suddenly feared not only for her own life, but for the Detective's safety.

Then the figure swooped downward, and Gayle knew that all of it, the pain and worry and heartache, was finally going to end. She would have been thankful if she didn't feel so damned guilty.

A hand that reached out and grabbed her own, pulled upwards.

Wants me to die on my feet, does it?

Gayle struggled to rise, but her injured legs kept giving way beneath her.

"I . . . I can't," she tried to say, but the gas from the canister filled her lungs, and she coughed violently. Strong arms reached underneath her, supported her ascent, practically carried her out of the cloud and onto the walkway beyond.

Blinking with irritated eyes, Gayle focused on the warbling image before her. A field of stars stared back, and, with a newly developed instinct, she quickly turned away before contact.

Ehat.

Silent as ever, he had saved her, was now supporting her on one shoulder as she hobbled away from the auto.

"Th . . . thank you," she exhaled more than spoke the words. "I was sure that you'd . . . that I'd . . ."

Engine sounds. The automobile was backing up, flattened rear tires thumping and clattering as it did so.

"I know this street," said Gayle. "One more block and we can reach a monorail stop."

One more block. It might as well have been four hundred million miles, the distance from Earth to Europa. Gayle's legs felt next to useless. Her body had given up, and her mind was shortly behind it. Ehat couldn't very well carry her for an entire block, certainly not while eluding their pursuer.

"I'm sorry," said Gayle. "I tried. I really did."

Ehat might have replied, but whatever he had to say was lost in the sudden din of an explosion a hundred meters above them.

All of a sudden, sound returned to Gayle's world with a vengeance. Shattered glass, helicopter blades, police sirens. Shouts and cries of heretofore unseen bystanders.

A silver shape was streaking across the sky, a silver shape tinged with blue. Several helicopters sped in pursuit, weaving in and out of the surrounding skyscrapers.

Gayle squinted. Was that the Silver Peregrine? The shape was already fading from sight, but the blue in her arms . . . could it be Thunderbolt? There was another shape in her arms as well, another figure, with fingers-touching his temples . . .

Then they were past, and Police helicopters raced on in their wake, spraying the air between them with high velocity shellfire.

The police . . . firing on members of the Superior Squad? What was happening? Had the war Gayle's pursuer had warned her about begun in earnest already?

The movement of a smaller gray shape caught Gayle's attention, almost fatally so, as she had lost track of the black automobile and suddenly its bumper was right behind them, nudging the back of Ehat's legs and causing the two of them to lose their balance. Ehat and Gayle tumbled to the pavement, and the auto stopped just short of running them over. The driver's side door opened.

Gayle twisted and craned up just in time to see the gray shape, suddenly much larger, rush into her field of vision and collide with the roof of the auto.

Her reflexes drove her face into her armpit barely in time to avoid a shower of metal, glass, and stone that erupted from the din of impact. Later, when she had time to think it over, Gayle would realize that stray shots from the helicopters' gunfire must have knocked loose a gargoyle or statue from one of the high skyscrapers.

For now, pure instinct governed the crawling motions of her arms as she dragged herself forward, stomach and breasts scraping painfully against the glass-strewn pavement, palms torn open and bleeding, away from the scene of the disaster. She didn't know if the driver or other occupants had gotten out in time. She didn't care. Nothing other than survival lived in her. Somehow, at some later point when conscious thought returned, she found herself, again supported by Ehat, walking through the monorail turnstile and onto a train car. The hiss of the train felt like the last escaping breaths of her life finally leaving her body.

He sat there, as impassive as ever, staring out the monorail window into the impenetrable night. She had commanded him to keep his eyes closed, so as not to reveal his true nature, but even with his shut he still stared, as if neither eyelids nor the reflections in the glass were obstacles. Gayle lay cradled in his arms, face pressed against his chest, glancing up at every stop in fear of the reactions of new occupants. But this was Mesopolopolis. It took more than a battered, bleeding, dust-covered woman in the arms of a slightly schizoid foreign looking man to attract the attention of this city's inhabitants, especially the ones who rode the rails at this late hour. Winos, party boys, the lonely, the disaffected, the street poets—they all had more important things to focus on as the train carried them to, fro, towards and away.

To where would Gayle and Ehat travel? The city's police had bigger worries than the two of them, if the Silver Peregrine and Thunderbolt were suddenly their quarry. But the Bloodhound Gang was commissioned to find Ehat, and the fact that most had died in the attempt just meant new Gangs were being assembled right now, no doubt composed of even nastier brutes. So long as they stayed in Mesopolopolis, they were marked.

Gayle's source, the mysterious man in the car, might have been her only hope. Why hadn't she at least met with him again, heard him out further? Why had she rabbited, with Ehat in tow? Now they had no one to turn to, nowhere to go, especially not once daylight broke, once Ehat started walking around with galaxies in his eyes.

No. There was one place where Ehat would barely attract any attention at all. There was one place where Gayle might find the resources to help her formulate a plan of action. There was one place where the police would have an awkward time at best conducting a search.

Gayle closed her eyes and began counting the stops until they reached the walls of Herotown.

Since the beginning of the First Heroic Age, there have been Supers who have placed their own personal desires above their responsibilities to the communities in which they operate. While this is not in and of itself evidence of "Super- villainy," it is widely regarded as the first step. From there on in, the rest is a matter of details and degrees.

—Preface to Scoper's *Supercriminology*

2

"You need into Herotown? Past the wall and the guards?"

"Yes."

"With the police and Peace Officers in pursuit?"

"Yes."

"Ah. But of course. That's why you came to me, isn't it. Me. A so-called Supervillain."

At first glance, the Rat didn't look like his namesake. The blond haired man in whose garage they had taken refuge stood tall, broad, almost regally, attired in a fine business suit. But something in his small eyes bespoke a beady and rodential intensity, something in the slight tic that tugged at his smile that twitched like a mouse's nose.

Craig had been right, bless him . . . wombats were not rodents. Rodents were far more frightening. Gayle had only heard rumors of this man back in Herotown. She was both grateful and resentful at finding them to be true.

"I don't recognize you, Madame. But you and your companion have become quite famous lately. Tell me again why I shouldn't just take the ample sums of cash you're offering me and turn you over to the authorities for even more reward?"

Gayle shrugged listlessly. "Because we take care of our own?"

"We? We? Who's `we,' dear? Supers? Ha. Tell me, if that's true, then why are your kind out hunting my kind, beating them senseless and throwing them in jail, like good little lapdogs, hoping if you uphold the Normals' laws then they'll give you a biscuit and a favored place by the fire? That seems to work for the Superior Squad."

Maybe not for much longer, thought Gayle.

"In the old days, when President Stevenson was running things," the Rat's nose seemed to twitch as he spoke, "when did any of you `heroes' protest the Annihilus Bay colony, the `home for the disaffected?' Only now, when President Lee comes along and puts you `heroes' behind bars too, do you start talking about `our own.' Please, spare me."

"Look," Gayle sighed, if you're not going to help us, we'll just leave."

"And find your own way back into the most heavily fortified area of the city, with its security now doubled thanks to the current crisis?" The Rat laughed. "You're welcome to try. But then, lacking the amazing tunneling powers of the Rat, I doubt you'll get far."

He drew closer, sniffed at Gayle's exposed neck. She didn't flinch.

"Oh, I do hear the Stoneman Facility for Metahuman Incarceration is lovely this time of year. Give my regards to the giant mutant spiders."

Gayle took a deep breath. She was in this far. "I can give you something the police can't."

"Oh?" the Rat twisted unnaturally at the waist, craning up to look in her eyes. She refused to meet his gaze. She could smell his breath, mint barely covering the stench of rotting leaves, wafting up to meet her. "Yes, I think we could arrange some, fair, amenable trade . . ."

His hand began to wander up her arm, to her shoulder, then down—

She caught it, gave it a twist, then swooped in with her other arm as she spun him and caught him around the neck. He coughed, hissing in shrill rodential tones.

"Stop! Stop! If you kill me, I can't help you—"

"You'll help me, all right. And I'll even help you. I have . . ." Her grip on him waned as her confidence did, and he slipped out from her grasp, scampering to a safe distance to hear the rest of her offer.

This is for a greater good, she kept telling herself, knowing all good villains swore by that line.

"I have the designs," she began again, "for the Peace Officer suits, weapons, and equipment. My benefactor created them. He has the specs and plans. With this information, you should be able to circumvent many of their defenses. At least until they catch on."

The Rat sniffed at the air, as if the scent of the molecules, disturbed by her voice, held the quintessence of truth or lie.

"That sounds decidedly . . . unheroic."

"I'm hardly the Silver Peregrine, now, am I? Besides, desperate times call for desperate measures."

"And how can I trust the accuracy of this information?"

"How can I trust you'll lead me back to Herotown, and not into an ambush?"

"Aha," the Rat smiled. "*Now* you're thinking like a Supervillain, my dear. Honor among thieves is so much Splen. Real alliances stem from mutual distrust. A balance of knives held at the back, so to speak."

"Whatever," said Gayle. Even moving her lips to speak seemed to take impossible effort.

Ehat stood by her side, impassive, oblivious to events. The Rat had made the mistake of pressing him to speak, and had spent ten minutes unconscious from his gaze as a result. He wasn't eager to repeat that performance any time soon.

And so the Rat opened up a drainage duct and led his two guests through a maddening series of burrows underneath Downtown, some smooth and polished, some dank and reeking of sewage, some ridden with stalactites and stalagmites far older than the city above it, than the ten cities that proceeded it.

"Let them all fight over the world on top," the Rat chortled. "When the dust settles, *we* will emerge and inherit the world."

Gayle wasn't sure she wanted to know precisely who "we" referred to. Supervillains? Or something even more sinister? At one point the three of them descended so far that Gayle could catch the primordial smells of the Earth itself wafting up at her, and she heard the scratching of other footsteps, or paw steps, or even slitherings. Once or twice Gayle could swear she heard the clank and thrum of machinery, and wondered who constructed these passageways, what worlds they led to. Inquiries to the Rat as to the nature of these only produced the response, "the answers would upset your delicate female mind."

Gayle's lame foot slowed their progress, much to the complaints of the Rat, who threatened on numerous occasions to leave the two of them behind. But he wanted his cheese as much as Gayle wanted her freedom, or at least, her return to a safer captivity, so they pressed onward. Just as she began to doubt the Rat's ability after all, he led them to a series of ladders that terminated in a manhole cover at the corner of Guardian and Marvel.

Herotown.

"They lock us away," Gayle shook her head as she surveyed the familiar streets. "They lock us away without realizing the cage has holes all through the bottom."

"Any good Rat knows his cage," said her guide, "and the passages from one cage to the next, and that's really all there is. One cage or another. You eventually find the spot with the best food, and stay. Which reminds me . . ."

"Your payment," said Gayle.

Was she really going to do this? Was she going to sell out the authorities? Well, what did she owe them, anyway? Especially now? So what if someone could get hurt or killed because of this information, so what if civilians or police died . . . police . . . even Roland . . .

"I'm afraid your payment's going to have to be modified a bit. I'll give you the money," she tossed him the cubit chit George had given her for emergencies, "but the designs are off the table."

"Whaat?" the Rat hissed. "Oh no, you don't. We had a deal, you little witch, and you're going to keep it . . . or else I'm just going to keep *you!*"

With that, he sank his fingers into her injured leg, fingers that had suddenly sprouted rodent talons. Gayle cried out in pain as she felt him drag her back, back towards the manhole cover, into the depths of darkness where no one would ever find her. She was being dragged away, and had no strength left to fight.

Her legs had already submerged beneath the ground when another force tugged at her arm. Ehat. He was straining silently, keeping her from the blackness, but the Rat had gravity on his side and Gayle felt the upper half of her body losing the tug of war.

She gazed up, saw the streets of the city that had been her hell and her home, pull away for the final time . . .

. . . and then she saw them.

One by one, poking heads out of windows and doors. Leaping off roofs, picking up shovels and broom handles, brandishing kitchen knives and old hunting rifles, hands sparking with fireballs and ice staves and bony claws. From every shop, every storefront, every crumbling tenement flat, they came, hearing the cry for help.

Heroes. An entire neighborhood of heroes. They were coming to the aid of the threatened, the imperiled.

The Rat saw them, heard them, smelled them, pulled with renewed desperation, but Ehat refused to let Gayle go entirely under, and by the time his grip began to slack, the others had arrived. Dozens of pairs of arms gripped Gayle, tore her from the villain's arms, hurled rocks and energy bolts and every curse word they could muster down the manhole at their foe. Their shouts of triumph drowned out the Rat's vows of vengeance, and then his squeals of pain and protest.

Ehat and a score of others helped Gayle to a shaky stand, stood with her, supported her. Gayle leaned on them, gasping for breath, dizzy from the fight and the enormous weight of the task ahead of her . . . but once again, bless and curse her soul, believing that completing her task was possible.

When we are young, we see the world through hero-colored glasses. Heroes are everywhere—in our families, in our books, in the news. Then as we grow older we change our hero-glasses for detective glasses, notice the clay beneath our heroes' feet, and one by one they fall, and we both cry and cheer. But when we finally don on the dark glasses of aged blindness, then, and only then, do we see the true heroes most clearly.

—Ella Ducharme, former State Poet Laureate

EPILOGUE

"Amazing," Marla shook her head slowly, as if even the effort to exert disbelief drained her. "They're being billed as heroes. Heroes."

"Those . . . Friday Knights . . . *did* try and rescue us."

"Did they?" she cocked her head slightly as Tenzin pulled at one of the wavy half-curls of her hair.

"That is what they kept claiming, Marla. And their actions seemed to support those claims. They fought Thunderbolt so the four of us could go free. Then they paid for it with their freedom, maybe even their lives."

Marla shifted, eyes scanning the morning edition spread out on the bed before her. "According to this, the so-called Friday Knights are being `held for medical treatment at an undisclosed location.' Peace Officers refused to comment on plans to prosecute the team for alleged operation without permit."

Tenzin nodded slowly, reading over her bare shoulder. The front page *Times* article painted the sketchy details of last night's battle. Some eager newshounds had snapped photos of the Friday Knights and performed some research. Suddenly, the particulars of the heretofore un-newsworthy "George Porgie" case leapt to the front page. The Friday Knights had been pursuing a sex-offender, who turned out to be a deadly criminal who, according to the police statement, freed accused space murderer Neville Shandon from jail. Then things grew hazy. Members of the Superior Squad and a Bloodhound Gang were somehow involved in the Knights' efforts to bring Georgie Porgie down. Casualties had mounted, and unconfirmed rumors indicated that Neville Shandon was among them. Similar rumors suggested "Porgie" himself was still on the loose. Let the frenzy begin.

Tenzin frowned. "Even Holloway would have trouble prosecuting these Friday Knights." he said. "Turning the populace against those who tried to save them from a menace still-at-large . . ."

"Grow up, Tenzin," said Marla. "The Lee Act allows for military tribunals in lieu of jury trials for Supers in violation of operational procedures. As much as liberals love `noble example' stories, within a week of Ehat's capture, everyone will forget."

"How can they forget what they didn't even know to begin with?" Tenzin considered how many details the story lacked. The fact that *Thunderbolt* broke into jail to kidnap Shandon, all to try and coerce this in fact seemingly harmless "Georgie Porgie," or Ehat, to do something for him. The fact that "accused space murderer" Shandon could have run away free, yet died to try and stop the Bloodhound Gang who, far from working with the Friday Knights, were apparently trying to kill them. And what about that commotion towards the end of the evening, when Tenzin and Marla could have sworn they saw a man with an enormous head step in front of the convoy, command the guards with his mind to release Silver Peregrine and Thunderbolt? Did she really see the three of them flee the scene, and Peace Officers in pursuit?

Marla closed her eyes, tried to lose herself in the grip of Tenzin's arms around her naked flesh. She failed. "I don't know what to believe any longer," she said. "I just don't. I can't trust the news, I can't trust my memories, or even my feelings—"

"No?" said Tenzin.

"No, I can't," she sighed, pulling from his grip, but not hard enough, earnestly enough, to break it. Everything since yesterday had been a blur. Shandon had led them out of the stadium, demanded they all run, and then charged back in to witness the action.

She had asked him why. He would only respond, "I've been forgiven, but I still owe a debt." It had made no sense.

Marla and Tenzin had sent Ehat on running, then doubled back— Marla had insisted, heaven only knew why, that they make sure Shandon was all right. They got back just in time to see him die.

When the Peace Officers stormed the Stadium, Marla and Tenzin were sure they'd be discovered. But they weren't. The troops were only looking for Supers. Now, she and Tenzin might well be the only two people free, the only two people alive, who knew the real story of what happened. Marla wasn't used to that kind of responsibility. Was this what it felt like to be a hero? Marla found the taste chalky in her mouth.

She couldn't handle it alone, not even with her newly awakened battle courage. So, following the words of Deacon Allbright, she sought out interconnectedness. She sought out the nearest, closest, most compatible connection—the man she'd loved two years ago. Was that it? She couldn't tell. Marla was beginning to realize that her life was starting to run away with itself. Going to law school, defending criminals, getting involved with Tenzin (twice now!), taking on the Shandon case, doing a 180 when she realized the significance of what was on the datadisk, and of course, joining the fray at the stadium . . . could it be that Marla just kept *doing* things, without even being sure why, except that she got them done? She never stopped to ask herself if she *wanted* any of these things or not. Did she keep doing them because of the challenge, because the process of pursuing and completing something felt good?

Entwined within Tenzin's arms, connected at last, Marla Arliss felt more lost than ever.

"You have indeed changed," Tenzin was saying. "Or perhaps you have not, and my perception has. What, in my younger days, I viewed in you as recklessness, as careless emotion . . . I now realize is passion, strength."

"I thought passion was a drug," Marla said, less hostilely than cautiously. "I thought separation from emotions was your goal, to move you towards enlightenment."

"The wise ones teach that the universe is a circle," he replied. "Perhaps, by traveling to the extremes of emotion, one can reach enlightenment via the other direction."

"That sounds like a load of splen to me."

"Perhaps," said Tenzin. "But I can think of no better explanation, save that I still love you, Marla. I love you for the fire you display, and want to stand by you."

"Be careful what you pledge," said Marla distantly, putting the finishing strokes on an image that had been building in her mind all morning. "I may be walking down some very uncomfortable roads shortly. Roads that will be very, very harmful to your career."

"So be it," said Tenzin.

Now Marla did tug away from him, twisted around, stared into his eyes with galaxies of shock.

"*What?*"

"After the events of this week, I . . . I am no longer sure that working with Holloway squares with my moral code."

"And you used to tell me my notion of `right' and `wrong' was primitive. Underdeveloped."

"Your fallibility does not somehow negate my own."

"You're not exactly winning me back," Marla harrumphed. She had to harrumph. Otherwise, she would have cried. "Well, I told you, after the events of this week, I don't know what's right and wrong either. I only know I need something more than what I have now. I thought the Church could fulfill that. But maybe . . . maybe . . ."

Tenzin smiled in self-satisfaction, looking to the world as jolly as the Buddha himself. "Maybe that is where I come in?"

"Yes. No. Maybe. Oh, I don't know." With a savage motion, Marla tore loose from the bed covers, rose to her feet and donned a bathrobe.

"Where are you going?"

"I'm going to call my boss," she said. "I'm going to pull in every favor, make every sacrifice I can . . . but I'm going to defend them, Tenzin."

"Them?"

"The Friday Knights."

"But . . . you . . ."

"Yes," she turned back to him, "I hate Supers. You know that. I know that. But the one thing I hate worse is not knowing. I need to get inside the heads of those Knights, Tenzin. Somehow, and don't ask me to explain how or why, I'm convinced that . . . whatever piece is missing from me . . . they have it."

"Nothing is missing from you, Marla," Tenzin stared from her to the bed again, impatiently, but she was already picking up the phone, searching.

* * *

Tenzin left Marla's Uptown apartment upon sunrise and took the monorail to Justice Plaza in the Federal District, then walked across the courtyard to the Attorney General's office. Every day he had passed gaggles of tourists rubbernecking at the seventy foot tall onyx statue of Lady Justice wielding her flaming sword high above. Today, however, he stopped, briefcase in hand, to look up with them. She didn't look a thing like Marla. Why did he think she should? How puzzling.

Doubts, however, did not keep one from one's duties. Not yet, anyway. Not until some alternate course of action could be formulated. Holloway's office had been abuzz ever since the rumors of Neville Shandon's death were confirmed. The Assistant Attorney General himself blustered hotly through the halls, shouting random orders to subordinates, doubtless looking for someone to pay for the loss of his chance at glory. Rumor had it he'd already fired a secretary this morning on the spot, for reasons yet to make themselves apparent. Tenzin wisely ducked into his own office and gingerly shut the door.

He expected to find his office empty, and found himself mildly disturbed to see the gangly, white-haired man in purple robes reclining in Tenzin's own chair.

"About time you got here. I thought you were never late."

"Ten minutes' tardiness hardly constitutes delinquent behavior," Tenzin said softly. "And I would imagine you would keep a lower profile."

"Why?" asked Tenzin's guest. "I have a valid permit. Unlike some people." He tossed a copy of the morning's *Times* into Tenzin's lap, the one bearing the picture of the captive Friday Knights.

Tenzin shrugged, trying not to show recognition. Did this man have something on him? Would he attempt blackmail? "Don't you want to know why I'm here?" the man asked.

"I assumed you would tell me eventually," Tenzin walked calmly to a table at the end of his office and, never quite taking his eyes of the visitor, activated the hot plate and began boiling some water for tea. The visitor smiled widely, blue eyes flashing in the morning light. "Consider this the `customer evaluation' portion of our arrangement. I'm interested in how you fared with my services." The water began to boil, and Tenzin softly dropped leaves into the cup. They floated gingerly, the water soaking their fibers and beginning the slow, inexorable drag that would take them to the bottom.

"Your agent . . . Buzz, was his moniker? . . . proved very useful," said Tenzin. "Ultimately, however, the information he gathered proved moot, as I'm sure you're aware."

"Yes, yes, yes," said the other man, "dreadful incident last night with Commander Shandon. My condolences to your entire office."

"Sarcasm ill-becomes a man's death."

"Why?" asked the visitor. "It's not like he'll care."

"The Commander leaves behind relations, albeit distant ones. Not to mention everyone whose life he has touched."

"Yes, yes, yes," said the other man. "Like you, and I . . . and oh yes, Buzz. He's still in the hospital, you know, thanks to your errand."

Tenzin frowned. Had they now reached the crux of this conversation?

Apparently they had. "If you were going to eliminate my agents after their usefulness had expired, Counselor, you should have told me. I would have sent you someone far more expendable."

Tenzin paused with his mouth above the teacup. "I . . . I do not know what you mean."

"Buzz checked in and told me mercenaries had attacked him right after the drop-off. He had no idea who they were, but I ran some checks of my own . . . they were hired with money I traced—not without some difficulty, mind you—to President Lee's office itself."

"I . . . I . . ." Tenzin stammered.

"Now, perhaps you'll tell me this is one of those cases where the left hand didn't know what the right hand was doing, and so forth. I might even believe you. But frankly, believing you would be bad for business."

The other man rose, and Tenzin took a step back, still holding the teacup. The water sloshed clumsily, spilling in drops upon the carpet. Was this man bold enough to attack him here, right in the Attorney General's office? Should he cry out? Attempt to defend himself? How?

"Relax, Counselor," the visitor said. "For the moment, you're too valuable for me to waste. For the moment, you and Holloway are the only two people in your office who know the contents of that datadisk, correct?"

Tenzin remained silent. Rhetorical questions didn't merit answers.

"Holloway is easy. Once he learns of the passing of Attorney General Halbert, I doubt he'll spend much thought on the potential for alien life. Besides, it wouldn't do a new AG's image good to start speaking such nonsense."

"Halbert is not dead," Tenzin said, feeling a nauseous wave creep up his throat despite the calming influence of the tea. "He is merely sick."

The other man shrugged and smiled with all the nonchalance in the world. "Don't argue with me. Argue with this evening's newspaper. When it hits the stands, that is."

"Who are you?" Tenzin hissed. "By what right do you come in here with threats and imprecations—"

"You're resourceful," the man interrupted. "That's why I picked you."

Tenzin felt his face flush. The floodgates gave way and admitted pride. "*You* picked? As I recall, I found you in the Herotowns—"

"Because I wanted you to, Counselor," said the man. "Because I knew that I could trust you with this knowledge. You, and your . . . associate, Miss Arliss."

Now the walls were down. Tenzin rushed the man before him, a growl deep in his throat, but where his hands reached out, only air remained. The visitor had floated out of his grasp, executed a spin in the air, landed behind him. Before Tenzin could even process the act, two swift blows rained on the back of his neck. Tenzin pitched forward, fell across his desk. His grip loosened on the teacup, which ignobly plummeted to the group, thunking meekly against the carpet, splashing its contents all over the desk's pseudowood.

The visitor clucked his tongue in disapproval as Tenzin struggled to his feet and spun around, murder in his eyes.

"I thought you weren't a man of violence, Counselor."

"If you hurt her . . ." he began.

"Pish," the visitor waved a dismissive hand. "I have no such inclinations. At least, not yet. Consider yourself on notice, Mister Myata. If I can't count on your sense of duty to enforce your silence, I can count on your sense of love."

Formless rage billowed beneath Tenzin's skin, a welcome lover embraced with open arms after so many years of rejection. "So what is it you want from me?"

"As I said, for now, only your silence. Eventually, I may ask more. Good day, Counselor."

With that, the visitor calmly opened Tenzin's door and walked out into the office, down the hall, into the elevator, and outside into the blare of the morning sun. Rough winds, engine noises, chemical smells . . . yes, Mesopolopolis proper sounded, smelled, and felt just like Herotown, give or take a few rads on the Geiger counter. The man adjusted his coat, ascended to the nearest monorail platform, and thought about love.

Love.

That buffoonish lawyer should thank his lucky stars that he forwent his ascetic ways and embraced love again. Without that hold of love by which the visitor could manipulate him, Tenzin Myata would have been dead right now, another loose end tied up. But death wasn't always the cleanest way to tie up loose ends. Especially loose ends like Gayle Fellman, aka Gal Friday.

As he exited the monorail, the man strode up to the battered remains of the jet-black automobile with the silver triangle hood emblem that waited for him loyally in the junkyard he had dragged it to last night. A setback, but a manageable one. He had found Gal Friday once before, and he would find her again . . . along with Ehat.

Knowing Gayle, he wouldn't even have to search. Eventually, she would come looking for him. Pulling Detective Roland's record, showing it to her, letting the natural course of heartbreak follow . . . yes, love was the rope that bound Gayle's loose end, the rope that would bring her back. Even roped, however, Gayle Fellman was not to be taken lightly. Especially not when hers weren't the only heartstrings that were bound.

Waley sighed as he tapped his fingers across the shattered chassis of his automobile. One thing at a time.

THE END

The Earth is in danger!

What will happen to Gayle, Ehat, and the Friday Knights?

This looks like a job for a hero . . .

. . . and the hero we need is YOU.

The sequel to this novel, *Red Lights on the Horizon,* has already been written. The author is depending upon the response of readers to *The Fragile Light* to create the kind of "buzz" necessary for a big-name publisher to pick up the *Herotown* series and spread it far and wide.

If you liked this book, tell a friend. Tell fifty friends. Hop on newsgroups and sing its praises. Tell everyone to visit **www.fragilelight.com** and order copies. If you know agents, editors, or publishers, bring the book to their attention.

Only you have the power to make the publication of the sequel possible. Be a hero and answer the call!